LOST & FOUND

THE LOST & FOUND TRILOGY BOOK TWO

VM RHEAULT

ABOUT THE BOOK

What would you give up to protect the woman you love?

Rafferty

I built a multi-million dollar e-zine with my own blood, sweat, and tears, and I won't give it up for a woman. Except, while I help Nic repair her reputation, she crawls under my skin and steals my heart.

When I find out how much trouble she's in, there's only one thing that will save her.

The very thing I said I would never give up.

Veronica

Resentful of a past relationship I had with billionaire Jack Durand, Raff hates to love me, and I can't ask him for his help. I'm alone, just like I've always been, and I do the only thing I can to protect my father: agree to marry another man.

Raff only prints the truth, and I believed all his lies.

Every single one.

CHAPTER ONE

*Rise and Shine,
Bridgeport!*

Veronica

"Still banged up from your little fall from grace?" Felix asks, smirking and sliding into the makeup chair.

It's been a hard few weeks since Jack's birthday party, and everyone knows it. No one is shy about ramming it into my face, either, but deep down, I knew it would happen. We didn't love each other. Maybe I could have—he's handsome, rich, and good in bed—but I knew he was in love with Emma Cox when we started seeing each other. I simply didn't think he would do anything about it.

Push came to shove, and shove he did—shoved me right out of his bed and onto the floor.

"You're such a dick, Felix," I say, meeting the reflection of his arrogant face in the long mirror attached to our makeup counters. I stick my tongue out at him, and he laughs.

Another fucking day on the *Rise and Shine, Bridgeport!* set. I'm so tired of this goddamned show, but I need the money, and the not-so-small amount of fame hosting the local morning program provides.

If I'm not a celebrity, I'm nothing, and I can't afford to be nothing.

He shrugs and grins. He's never liked that between the two of us, I was always the more popular, paparazzi swarming me the second I step outside. Dating Jack helped with that, landing a fish that wouldn't be caught, and now instead of wanting the dirt on my love life with him, they want to know about my love life without him.

Rafferty Clark says any attention is good attention, but when the paps call me a jilted bride, I don't know how true that is.

"All I'm saying is, maybe let someone else have a turn."

I grimace. "I'm not stopping you."

"No one gives a fuck about me."

Reaching for a makeup wipe to clean the gunk off my face, I say, "Then figure it out. You're single and good looking, date somebody."

He brightens hopefully. "You wanna? The producers would love that."

Dating my co-host would not be conducive to my situation. Felix Rivera may be smart, charming, and good looking with his dark Latino looks, but he doesn't have the clout and bank account I need to get out of my mess. "Sorry."

I scrub the makeup off my face revealing the bags under my eyes and my skin's pallor.

"We could hit up the fundraiser for the Bridgeport's Women's Reproductive Health and Resources Center," he says, mimicking my motions, only he looks the same under the layer of makeup caked onto his skin.

"That's the last thing I'm going to."

Jack Durand and his family are huge supporters of the

resource center, and it will be the first big event Jack and Emma attend as an engaged couple. The measly charity events I've had to go to since Jack dumped me have been bad enough, and having to go alone, no less, since I refused to jump from Jack to someone else days after we broke up.

I'd rather appear dumped than desperate, even if that's what I am.

"Mike won't let you skip that," he says, balling up the wipe and throwing it into a trash can under the counter. "We dedicate a huge section of the show talking about who wore what, who went with whom. Everyone is gonna wanna know who you're going with, V. Mike will fire you if you don't attend."

The worst part is, he's right. The producers force us to go, the expectation written into my contract when I accepted the position. *Rise and Shine, Bridgeport!* is all about everything Bridgeport, and Jesus Christ, if I have to attend one more Home and Garden show at the Bridgeport Arena I'm going to puke. I don't have a garden and don't want one. Don't have a home, either, but let's not get into that.

At least the rumors I started about Jack and me weren't around long, otherwise, I would have attended the Bridgeport Wedding Expo that was held in February not only as a host of Bridgeport's most popular morning talk show, but also as a future bride. Watching those models walk down the runway in all that froth burns me up with jealousy. A woman with a history like mine doesn't get married. Not happily.

"I'll handle it."

"Maybe we'll get some new blood," Felix teases, sliding from his chair. "We could use some around here."

If Felix doesn't watch out, it won't be my blood that will need replacing, it'll be his. "Fuck off."

He chortles on his way out the door.

Alone in the dressing room, I slump against the counter.

We have a makeup artist slather it on, but washing it off is our own responsibility, and pulling another wipe from the dispenser, I'm happy for a few moments to myself.

My phone vibrates near a compact of blush and my dad's name glows on the screen, but I let it ring. I can't talk to him now. His choices fucked up my life, a realization that becomes truer with every passing second.

I linger, reluctant to leave the safety of the building, but I hate this job and don't want to be here for longer than I have to be.

Wearing summer dress slacks and a sleeveless blouse, I step out of the building and onto the sidewalk into the early afternoon sunshine.

I wish I could run away and disappear, but there's too much at stake and I do the only thing I can do. Glue a smile onto my face, greet the paparazzi like nothing is wrong, and breakdown when I get home, like I've been doing every day since Jack Durand told the whole world I wasn't good enough to marry.

No one believed him more than me.

CHAPTER TWO

Rafferty

"Y̶ou've been avoiding me," Emma says, not giving me the chance to even say hello.

"Not true," I deny, though we both know it is.

One of my bloggers didn't need five seconds to report the big rock Jack Durand slid onto my best friend's finger the weekend they went away to a little B&B on the outskirts of Bridgeport and came back happily engaged.

That was two weeks ago, and since then, I've made myself scarce. Emma would defend our friendship as if her life depended on it, but things change and time moves on, and if you don't move with it, you get left behind.

"What have you been doing?" she asks.

I lean back in my office chair. I was tweaking an interview with an up-and-coming rockstar who performed at the Bridgeport Arena last night to a sold-out house. He wanted to set the record straight about his drug use, and after his concert, we met for drinks and conversation in his hotel room. His manager gave him a list of potential people he could talk to, and I was his first choice. He knows my reputation for only printing the truth, and what he'd say on my record everyone would believe. "Aren't you at work?"

"Yeah, but I have a second to talk to you. I know somebody."

"Funny." She knows two somebodies, and both of them are very, very happy. I caught Ronald Durand out on a Friday night, and the crusty old man actually smiled. On camera. Only Emma and Jack's engagement could make the old goat do that.

"So . . ." she wheedles.

"So, I'm still helping Nic tread water. Same shit, different day." I try to sound nonchalant. She doesn't need to know that the two Sundays she brought Jack with her to her mother's was a change I hadn't been prepared for, and visiting Aunt Caro, while nice, wasn't the same. Emma and I never had anything romantic, but it's difficult to find a new routine when you're used to someone being in your life practically 24/7 and then she suddenly disappears.

Helping Nic has been a blessing in disguise, but only writing articles and trying to spin things in her favor has stopped working. She needs to go out and show the world that Durand didn't hurt her. She's feeding into the rumors he broke her heart. Maybe he did, but she can't let them know it.

"How can I help?"

It's ironic she would ask considering it's her fiancé who made the mess in the first place, but to me, it's proof Emma has a good heart. She doesn't hold a grudge against the woman Jack dated for two years before he proposed to her, and I admire her all the more.

"I don't think she has any friends, Em."

"Really?" She sounds surprised, and after helping Nic for nearly a month and coming to that conclusion, so was I.

"Really. Jack would know more," I say reluctantly, "but from what I've seen working with her recently, all she does is go to work and then goes home. The show expects her to attend the odd charity event, but she doesn't do lunch and shopping with the girls, that kind of thing."

"I can do that."

I open my mouth to ask what, exactly, she can do, but she says quickly, "I was really calling to tell you the parties are starting."

I wince. "Emma."

"I know, but you can't not be there. Especially since you told Jack you'd be a groomsman. Which was really sweet, by the way, and I appreciate it."

I didn't agree to be a groomsman. Durand asked, and I . . . didn't tell him to fuck off like I should have. Christ. I wouldn't have done it anyway, even if the words had been on the tip of my tongue. I'd rather chop my arm off than hurt Emma.

"When is it?"

"You can choose."

"Fuck." I sigh. "I can't choose. When's the *first* one?"

She laughs. "Heath and Zoey are throwing us something at their house after the fundraiser, but honestly, you don't have to go to that one. Ron's hosting a garden party at the Bridgeport Hotel tomorrow evening. Drinks, light appetizers, dessert. I think it would be a good idea if you brought Veronica. Jack and I talked, and he knows he was an ass and he'd like to apologize."

"You mean, you're making him apologize," I say dourly. Apologies don't mean shit if they aren't sincere.

"He knows he needs to admit a few things, and he's doing it voluntarily. I'll leave it at that."

"Fine. I can ask, but something's up and I don't know if she'll go. What time is it?"

"Five to nine."

"Isn't all this a little early? Do you have a date set?"

"November. We decided to keep trying if I'm not pregnant yet. I'd like a dress to hide it if I'm showing during the ceremony, but we both agreed we'd like to be married before the baby comes."

"*A* baby, you mean."

"Yes, any baby," she says, amused.

I love how happy she sounds. Emma looked like death warmed over the night Durand was supposed to propose to Nic at his birthday party. I might have told him it was nothing, but I was worried for her, too. I'd never seen her look so torn up about anything, even when her father passed away. The rumors and proposal came out of nowhere and never in the time Nic and I were putting out the fires did she ever explain it.

"I'll be there. I can't accept on Nic's behalf, but I'll ask. Are you sending out invitations?"

"No. It's something Ron thought of at the last minute. He and Jack are still figuring things out and Ron wasn't sure if Jack would appreciate something like this."

"Does he?"

"I don't know. I think it would be easier for him if Claire were on board, but Jack told her we were engaged and the next day she flew out to California. She's been spending time at their beach house in Malibu. She won't be there tomorrow night and that hurts him. He doesn't want to choose sides, but if he forgives Ron, it will feel like he is."

I like Claire, and I scowl. "Why would he take his father's side? What Ron did was really shitty. If Jack hadn't fallen for you and fought against everything his father led him to believe, he would have spent his entire life alone."

"Jack said he understood the jealousy, that he could relate."

I know exactly what she's referring to, and it pisses me off. Durand chose to believe what he wanted to believe about my friendship with Emma—he was too big of a coward to accept the truth.

She continues, "He's ashamed of it, and it's big he can take ownership of his feelings. I'm proud of him, Raff. He had to overcome a lot to ask me to marry him. Sometimes it all still feels like a dream and I'm going to wake up."

"You deserve every happiness, baby girl," I say, the endearment slipping out of my mouth from years of habit. I need to stop. Jack won't be happy if he hears it no matter how innocent it is.

"Thanks. So, you'll be there? Invite Veronica. I need to get going. I'm training in Jack's new PA."

"I'll do my best. See you tomorrow night." I disconnect.

Propping my feet up onto my desk, I roll this around. I was thinking Nic needed to be seen out and about, not hiding like a kicked puppy that peed on the carpet.

It doesn't hurt that I haven't seen her in a couple of days, and (taking a cue from Durand) if I have the guts to admit it, I miss her. The wall I asked him about is still there, but I haven't done anything to climb over it, much less tear it down.

Maybe it's time I try and see how far I get.

What are you doing tomorrow night? I text her. *Rise and Shine, Bridgeport!* was done filming a couple of hours ago, and she's usually home by now.

What I'm always doing. Not a damned thing.

Come with me to Jack and Emma's engagement party at the Bridgeport Hotel, I respond.

Hell, no. You're kidding, right?

I grin and my cock stiffens. She's feisty when she's mad, and I love it. Instead of texting, I call her. She answers but doesn't say anything. "Nic, come on," I say over the silence. "We talked about this. You have to stop wallowing." I don't know if wallowing is the right word, but she's been doing something these past few weeks since Durand dumped her.

"How would that look?" she asks, and she has a valid point for someone who needs to keep a thumb on the pulse of her career. If they didn't think she's washed up, there are several talk shows taped in Bridgeport she could possibly land a spot on if *Rise and Shine, Bridgeport!* ever let her go, but that's a big if considering she was in a relationship with one of the country's richest men and he ended it in front of five hundred people.

"Like you don't give a rat's ass Durand broke it off with you."

"I think that ship has sailed," she says tartly, and I can imagine her frowning and crossing her arms over her chest the way I've seen her do hundreds of times.

I can't disagree. I had a helluva time spinning the pictures of her crying at Durand's birthday party. "Then let it go."

"That's easy for you to say," she snaps. "I had a lot riding on—"

I lower my feet to the carpet. "You had a lot of what riding on your engagement to Durand?"

"Nothing. It's nothing that concerns you. I'll go. What time?"

"I'll pick you up at five. It's an evening garden party."

Nic disconnects without a goodbye, angry I'm right and there's nothing she can do about it. Her little slip up started the wheels turning, though. What in the hell could she have had riding on Durand's proposal? Only his proposal? Or the marriage?

I think back to what Emma said. For someone with such a public occupation, there's not a lot we know about Nic.

It's my nature to dig, sniff out news, good and bad, but I resist reaching for my keyboard.

What I want to find out about Veronica Chapman, I want her to tell me herself, preferably in bed, under the covers, as we both catch our breaths.

CHAPTER THREE

Veronica

I stand in front of my closet, my hands shaking. What the hell does someone wear to a party like this? Finally, I choose a little silver cocktail dress that's held up by thin straps and skip the jewelry. It's not going to matter what I wear —I'm going to feel like a fool no matter what—and I don't do anything with my hair, either. Parted severely down the middle, I let it hang in a sharp sheet to my shoulders. I don't carry a coat, though the evening may turn cool. I've seen Emma with Raff's suitcoat draped over her shoulders enough times to know if I get cold, he'll easily give it up. The last thing I add is a small silver purse that dangles from my wrist by a narrow strap. All it has room for is some cash in case I find myself in trouble and a lipstick. A condom, too, but I skip that.

Outside, the paparazzi are going crazy, and they start throwing questions at me the moment I step onto the stone steps in front of my building. They know exactly where I'm going, and they drool, begging, wanting to know who I'm going with. A limo glides to a stop near the curb, and Raff climbs out to help me inside.

I gingerly navigate the stairs in my heels, step toward him, and nervously lick my lips. He's gorgeous dressed in taupe pants and a robin's egg blue dress shirt, a brown and blue tie knotted loosely at his throat. No suitcoat though, so I guess I'm on my own if I get cold.

"Hey, dollface," he says.

I move closer, and he snakes his arm around my waist. The paparazzi snap pictures and film us, and they eat up his nickname for me. Even my skin flushes. The first time he called me that, all the thought flew right out of my head. Plenty of people have called me by a nickname, but only Raff's has ever held the affection I crave.

Raff slants his mouth over mine, and I stiffen in shock. Only four weeks ago I was hoping to be engaged to another man. I've been called a jilted bride all this time, now they'll call me a whore.

He shoves his tongue into my mouth, and I have no choice but to wrap my arms around his neck and let him ravage me.

Time slows, the paparazzi's shouting fades, and there's nothing but me and Raff on the sidewalk. I'm seconds away from suffocating, and it's as if he knew I needed air. He pulls away and searches my eyes. "Get in the car."

I drag in a ragged breath and slide onto the rich leather bench, my skin slick with perspiration.

Raff's sits next to me and the driver slams the door shut.

"What was that for?" I ask. "Wasn't that a little OTT?"

He rolls his eyes. "Are you thirty or ten?"

"Now everyone will think I'm a slut."

He pours a glass of whiskey and offers it to me. "Now everyone will think I wanted you and I'm taking my chance."

I sip to wet my mouth and narrow my eyes. If Raff's felt

something for me other than pity, he's been good at hiding it. "Are you?"

Tilting his head, he says, "One day I'd like to know if the curtains match the rug."

I scowl. "For Christ's sake, of course not. Now who's ten?"

He chuckles and pours more into my glass. "Drink up."

"Why?"

"I want you buzzed so you can enjoy yourself. No one is going to call you a slut. You have a right to move on."

"*Pfft.* A lot you know." I down the second glass and hold it out for more.

"I said I want you buzzed, not drunk."

I'm scared, and I'm nasty to hide my fear. "Don't want to carry me out of the hotel like Jack did for Emma?"

He pours more into my glass, but only half the amount of the first two drinks. "I have it on trustworthy authority that when Durand brought her back to his penthouse, he let her sleep. If I carried you home, you would not be afforded that luxury." He slides over the bench and his lips graze the shell of my ear. "Have you ever had drunk sex? It's supposed to be very good."

I bet any sex with Rafferty Clark is good. I bet he knows all the right buttons to push at exactly the right time, and he wouldn't let up until I couldn't move. "Is that what you're getting at? You want drunk sex?"

"Not tonight. I like a side of consent along with my main course, and if you're drunk, you can't give it."

He pours a drink for himself and stores the bottle in the bar's cabinet.

"What if I give it now?"

"Consent now doesn't mean consent later, and any gentleman would know that."

"Then how does one go about having drunk sex? Sounds like it's impossible."

Raff caresses my cheek. "When you know, without a shadow of a doubt, that I would never, ever hurt you. You don't know that yet—I haven't earned it."

Oddly enough, I do. For all the help he's given me this past month . . . and not even the help. I never cried in front of him, but somehow I know if I'd broken down, he would have rubbed my back, offered me a tissue, and simply been the rock I needed him to be.

"I know, Raff."

"Do ya, dollface?" he whispers, his thumb brushing over my bottom lip.

"Yeah, I do."

The limo glides to a stop in front of the hotel.

"Then, come on."

The driver opens the door, and I grab his hand. "Why are you doing this?"

He tangles my fingers with his and says, "I love Emma, as a friend, with all my heart, and I would never, ever tell her this. I think Jack Durand is a piece of shit for what he did to you. You deserve better, and I want to be the one to give it to you."

There's not a chance for me to say anything. He gently tugs on my hand, urging me from the limo and onto the sidewalk in front of the Bridgeport Hotel.

The paparazzi shout at us, whipped to a frenzy we're together. They've already seen the footage of him kissing me outside my building, and Raff eggs them on, wrapping his arm around my shoulders and holding me close.

"Are you together?" one reporter yells.

Raff smirks. "Obviously," he says, enjoying standing on the other side of the camera.

Everyone laughs.

"We can see that, but you know what it looks like."

Raff stills and anger rolls off his body. Velvet ropes prevent the reporters from stepping onto the hotel's property, but I doubt the forced distance keeps anyone from feeling the rage that burns hot. "I do your job seven days a week, fifty-two weeks a year, and trust me, *nothing* is *ever* what it looks like. You remember that because if you don't, I will remind you, and you won't like how I do it."

The paps quiet, some taking our picture, but most are frozen, their cameras filming us and the furious tension still radiating off Raff. He nudges me toward the hotel's gleaming glass doors.

"Was that necessary?" I ask breathlessly, caught up in his heartfelt defense of my reputation.

"I will not let them turn you into a pariah because a billionaire decided to be an asshole," he says, striding briskly across the polished lobby floor.

"It wasn't all him," I say, trotting in my heels to keep up.

He turns swiftly, fury still written all over his face. "Do you love him?"

I skid to a halt. "W-what?"

"You heard me. Do. You. Love. Him?"

Do I love Jack? I needed him. Needed the shelter our relationship provided. Needed what being married to him would have given me. But I never loved him.

"No, I don't love him. Why are you so angry?"

He deflates, the tension seeping out of his shoulders. "I don't know, Nic. I don't know. He hurt you."

"It's not your responsibility to be that mad. Like you told me, let it go, or you'll lose Emma's friendship. You can't be like that toward her fiancé. She won't tolerate it, not even for you."

"You think if I walked into that party right now and told her to leave him, she would say no?"

"Yes, she would say no."

"You know that for a fact."

I step closer to him, search his face, his blue eyes razor sharp. I don't know why he's angry, don't know why he's chosen to take my side when there aren't any sides. I'm as much to blame as Jack, maybe even more so. "Yes, I do."

"How?"

"If I loved a man as much as Emma loves Jack, I wouldn't leave him for anything in the world. Let it go, Raff. Please."

He grits his teeth. "Okay, but only because it's none of my business. Damage control, fine. The cause of it, none of my business."

"Thank you."

He's calmer, gripping my hand, and we walk through to the rear of the hotel. The gleaming glass doors open into a huge garden, a magical wonderland hidden in the middle of downtown Bridgeport.

Raff and I pause on the stone stairs that lead down to a matching path, and everyone stops their conversations to gape.

I recognize the faces and know the names of the guests chatting over champagne and canapés, but I feel like a stranger, and an unwanted one at that. Raff squeezes my hand, and there's not one person who misses it. I don't know what his game is, but I think he's winning.

Emma breaks away from the group of people she was talking to and floats across the grass to us. She's radiant, and I've never seen her look so happy. A gorgeous diamond glints on her left hand nestled into a platinum setting, and I can't help but think the ring should have been mine. The day after Jack's birthday party, I called the jeweler the Durands use, and he said Jack never showed for the appointment I asked Emma to enter into his planner. Jack knew long before the party he wasn't going to ask me to marry him. He knew the day he met Emma he wouldn't marry anyone but her.

"You two look wonderful," she says, standing on the bottom step, her head tilted up at us. "Did you come together or arrive at the same time?"

"Together," Raff says, and over him, I say, "We met in the lobby."

"Shut up," he says, frowning.

Emma's mouth drops open. "Raff. Don't talk to her that way."

"What? She's lying. I picked her up, we came together, and we'll leave together, too."

"I'm sorry, Emma." My hand still trapped in Raff's firm hold, I lean toward her and air kiss her cheek. We're not close enough for me to do that, but only saying hello felt too little. "He's been in a mood all the way here."

"I may have an idea why," she says, her eyes twinkling and her tongue poked into her cheek.

Raff scowls.

Jack walks across the garden toward us.

"Oh, here comes the reason now," she says.

I'm surprised Emma can joke about something that a few weeks ago would have brought both of us to tears. I hope Raff can keep his disapproval of Jack under control. We may not be one big happy family, but he'll always belong to the same group of friends, and I don't want Raff to lose Emma's friendship over something that's mostly my fault.

This time, I squeeze Raff's fingers, and we meet Jack on the grass.

"Veronica," he says, kissing my cheek, a real one, his lips grazing my skin. "Clark." He holds out a hand, and Raff grudgingly shakes it. "Thank you for coming. It means a lot to Emma and me that you're here."

"Wouldn't have missed it," Raff says, smoothing his palm over the back of Emma's head.

Jack frowns.

Raff drops his hand.

Emma sighs.

There's going to be a lot to get used to in the coming months, and I can picture Jack and Raff going head-to-head like a pair of bucks fighting for territory. I'm not sure who would win if it came to blows. Jack has more money than God, but Raff, Raff has street smarts he honed from somewhere, a cunning that might be sharper than Jack's ruthlessness.

I want to get the hard part out of the way, and I turn to Jack. He looks good dressed in charcoal grey slacks and a black dress shirt, a black and silver tie knotted loosely around his neck similar to Raff's. I can be honest and say that Jack looks more at ease, more content, than I have ever seen him, at least when we dated, even after a marathon of hot sex. I could feel slighted and insulted, but he was with the wrong woman for the wrong reasons. I was with the wrong man for the wrong reasons as well, and now it's time for comeuppance.

"Can we talk?" I ask him.

His eyes flick to Emma, but it's not Emma who's reacting badly. Raff grips my upper arm, his fingertips sinking into my flesh. I understand Raff doesn't want Jack to hurt me anymore, but I've been fighting my own battles my entire life and this is one more I am not going to win.

"Yeah. I think it's time," Jack says, stepping to the side.

"Please don't," I tell Raff, and he loosens his hold.

"Let's go get a drink," Emma says, and she wraps her arms around one of his and leads him away, looking like they have so many times online whenever one of his bloggers would live stream them walking down a sidewalk.

"They should be together," Jack says, his voice cracking.

"Don't say that. Emma loves you."

I walk with him deeper into the garden, my heels sinking into the grass. I'm not a stranger to this part of the hotel, and I find a bench near a bird bath spouting water. We disappeared from sight, and we're alone, only the two of us and the two years we should never have been together.

He sits heavily on the wrought iron, but it does nothing but hold him up. Much like Emma does, I suspect. "I don't know why. Christ, I feel like a fucked up little kid all the time."

"We're all a little fucked up," I say, sitting too, resting my elbow on the back of the bench and propping my head in my hand. "It doesn't help we were dating when we had no right to be."

He huffs a laugh. "I was using you, plain and simple. I owe you an apology for more than my birthday party. I should have told you I wasn't going to propose, should have talked to you about it like an adult. I didn't know how big of a fallout you'd have to deal with, and I am really sorry about that. Is the show still giving you a hard time?"

"Yeah, but something else will happen and I'll be old news." I lift a shoulder. "I was using you too, running from something I can't run away from. I was hoping that if we married I would . . . well, it's not your problem. You're not fully to blame for what happened, Jack. I tried to manipulate you, and that was a mistake. We have to forget about it."

"It was a good two years," he says.

I laugh. "No, it wasn't."

He chuckles. "No, I guess they weren't. Emma was under my nose the whole time. I'm lucky she hung in there."

"She loves you too much to give up."

"Yeah," he says softly. "You and Clark?" He brushes a piece of hair out of my face. We all have habits that will be hard to break.

"No, I don't think so. I need time to figure things out."

"He asked about you, you know. I confronted him and told him I was going to ask Emma to marry me. He told me a few things I needed to know, but he wanted to know about you, too."

"He's been really sweet, helping me with the gossip. I think *Rise and Shine, Bridgeport!* would have let me go if it hadn't been for his . . . he calls it damage control. Maybe it is, but because of his scrambling, our ratings went sky high after your party. I don't think the producers wanted to admit it."

"Then it wasn't a complete shitshow."

"Not entirely." I meet his eyes. "Be happy with her, Jack. Don't turn into your own worst enemy. If you're an ass and act like you don't deserve her, you'll turn into an ass who doesn't deserve her. She loves you, you love her, and really, if you let it, it can be that simple. I'm happy for you."

"Thanks."

"I'm sorry for my part in how our relationship ended, for the things I said in your lobby."

He slides closer, wraps his arms around me, and I rest my head against his shoulder. His embrace used to symbolize safety, a security net. He never acted like he didn't care, and while we were dating, he always checked in, made sure I had everything I needed. He wasn't as callous as he wants to believe he was, but it wasn't enough for me. Couldn't be enough for me.

"I'm sorry too, but I have to thank you. If you hadn't done what you did, I never would have confronted my feelings and Emma and I wouldn't be engaged. If you ever need anything, ask. We'll always be friends, whether Clark likes it or not."

Sitting up, I say, "I think he thinks the same about you and his friendship with Emma."

Jack blows out a breath. "Yeah. I have to do better. I know I need help, and we're starting couples therapy. I have a lot to deal with. Forty-one years of thinking my wife will eventually leave me for another man and abandon our children. I gotta get that under control."

"That's great. You trying will make every bit of difference. Come on, we better get back or they'll think we ran off to Vegas to elope."

He laughs. "Christ, after all this, that would be something."

Jack has made drastic progress if he can appreciate a joke about eloping with me and enjoy it for what it is. Emma's changed him for the better, and I'm not bitter enough to resent him for that. We all deserve to be happy and find love.

I'll never be able to. That's something I'm coming to terms with. I fought against it, but I won't make another mistake like I made with Jack.

Nothing can save me.

I know that now.

We step into the clearing, and Raff's involved in a bubbly group conversation with Mia and Haisley, Emma and a woman who looks like she could be her mother, Zoey and Heath, and Jack's dad who is positively glowing standing next to his future daughter-in-law. "Hello, Mr. Durand. This is a lovely party."

He appraises me, his eyebrows raised in surprise. I've always avoided him, his gruff nature more than I wanted to deal with, but now that his secret is out in the open and his son is happy, his abrasiveness has worn off. "Miss Chapman. It's nice of you to come."

I smile at him, he smiles at me, and a truce is born.

Jack shakes his head in amazement.

Emma introduces me to an excited woman who does turn

out to be her mother (blushing, she asks me for an autograph I scrawl on the back of a grocery receipt she dug out of her purse), and we sit at a large table covered with a stark white tablecloth and nibble on a sampling of chocolate desserts. We chat about Jack and Emma's wedding ceremony and the bridal shower Mia and Haisley are throwing for her. I don't know if I'll be invited or not. I don't feel on the outskirts of the group, but I wouldn't be here if Raff hadn't insisted on bringing me as his date.

I'm content, laughing, my hand on Raff's knee under the table, his fingers playing with my hair. Mia, Haisley, and Zoey include me in conversation, Emma suggests shopping before the big fundraiser, and a ball of something sad burns in my throat.

I can't have this.

Raff will find out the kind of debt I'm in, and he'll run.

We're both quiet on the drive to my apartment. The limo glides to a stop in front of my building and idles double-parked next to an SUV and a convertible. Raff says, "Invite me up."

I want to, but why pretend I can have something I can't?

"I wish I could, but I have an early morning, as usual. Raincheck?" I ask, forcing cheer into my voice. At least I have a valid excuse. It's past my bedtime, and he knows it.

The driver waits by the limo's door to open it, and Raff studies me through the dim light of the car. "Will you go with me to the fundraiser for the women's center? I've always been a huge supporter."

If I can consider spending time with him a professional move instead of turning it personal, then there's no reason why we can't do things in public. As Felix pointed out, the show expects me to go and having a date will help. "Okay. Thank you."

I turn toward the door, and the driver opens it to allow me to place my foot onto the street.

Raff grabs my wrist, his grip like a vise. "You never loved him."

It doesn't matter if I ever loved Jack or not. I can't have a relationship with Raff. I can't.

Tears threaten to fill my eyes, but I've had years of experience pushing them back. "I never loved him, Raff."

He doesn't loosen his grip on my arm. "Let me walk you up."

"No. Then I'll want you to stay, and I need my job."

Grinning, he says, "I'll let you off the hook this time. Goodnight, Nic."

"Goodnight. Thank you for tonight." I lean over and press my lips to his stubbly cheek.

He turns his head, and our lips meet.

I sigh.

When he said he wanted to spin Jack's dumping me, I had no choice but to accept. It helps Raff and I have always gotten along, boosting each other's careers over the years while we shared the same love of whiskey, thriller authors, and movies, and working with him to put out the flames of my reputation felt natural.

But it never went further than that. Until the night of Jack's party, I assumed, like everyone else, he and Emma had a thing.

"I can't."

He rubs his thumb over my lips. "I'm a patient man."

I smile sadly and slide off the bench and out of the limo. I push through the doors and step into my building's lobby. I don't look back.

The elevator carries me up, and I slip off my heels. There's one good thing about looking like shit: when you look like more shit, no one notices.

I don't turn on the light in my apartment, dropping my shoes and purse in the hallway. I need to wipe my makeup off, drink a glass of water, and go to bed. The makeup artist on set can only do so much.

Shuffling by the living room on the way to my bedroom, I feel him, his presence heavy. He sits on my couch, his ankle propped onto a knee, the red tip of his cigarette glowing hot.

"Hello, Veronica."

CHAPTER FOUR

Rafferty

I don't get any sleep. Not after a shot of whiskey, not after a hot shower where I take care of the want, the need, that built up at Emma and Jack's engagement party.

There's not a lot of opportunity to sate my sexual appetite, for lack of a better term, not discretely, and that matters most. I've had to tamp down the natural urges all humans have. It would have been easier for me if Emma and I had had a benefits part of our friendship going for us, but I'd try to think of her that way and my dick would hang limper than a deflated balloon. Even if she'd been willing, there was no chance.

Sitting next to Nic at the party, the breeze teasing me and blowing the delicate scent of her perfume my way while Heath and Zoey made gooey eyes at one another and Emma and Jack pawed each other, ramped up my sex drive to a very uncomfortable level. Heath and Zoey were particularly affectionate, still riding the high Paige was safe after she fell asleep in a closet and disappeared for over two hours during a frightening game of hide and seek.

It would have helped a lot if Nic had invited me up, but I also don't want my first time with her to be a desperate fuck. I want to enjoy her—I've craved it long enough.

Jack Durand hates me for my friendship with Emma, well, right back at him, the prick. If Nic and Durand had gone through with their engagement, I would have been as bad off as Emma—I only hid it better.

Drunk sex. I should never have brought it up.

The sun comes up, persistent like that, though I try to block it out, pressing a pillow over my face. It doesn't work. Blurry, I stumble down the stairs. Coffee's my best friend, and I wait impatiently for it to drip. Most of my day will consist of watching the social media sites and measuring the responses Nic and I going to Jack and Emma's party will elicit. Inevitably, the jokes we swapped partners will start, maybe even a four-some rumor here and there.

Emma's a sweetheart and Durand is a lot softer, easier to be around, and the social media feedback on their engagement has been positive, if not laced with surprise as neither hinted at any kind of attraction toward each other.

I don't have enough feedback to know what people think about Nic and me or how that public perception will affect her job. I'll keep a close eye on it for the next little while. I don't want anything we do to hurt her.

Undoubtedly, some people will think I picked up Nic because Emma suddenly became unavailable, but the fact is, I've had my eye on Nic for a long time. She might have eyed me back, but she was happy with Durand. Maybe I'll never know why she was willing to settle if she didn't love the guy.

Coffee helps clear the fog in my brain, but the handjob I gave myself last night far from satisfied me. A man doesn't find long-term gratification unless he's getting the real stuff on a regular basis and I'm nowhere near that. Booze will have to do. After noon, of course.

I get out of the car five blocks from the office. I need to stretch my legs, but my house is too far from *Talk of the Town* to walk the entire way. I don't need a penthouse like Durand, nor a yard like Emma's little apartment offered where she enjoyed sitting with a glass of wine and a book. I live in an abandoned warehouse I purchased years ago. High ceilings, spacious rooms. I bought the entire building for cheap, converted it into an enormous luxury house and host lavish dinner parties. No one knows I'm lonely as fuck. Emma filled in some of that, like I did for her, but there's nothing like waking up to a woman you love, who you know loves you back.

I catch my reflection in a women's boutique window, and I straighten the knot in my tie, a scantily-clad mannequin looking on, her eyes blank.

My cell chimes, and my brother's name glows on the black screen. The little green button to answer the call mocks me. Reese and I get along okay. I've been called a scumbag doing what I do, and he's a scumbag of a different variety.

"Reese."

"Yo, bro," he says, full of jovial good cheer. Life is good for Reese Clark. Family favorite, killer looks, money to burn, and though I would never admit it to his face because his ego is already the size of Texas, smart as fuck.

I grimace. He's a couple of years younger than me, Mom popping us out one after the next and calling it good. I'm surprised she took the time at all, though rumor has it she was on the phone while pushing me out, and she gave birth to Reese on the family jet thinking she could squeeze in a dinner at the White House before she went into labor. At least I was born in a hospital, and I've always used it to gain the upper hand when being the older brother didn't help.

Trying to refrain from resorting to my usual rude behavior, I say, "What can I do for you?"

"You still going to the mud factory?"

"It's not slinging mud if it's true," I calmly reply.

"So you say, but I doubt you want your secrets all over the interwebs."

"Don't do it if you're ashamed of it."

"Ah-huh. So that's a yes, then."

I sigh. Did I mention my parents hate I started *Talk of the Town* from ground, er, mud, up? They're not proud of me and what I've created from scratch.

"You're not any different. What's up?"

"Calling to tell you I'm engaged. You wanna fly out here for drinks?"

"You and Belinda?" I ask, not surprised.

They met at Harvard, and she's as ambitious as our mother, her phone surgically attached to her ear. At least that's something I can appreciate about Nic. She's ambitious too but knows how to unplug and live life. Never once at Jack and Emma's party did she check her phone. Hell, I'm not sure she could have fit it into her tiny purse. She was in the moment, laughing with Mia and Haisley, talking wedding dresses and boutiques with Emma and her mom, who was delighted to finally meet her. I appreciate a woman who knows when she has to turn it on but can be self-aware and kind enough to turn it off. I already feel sorry for Reese and Belinda's kids.

"Melinda, and yeah, the 'rents are thrilled."

Shit. I feel sorry for Reese and *Melinda's* kids.

I'm sure Mom *is* thrilled Reese is marrying her clone. I can't wait to see them for Christmas.

I love my family, but goddamn, there's more to life than work.

"Yeah, sure, one of these days."

"You just don't want to hear Mom bitch at you. She's not happy with what you've been doing. Especially since you're not BFFs with Emma anymore."

"How'd you hear about that?"

"CNBC. Did a whole thing on Jackson Durand. Had an analyst dissect what his marriage will do to Variant. Now there's a rich fucker."

"Just because you're rich, that doesn't mean you're happy," I say automatically.

"He is now that he's engaged. Emma's a cutie. You sure you never tapped that? What are you, gay?"

"Would that bother you, Reese? If I brought home a man?"

"Hell, no, I'm woke."

"Really? I had no idea you cared about Black Lives Matter."

"Bro, *all* lives matter."

Jesus Christ.

"Is this the only reason you called? To rub my nose in yours and Emma's engagements?"

"Nah. I wanted to say hi, and to tell you Dad's planning to call in a couple of days."

Fuck. Reese's call was only the tip of the iceberg. If Mom really has decided she's not happy with me running *Talk of the Town*, she won't let up. Dad will call next, then she'll call me herself, or God forbid, she'll fly out here to talk to me in the guise of visiting Aunt Caro. Shit.

"What the fuck does Mom want me to do?"

I'm still standing in the middle of the sidewalk, four blocks from my office, all my cussing earning me dirty looks from pedestrians on the way to their own jobs. I pinch the bridge of my nose. I feel a headache coming on, and I only wish it were due to lack of sex.

"You know what. Come home and work for the family firm."

"Reese," I say, dread building in my gut.

"I know, but you were friends with Emma and she was giving you a pass. She was hoping you'd marry her and move up here, but that didn't pan out. You sling mud for a living, man, and she's done with it. Listen, I gotta get going, I'm having breakfast with Judge Chamberlain, but Dad's up next, and then you know what happens, and ain't no one wants to deal with that."

Yeah. She'll peel the skin off my bones. You thought Ramsay Bolton was bad? He doesn't have a damned thing on my mom.

"Thanks, Reese," I say, sincerely. It's always nice to have a heads up. "I'll visit when I can. Congratulations to you and Melinda."

"Thanks. I know you won't tell Mom. She's already knocked up. We need to get married fast, and I hope you'll be there and stand up with me."

"Yeah, yeah. Sure. I'm already doing wedding sh—stuff for Jack and Emma. Count me in."

"Thanks, bro. Talk to you later. Be a good boy."

The line disconnects.

You know what hits me harder? It's not that Mom is going to call me in a few weeks and bust my balls, it's that my little brother has what I want. Not so much the job, though he's a famous criminal defense attorney in his own right. No, I don't know Belinda, I mean, Melinda, well, but my brother's gonna have one big happy family and I'll be slinging mud and exposing assholes who can't keep it in their pants.

At the office, my bloggers who work for me are typing away, throwing their own handfuls of mud.

I dive into looking for news about Nic, and for once in a very long time, I sit at my desk, unsettled.

————

Nic's doing her thing, and I do mine. I try to resist turning on *Rise and Shine, Bridgeport!* but it's background noise, and I like hearing her voice.

A handler for a couple of soap stars who are traveling through Bridgeport and have a slot on Nic's show tomorrow morning calls and asks if I want access to interview them. I say sure because I never turn down an interview that will drive traffic to the e-zine. They're the infamous couple of the hour. Life imitating art, they play a married couple on *Shattered Yesterdays*, and recently he was caught with his pants down like his character, Remington Harris, a man with the worst luck I've ever seen. Everyone wants him dead—on the show, as far as I know. Not that I watch *Shattered Yesterdays*, but when you narc for a living, sudsy soap news isn't that far behind.

I catch a short break for a late lunch, eating a ham and Swiss cheese croissant I grabbed from the deli down the street. My computer monitors are up and running, just like they always are, and Justin, one of my streamers and jack-of-all-trades, spots Nic walking down the sidewalk to her building. After a morning of filming, she looks tired, but we did stay at Jack and Emma's party later than I expected we would. There's a slump to her shoulders, and I want to cuddle her in my lap, smooth her hair, and tell her to go to sleep. She wouldn't let me do that, and a phone call will have to suffice.

On my screen, in real time, I watch her dig her phone out of her bag and look at who the caller is. She reads my name, and Justin's close enough I can see the slight smile.

Before she answers, I text him. *Keep your camera on her.*

For sure, boss, is his quick reply.

"Raff," she says, having no idea I can see her.

Exhausted but gorgeous, she's dressed in black heels, a black pair of slacks, and a white blouse that looks like it could have grey pinstripes in the material. Justin's close, but far enough away she doesn't know she's being watched.

"Hey, dollface."

She presses a finger to her lips. "Hi."

Her mouth moves on my monitor faster than her voice comes through my phone.

"Thanks for last night," I say, watching her step toward the building and lean against one of the cement rails that lead up to the door.

"I had a good time. Emma doesn't need to be nice to me, but she is. I don't know her well, and I was surprised."

The shifting dynamics will take some time to get used to, and I say, "She's not like that."

"I know that now, and I appreciate it. Are you at work?"

"Yeah. There's a reason for this call, not only to hear your beautiful voice."

She smiles wryly, and Justin zooms in a bit. It will be interesting to hear the gossip speculation from anyone who's watching the streaming and wondering who Nic's talking to.

"And what's that?"

"I'm interviewing Tamara and Damian tomorrow afternoon for the 'zine. Their agent suggested the four of us go to dinner tomorrow night being they've got a couple minutes on *Rise and Shine, Bridgeport!* and somehow he found out we're a thing. Photo-ops, you know, not to mention, it would be good for you to get out and do more without Durand."

"We're a thing, huh?" she asks.

"I'd like to be."

She steps up two of the stairs and looks over her shoulder. She catches sight of something that's outside the camera's view, and she stumbles, her hand grappling for purchase against the handrail.

A gentleman trotting down at the same moment catches her arm and steadies her.

I text Justin, *Don't take your camera off her. What did she see?*

"Thank you," she says, and he nods and continues down to the sidewalk.

There's someone leaning against a light pole a block down, smoking.

Man or woman? I ask.

Male. Tall. He's got his eye on her.

"Raff, I can't. I can't move this fast."

"Dinner then, nothing more."

Do you know who it is? I type quickly.

"All right. But only because the producers will be happy."

I've never seen him before.

"I'll take what I can get. Get some sleep."

"I will. Raff . . ."

"What is it, dollface?"

"Thank you."

She's standing on the middle step of the staircase leading up to her building's front doors. Her silver hair is blowing in the breeze, the afternoon sun warming her back.

I lose a little piece of my heart in those few seconds we're connected on the phone, watching her unfiltered movements, her reaction to my voice.

"Anytime, Nic. I mean that."

"I know."

She looks over her shoulder again, disconnects, and hurries into the building.

I call Justin. He's one of the several guys on my team who walks the streets catching Bridgeport's elite going through their daily routines. I have more footage of Durand and Heath Novak walking from the gym to the pub next door than I know what to do with.

"You don't know who that was," I ask to be sure. Whoever it was scared Nic, and I don't like it.

"No. He's not a celeb."

"Okay. If you catch him again, get as close as you can. She knew him, didn't like him, and I want to know who it is."

"Got it."

I spend the rest of the day reading articles about Tamara and Damian (or as the sleazier rag mags like to call them, Tamian), the allegations he's cheating and his denials, claiming he was "in the wrong place at the wrong time" when the photos were taken. I rub my hands over my face.

They call it mudslinging for a reason.

Everyone's dirty.

———

I sound like a user when I whine about not having Emma to hang out with anymore. Christ, if we weren't at work, we were together, and even after a month, I still haven't adjusted to attending events alone or spending an evening by myself.

I'm never alone, *alone.* The second I step into a venue I'm swarmed by people who want their fifteen minutes of fame on the e-zine. Being famous for being famous, as Reese loves to accuse me of, definitely has its perks, but I've always been one who can be lonely even if they're standing in a room full of people and searching out a celebrity's bar's grand opening hoping to expand his career off the screen or scouting a gallery showing to write about who buys the most expensive pieces doesn't quite fill the hole Emma's engagement made the day Jack Durand asked her to marry him.

Nic helps, but if she decides she doesn't want anything with me, I won't have an excuse to stay in Bridgeport. My mother, if she can look up from her phone for five seconds, will admit she's a romantic, and she was pulling for Emma and me to get married, something I told her many times would never happen. She decided she'd rather hope for that than give me permission to stay in Minnesota and run my mudslinging business. My time is running out, but short of telling her to shove it where the sun don't shine like Aunt Caro told their parents, I'm out of options. It's expected I use my law degree, and Mom won't rest until I am in some capacity.

Right now, the only thing I use my law degree for is keeping *Talk of the Town* out of hot water legally, but that's not good enough for my family.

I spend an uncomfortable, and unwelcome, evening alone sipping whiskey and trying to read (even I need a screen break sometimes), and having a full day ahead of me is a godsend.

The next morning, drinking coffee at my desk, the reassuring clicking of keys echoing to me from the bloggers' cubbies, I watch Tamara and Damian chat with Nic and Felix. They don't touch on Damian's alleged cheating, but the couple won't be so lucky with me. Their agent gave me permission to ask whatever I want, and I want to know the truth. If he's lying to me, I'll be able to see it on his face, and I scribble notes about his body language and hers. They both hold large, sturdy coffee mugs decorated with the show's logo and gossip with Nic and Felix about their careers and their longevity on the show, both of them having started out as teens and growing up literally, on screen.

Nic, for all the shit Durand dumped on her in the past few weeks, looks better than she has in a long time, but I don't know if I can take credit for that. She might have popped a sleeping pill and slept from the second we said goodbye yesterday afternoon to the minute she had to wake up this morning, and if she did, I'm glad. Her skin sparkles and her eyes are bright. Her hair glitters in a sheet of silver stopping at her shoulders, and for a moment I imagine wrapping my hands in it and tilting her head in the exact way I want to devour her mouth.

Tamara and Damian stop by my office after their guest spot on Nic's show. I don't film them—they've already been there, done that. My interviews, the big ones like this, are text only. I record our conversations as backup to my memory, and tonight at dinner if one of my guys grabs a decent clip of us eating, I'll add it to the interview as bonus content, but there is something to be said for pen and paper.

We settle into my office's conversational area, water bottles and a fruit tray sitting on the table between us.

"You looked good on *Rise and Shine, Bridgeport!*. What brings you to the city?" I ask to get us started.

We chat for over an hour, and I click off the recorder, my mouth dry from all the talking. Damian stands with his arm outstretched for a handshake and says (off the record), "Thanks, man. You know, not one fucking person listened to me the way you did. They already had their judgments lined up in a row, so ready to knock me down."

Shaking his hand, I say, "You told me the truth, and that's all I wanted."

"Not everyone wants to believe the truth," he says, tangling his fingers with Tamara's and nudging her toward my office door, eager to leave now that the interview is done, "but you did. Dinner's on us tonight. You and the woman from the talk show this morning, right?"

"Not like that," I say.

Tamara pouts. "Too bad. You guys would look cute together. I need a nap. Damian?"

"I got you, honey. Let's go."

Their handler meets them at the elevator, and I watch them disappear, the doors gliding shut, hiding them from view. I spend the rest of the afternoon typing up the interview from the recording and my notes.

I stay at the office until it's time to meet the soap star couple at the restaurant, and I pick Nic up at her building, starving for more than only a meal. She's downstairs waiting for me again, and I'm tempted to ask if she's being polite or if she doesn't want me to come up for other reasons. When we were dumping water all over the fire Durand made of her career, I wasn't thinking with my dick, and she wasn't thinking *about* my dick. If she doesn't want me in her apartment because there's a bed in there, she's thinking of me as more than her PR manager, and I'll take it.

I double park and round the hood to let her in.

"You're driving?" she asks, sliding into the seat of my SUV.

"Sure. Sometimes I do, for fun." I lean in and rub my nose over the shell of her ear. "What I'm really hoping for is after dinner we drive out of the city and find a dirt road and park."

"Park and do what?" she asks, her mouth twitching.

"We can move into the backseat . . ." I murmur, my hand to her cheek, "and play checkers."

"Only if I get to be black," she whispers and turns her head, brushing my lips with hers.

"Anything you want, dollface," I say, slipping my tongue into her mouth.

Nic sighs and sinks into the kiss, threading her fingers through my hair.

The emotions I felt watching her talk to me yesterday

swamp me, and I wrap my arm around her back, pulling her as close to my body as I can.

Too many minutes later, I reluctantly pull away. Tamara and Damian's interview will bring in a lot of traffic from the soap crowd, and I can't afford to tick them off because I want to neck with my, hmm.

"We'll have to reconvene at a later time." I slam her door shut and walk around the truck's front. Settling behind the wheel, and I fasten my seatbelt.

"Do you watch *Shattered Yesterdays?*" she asks.

Chuckling, I meld into the sparse traffic on her street. "No. You?"

"*Rise and Shine, Bridgeport!* is on the same channel, and sometimes it will play on the TV in the dressing room while we change. Do you ever feel like you're in a soap opera?"

"Rich people fucking around? Not especially, though I can see the similarities."

"I think Emma and Jack's surrogacy plot happened last year," she says.

Twisting my lips, I flick her a wry glance. "Really? I can't imagine that ended well."

"Not for the characters, no. Sperm mix-ups, labor complications. They really strung it out."

"I can see that. It's a shitstorm in real life. How about you? Your life OTT?" I ask, teasing her.

I thought it would bring a smile to her face, but she casts a glance down at her lap.

"Sometimes I wish I could leave it all behind."

Tangling her fingers with mine I say, "Nic. You can't run. Everything will follow you. I learned that the hard way."

"What are you running from?"

"Family. Responsibilities. The best you can hope for is that you find someone to share those things with, so life isn't so hard."

"What if that's impossible?"

I don't know what she's getting at, why she thinks she has problems she can't escape from. It can't have to do with money, but maybe it does. Nic does well financially, hosting the show for the past handful of years. She doesn't seem like she spends a lot— her work schedule keeps her from jetting off on vacation every other weekend. Unless she has a jewelry collection that would put the Queen to shame, it's not money that concerns her.

"Think like a character in a soap. What would they do?"

"They would go through with it. The writers have set it up for them to have no choice."

Go through with what? I want to ask, but I know enough about soaps and their characters' impossible choices to say, "Then maybe you should. See where it leads."

"If I ever disappear, then that's what I did."

Christ, I think my heart stops. "Nic."

"No. You're right. Sometimes you have to do the hard part."

I pull under the restaurant's canopy and a valet doesn't waste any time opening Nic's door, stealing the precious seconds I needed to ask what the fuck she meant.

I surrender my keys, and pressing my hand to her lower back, I escort her into the restaurant. It's classy, cream and cherrywood, water dripping down glass panels, the sound trickling over classical music, chandeliers that resemble lit-up piles of sticks casting a dull orange glow over the room.

Tamara and Damian are already sitting at a corner table, and seeing us approach, Damian sets his napkin aside and stands.

I hold out the chair across the table from Tamara for Nic, and she sits, smiling at me in thanks over her shoulder.

"I love your hair," Tamara gushes over a basket of rolls. "I wanted to tell you this morning, but I didn't have the chance. Is it easy to maintain? How did you decide to try it?"

I want to hear the answer too, and I sit and lean in, resting my arm on the back of her chair.

Damian picks up a small leather menu, and he splits his attention between the wine list and Nic's answer.

"Oh, well, thank you. It's kind of over the top," she says, quirking her lips at me, "but I grew up poor in a little town quite a few hours north of here. When I was twelve, I won a gift certificate to a local salon. I went to redeem it, and she asked me what I wanted. I didn't know. I was so tired of being an outcast, passed over. I said, 'I want to be different.' 'I can do that,' she said, and two hours later, I had silver hair. I was a blonde before, so maybe she didn't have to put too much effort into it, but I do know the total would have cost more than the gift certificate was worth. I saw what she did, and I cried. She was afraid I hated it, but I thought she turned me into an ice princess, and from that second forward I promised myself I would never change it back."

Durand had it half right when he warned me about Nic's wall. It's not only a wall, she's locked herself in a castle's turret, high above anyone who can hurt her.

"I love it. It suits you."

"Thank you. I had to babysit, clean houses, anything I could to earn money to keep it up. I never had enough, but the stylist never said anything. I think somehow she knew I needed her. It gave me confidence. I did better in school, and I won scholarships to go to college. I majored in journalism and bounced around a few smaller morning talk shows before I landed *Rise and Shine, Bridgeport!*. That stylist opened up a whole new world for me."

A server interrupts our conversation and asks what we'd

like to drink. Damian orders champagne. Tamara wiggles happily, and he pushes back a smile of amusement.

We wait in silence for the sommelier to return with the bottle, and Damian sips first and nods his approval. The sommelier fills our glasses and leaves the bottle in a champagne bucket at the edge of our table.

Tamara resumes our conversation, saying, "I love stories like that. We got into acting similarly. We were both in the school play—"

"Plays," Damian interrupts, brushing his wife's cheek with his thumb.

She laughs. "Plays. And our director always said we would go on to be famous. I don't think without his support and encouragement we would have had the guts to try."

Damian nods. "We did the same thing you did. Moved to LA from a sleepy little beachside town. I was so in love with Tamara by then, I said, if I don't make it and you do, I will support you no matter what."

"Chivalrous," Tamara says, picking up the story, "but I had the same fears. I mean, look at him. There's no way he wouldn't have *not* made it. We auditioned for *Shattered Yesterdays*, and it was like a dream when both of us landed roles. They were small at first, walk-ons, and we had to wait tables and bartend to pay the rent, but we grew older and our parts got bigger, and now we're members of the show's anchor cast."

"How does that feel, to grow up and into a career together?" It's not the same question I asked during my interview with them earlier this afternoon, but it's close.

Tamara sips her champagne. "I think, if we couldn't have traveled the journey together, our relationship would have suffered. That thing with him, I know what it's like. It's not the first time either of us has been accused of cheating, and it won't be the last. But we know how it works, we know what to believe and what we shouldn't. Damian would never cheat on me, but if I wasn't part of *Shattered Yesterdays?* If I wasn't on set with him every day? Maybe there would be doubt there because how do you know?"

"You have to decide to trust the other person," Nic says. "If you can't, there's not much of a relationship, is there?"

"It helps to know the environment, the landscape, but yeah, I don't think Tamara gives herself, or our relationship, enough credit. The second those pictures came out, she said, 'Who's setting you up?' Not one damned thing about blame, or why I was there in the first place. 'Who's setting you up?' It was that simple with her." Damian looks away and clears his throat, sighing in relief the server chooses that moment to place our meals in front of us.

Nic cuts into her fish. "What if one of you would have found success but the other hadn't?"

With her time on the show, she knows how to keep a conversation going, and I relax. It's nice not having to lead, and listening to them chat, I enjoy the steak I ordered.

Under control, Damian says, "If I would have, and she hadn't, I would have given it up. Moving to LA was a lark, fame and money a byproduct of having a good time. But I wouldn't have those things without her. Raff says you aren't together, but you feel together. Wouldn't you give up *Rise and Shine, Bridgeport!* for him?"

Her lips tremble.

"Don't answer that, Nic." I grin at Damian. "We're a little newer at this than you and Tamara. Talk me through what your PR firm did for you. I might pick up some tips."

I rub Nic's thigh under the table. I don't want her to give up anything to be with me, and I don't want to give up anything to be with her. I like where I am, what I'm doing. I don't want to be a workaholic like Reese, marrying my mother's clone.

I'll fight to keep *Talk of the Town* until my hands are bloody. Aunt Caro didn't need our family's money, and I don't need it, either. She and my uncle lived simply, and once *Talk of the Town* brought in more than I could spend, I would (and still do) slip her cash to buy whatever she wanted to treat herself.

The topics turn to lighter things after that, and Nic shakes off the tension Damian's question caused.

Nic and I order different desserts, and keeping in mind this dinner is as much for her and her reputation as it is for *Talk of the Town*, I feed her a bite of my cheesecake. She reciprocates, and I nibble at a bite of a chocolate concoction from her fork, wishing it were her lips instead. Damian and Tamara smile over coffee, and people sitting close to us try and fail to discretely snap pictures.

Tamara tells Nic a story about a snotty makeup artist on the soap's set, and Nic laughs. She lifts her coffee cup to take a sip, her eyes roaming the dining room, and blood drains from her face.

I quickly look in that direction, but I don't see anything, or anyone, out of the ordinary. "Are you all right?"

She shakes her head as if to clear it. "Yeah. I thought I saw someone."

"We have a couple of guys outside. You're safe here," Damian says, signaling for the check. "We really appreciate you talking with us today, Raff. I've done a lot of interviews since this whole thing, and no one listens. They hear what they want to hear. Your interview will hopefully put it all to rest. Tamara and I might know what really happened, but dealing with it is still stressful."

"You're welcome. I'm not about the money or traffic to the site. *Talk of the Town* is about the truth and always has been."

Damian signs the slip, and we all push away from the table.

Outside, we pause under the canopy and wait for the valet to retrieve my truck.

It's another late night for Nic, and she looks exhausted, lines pinching her mouth and eyes.

We say a round of quick goodbyes, and a limo sweeps Tamara and Damian away.

"You okay?" I ask, wrapping my arm around her.

"Yeah. Tired."

I kiss her temple. "I'll get you home."

She's quiet in the truck, and I double park around the corner, the vehicles' owners most likely in for the evening. "Let me walk you up."

"Raff—"

"I won't ask to stay." I can hear the frustration in my voice, and Nic can hear it too, but all she does is smile sadly.

We're silent in the elevator, and at her door, I trap her against the wall, my hand cradling one side of her face. "Are you afraid of me? I would never hurt you."

"You don't understand," she cries, trying to push me away.

I don't budge an inch. "I want to, Nic. What are you so scared of?"

She meets my eyes, tears clinging to her lashes the way I want to cling to her and beg her not to shut me out.

Her voice is barely a whisper and I hear it with my heart more than my ears.

"Everything."

She ducks under my arm, unlocks her door, and there isn't a sound on her side besides the soft *snick* as she slides it back into place.

CHAPTER FIVE

Veronica

I lock up. I can feel Raff standing on the other side of my door, but I don't break down and cry. If I do, I'll never stop. I clean off my face, drink two glasses of water to counteract the champagne I drank at dinner, and go to bed. The extra sleep I was able to get last night didn't do any good. I could sleep twelve hours a night and it wouldn't do any good. My life is fucked, and it shows with every stress line on my face.

Tossing and turning, I try to fall asleep, but I don't feel safe. I should have let Raff inside. He wouldn't have wanted sex if I didn't want to give it to him, content to be with me, but I don't want to use him because I'm scared. I don't know how Blaise Barker broke into my apartment. How many times he did before that I don't know about, or how many times he will now that he knows I know he can. The night I found him on my couch, he scared the shit out of me, dark and dangerous, the power of his family behind him, my father promising him I was his.

He's giving me time to come to terms with the arrangement, but I never will. He'll have to carry me out of my apartment, out of my *life*, kicking and screaming, and he's powerful enough to do it.

I swear I saw him tonight at dinner. He blended in with the other patrons wearing his dark, expensive suit, his hair swept back revealing features that are sharper than a hawk's, but I did a double take, and then he was gone.

Tamara and Damian's security wouldn't have been a match for Blaise Barker.

I have a crappy night's sleep (but what else is new), and I drag my ass out of bed. Somehow, I find enough calm and grace to film today's show, Felix asking me on air about the dinner with Raff, Tamara, and Damian, the producers flashing paparazzi photos of us laughing and sipping champagne. He's resentful that with my connection to Raff I'm invited to things like that. It boosts my career and the show, but not him. He tries to control it, but luckily, his scowl when he speaks to me looks sexy on camera. He needs to find his own leverage. He's good-looking and friendly and he should have no trouble finding a high-profile woman to date if that's what he wants.

I catch a taxi home, but I don't linger on the sidewalk. The sun is warm, and I want to stand outside and absorb it into my bones. I'm cold, always so cold, and the only time I'm not is when I'm with Raff. I spend a quiet Friday night alone, but I'm jumpy, and even a hot bubble bath and a bottle of wine doesn't help me relax.

The sun starts to shine behind the blinds, lightening my bedroom, and I'm still awake. I didn't get an hour of sleep, though I went to bed as early as I usually do, and I'm tempted to lie in bed all day. Raff texted me right before midnight and reminded me of the fundraiser next weekend and asked if I was still willing to be his date.

Honestly, with Blaise breathing down my neck and my father egging him on, I don't know if I'll be around for it.

I use the free Saturday to run errands—dropping clothes off at the dry cleaners, stopping at the grocery store on the corner, picking up more vitamins at the pharmacy. I pay bills online and book a hair appointment to freshen my color. I should text Raff and thank him for asking me to dinner with Tamara and Damian, but I don't. I don't want to need him. I needed Jack and now my life is tilted sideways. A woman needing a man will always bring trouble to her door. It's a lesson my mother tried to teach me, but I was too young to understand. I do now. A woman can't count on anyone but herself.

My father calls, interrupting me eating an unappetizing salad for dinner. I didn't have the motivation to fix a real meal. I should have found a place to go—especially since I didn't go out last night. A quick glance at *Talk of the Town* would have given me ten different choices, but I'm too tired to pose for the camera. Any camera. Staying home in my pajamas on a Saturday night is a luxury I won't be able to enjoy for much longer.

Against my better judgment, I answer. "Hello." My voice is flat.

"Annie," my father says.

"Don't call me that. It's not my name."

"Because you're too ashamed to be associated with your own goddamned family."

"You got yourself into your own fucking mess, and you expect me to get you out like you always do. I'm tired, Daddy. I can't do this."

"I want out, and they won't let me without your help."

"Maybe you should have thought of that before." I dump

my salad bowl and its remains into the sink. I'm not hungry anymore.

"I was doing what I had to do to take care of you. You're punishing me for doing my best." Bitterness fills his voice, but I don't buy any of it.

"You weren't doing it for me. You were doing it for the fame, the power, and the money, and you thought if you wanted out all you had to do is say 'I retire' and submit your form to Social Security. Guess what? It doesn't work like that. They want me so you keep your mouth shut."

"He'll treat you well, you know that."

"Like hell I do."

"He told me he went to see you. Did he hurt you?"

Blaise sat on my couch, calmly smoked his disgusting cigarette, and leered at me through the dark. "I'm getting impatient. You thought you could squeeze your little ass out of this with an engagement to Jack Durand, but that didn't work, did it, sweetheart? Now you're hanging on someone new, but let me tell you, Veronica, there's nowhere for you to go. Ma doesn't like this. She's getting antsy, and we might stop cooperating with your daddy dearest if you can't take this seriously. It's not a game, and I am more than willing to prove to you it's not."

He stood from the couch then and letting his cigarette hang from his lips, he framed my face in his hands. He's Jack's age, and years ago, when my father first started working for Mollie Barker, I had an eyewitness account of how cruel he could be to helpless things.

I am helpless, and he knows it.

His eyes never leaving mine, he slowly pulled his cigarette from his mouth using his thumb and three of his fingers. My heart thumped so hard it felt like it was going to leap out of my chest. He'd have no qualms using it for more than a nicotine fix.

Blaise kissed my forehead. "I have a soft spot for you,

Veronica. I won't hurt you unless you give me a reason. Don't," he said, and with that, he let himself out of my apartment and I dropped to the floor in a pool of fear.

"No, but you know he could. Do you know what happened to his first wife, or his second?"

He doesn't, and my father's silent. Susie Q, Blaise's first wife and rumored high-class escort, disappeared one dark and stormy night. The "official" story is she was driving herself home, and speeding on the wet road, flipped into a ditch. That would have made sense on a night like that, but her vehicle and body were never found. Blaise leveled up and Layla Barker, his second wife and runway model, disappeared without a trace. Her "official" story is Blaise filed for divorce and Layla moved to Paris. Only, no one can find her there, and no one wants to look too hard. No one knows what really happened to those women, but whatever did, that will be my fate when I marry him.

"I need to go to bed," I say over the silence.

"Stop fighting this. I want out."

"Maybe I should let them kill you. You seem to have no problem offering me as a sacrificial lamb." I say the words, but I'm no more likely to go through with it than Blaise letting me go free. I love my father, and until he tangled with the Barkers, he did his best by me. He kept me after Mom took off, but he could have disappeared too, leaving me to grow up in the system. He loves me, he just loves himself more.

"You wouldn't do that."

I sigh. "No, I wouldn't. I need time to . . ." To what?

"I'll keep working for Ma, but your time is running out, Annie. Blaise wants you, and once he sets his eyes on something, you know he won't stop until he gets it."

"I know. I love you, Daddy. Be safe."

"Thanks, sweetheart. You do the same."

The conversation ends on a strangely normal note, a father and daughter catching up.

My phone's screen is blank for two seconds, and then it lights up with a text from an unknown number. *When do you have time to shop this week?*

My mind is already saturated with the nightmare of marrying Blaise Barker, and desperate and delusional thoughts of who would turn a simple, innocent shopping trip into something dangerous fill my brain. My fingers shake, and I have to retype the text three times before I can send it typo-free. *Who is this?*

Oh, sorry! Emma. Jack gave me your number.

My lungs release a shuddery sigh. For as long as Jack and I dated and Emma was his PA, there was never a reason for me to need her cell number. If Jack wasn't answering his cell or office landline, I called Emma's desk phone at Variant. If he didn't answer after business hours, I waited until he texted back. Our relationship was casual enough we didn't keep tabs on each other. I was a fool to think he'd marry me.

Emma will never know the panic she caused, and I try to keep my response light. *That's okay. Shop for what?*

Dresses for the fundraiser. Aren't you going with Raff?

I won't back out. I said I'd go with him, and I will. Not because the show expects me to, but because I like being with him. I'm skittish, and he thinks I'm still recovering from Jack's dumping me, but that couldn't be further from the truth. I don't want him getting tangled up in my dad's web, and being associated with me, that's exactly what will happen.

I have a dress.

I don't know what prompted me to shut her down. I'm not jealous she's with Jack. When we started dating, I knew he was in love with her. I didn't know then he wasn't acting on it because of his mother and what his father did to her, only grateful he was giving *me* his time and not her. Jack's a nice guy, we got along and he's good in bed, but he used me to hide from his feelings for Emma and toward the end, I used him to run from Blaise. There was nothing else between us.

There's a long pause, and then she types, *Oh, okay. I'll see you at the fundraiser then.*

Her tone sounds like I hurt her feelings, and I don't want to do that. Raff won't interfere if I don't want to play nice, but he'll be disappointed. What I want from him, I can't have, but that doesn't mean I need to alienate everyone in my life.

I sigh. *But that doesn't mean a girl can't have another, right?*

A dress for a fundraiser like this will cost a grand at least, but I can expense it to the show. They're the ones who want me to go. They can pay for it. Besides, it would be fun to have something new. The dress I planned to wear is a couple of years old and has already seen an event or two.

Emma sends a smiley face, but nothing more. Yep, I hurt her feelings.

I can shop after taping the show Wednesday. I could have said any day of the week, but Sundays are always off the table—Raff's told me Emma spends that day with her mother. Suggesting Monday or Tuesday and I would come off too eager, any later than Wednesday and we wouldn't have time to try again if we don't find what we're looking for.

I rub my forehead. Christ, Veronica, it's only shopping with your ex's fiancée. Get a grip.

Can we do a little after 3:00? she replies.

We? Who's we? *Who's we?* I ask.

What do you mean? Zoey, Haisley, and Mia are going with us but we all work later than you do.

I'm stupid. I'm stupid and tears fill my eyes. I've never had a group of girls to do things with. My ice-princess hair might have set me apart in a good way, giving me the confidence to do what I needed to do to get out of that shitty little town I grew up in, but it set me apart in a bad way, too. Kids went from calling me a poor tramp (they didn't understand that everyone in that godforsaken town was poor) to a snob, and then after, when competition for crappy talk show positions at small-time stations was fierce and no one took kindly to a pretty woman with silver hair. I didn't think much of it. I grew up alone, spent most of my adult years without a friend. *Rise and Shine, Bridgeport!* shoved me into the spotlight and I have enough acquaintances to fill a telephone book, but true friends. Nope. Can't say I've ever had one.

I take too long to answer.

Is that okay? she texts.

Yeah. Thanks for inviting me.

It's no problem. Zoey wants to meet at Saks. Around 3:15?

A later shopping trip will turn into drinks and dinner. I want with all my heart for this to be part of my life. Raff. Friends.

Perfect, I respond, my vision still blurred.

See you then.

Emma sends that text, and three more dots appear. I wait. They disappear, and I think I'm reading too much into our conversation, then they reappear. After a moment another text pops: *I'm glad you're coming with us. You have a lot of reasons to hate me.*

I laugh. Nothing like putting it out there. *I suppose my reasons are yours, too, so again, thanks for inviting me.*

She sends me laughing emojis. *I didn't think of it that way. Truce?*

Truce.

See you Wednesday.

With that, the texts stop, and I know she's done.

I could hate Emma Cox for being engaged to Jack, and I

could hate her for being best friends with the man I'm falling in love with. I could let that fester and drive an uncomfortable wedge into their (our?) entire group, or I can accept that she has relationships with both while she accepts I dated Jack for two years and that Raff and I are spending a lot of time together.

I'll enjoy her friendship, and Zoey's, and Mia's and Haisley's, and treasure it for what it is. Once Blaise makes good on his threats, and make no mistake, he will, I won't have the chance to hang out with friends, with anyone, ever again.

CHAPTER SIX

Rafferty

"**H**is name is Blaise Barker."

I'm sitting at my desk in my office, something I've started doing if I don't want to be alone but don't have any plans or anyone to do them with. I need to stop or my bloggers will think I'm accessible 24/7. My private life might be public for the sake of *Talk of the Town*, but I have limits, too. Sundays used to be my day to relax at Emma's mother's, but that privilege now belongs to Durand.

Not that I mind. I'll still see Marti Cox occasionally, and from what I've heard, he gets along with Marti as well as I do, which will thrill Emma. She wouldn't handle it well if her fiancé and her mother didn't like each other. If I'm being fair, there's not a female Durand couldn't charm, but I don't like him enough to admit it.

"Who the fuck is that?" I ask Justin. He knows his way around the internet and has skills that rival my own when it comes to ferreting out information he shouldn't have. If there's ever a piece that sounds not quite on the up-and-up but I'm already researching something else or in other ways occupied, Justin is my go-to for checking legitimacy. I'm not surprised he came up with something so quickly.

"Two-bit arsonist. Not much about him online, some newspaper articles, that's about it. Owns a few warehouses and a couple of shipping boats up in Fairfax near Cavern Lake."

"Arsonist?" I don't like the sound of that. Arson is personal and it hints at offense taken and revenge planned.

"Kid stuff."

Still don't like it. Kids grow up into adults.

"What about him and Nic?"

"No connection as far as I can tell, but that doesn't mean he's not a sick member of her fan club."

I wouldn't have considered that, Nic's job a pretty commonplace fact in my life, but now that Justin brings it up, it could be any deranged asshole who gets off watching her spar with Felix Rivera over coffee and Bridgeport gossip.

"Okay. Maybe he was only minding his own business."

"That's what I think," Justin agrees. "There's no way they could know each other."

"If you spot him on the streets again, let me know."

"Will do." He hangs up.

The chances of Justin seeing him are slim to none, even in the unlikely event the scumbag is stalking Nic. Justin isn't assigned to her (I would never do that now we're more than friends) and it was simply a freak thing he happened to be on her street after she was done taping her show.

I don't think it's anything, but it's puzzling why Barker's hanging around Bridgeport if he has business near Cavern Lake. Fairfax isn't far, but we're not close enough the drive would be a comfortable daily commute.

A half an hour later my cell chimes again, the ringtone I

assigned to Emma filling the entire floor. No one works on Sundays, not even my most dedicated (kiss ass) bloggers.

I tear my eyes away from an article I'm scanning that's more than thirty years old about a teenaged Barker caught doing things he shouldn't be doing. "Hey, baby girl," I answer, and then I wince. I need to stop calling her that. Durand's giving us a grace period, either by his own intelligence or Em telling him to back off, but it won't last long.

"Hey," she says, unaffected by my slip up, "I texted Veronica last night. She didn't seem keen on the idea of shopping with us, but I turned it around."

I can imagine what Nic was thinking when Emma asked her out for an afternoon of shopping. You know those videos of caged animals that feel grass or water for the first time? That will be Nic, joining Emma for an afternoon of shopping and later, drinks. Wait. "Us?"

"Now you sound like her. I can't go shopping for something like the fundraiser without Zoey, and Mia and Haisley."

I chuckle. Yep, I'd pay money to watch Nic go out for an afternoon. "Right."

"They'll be a good buffer. I doubt she would have said yes if it had been only the two of us. I don't think she likes me, Raff, so you can't be disappointed if nothing comes of it. She's her own person and can choose her own friends."

"It will help you're giving her a chance. The whole situation is awkward." And if I let myself, I still get royally pissed at Durand for letting it happen.

"Yes, well, we'll see how it goes. We need to clear the air, and once we do, maybe things will settle. Jack told me what he and Veronica talked about, and they admitted to using each other."

"What would she need him for?" Besides the money, and we've already been through that.

"Boosts her career, that's what he told me, and he was happy to help her."

"Jack never said why Nic wanted to marry him?"

Emma's silent for a moment, and I tense. Maybe Nic lied to me, and she's in love with the bastard after all.

"No, but I think he took it at face value. There's not a woman in the country who doesn't want to marry Jack, Raff."

I hear the fear. "He loves you, Em."

"I know. It all seems like a dream, but it helps he has the same fears as me. He checks up on me even if he won't admit to it."

"As long as it doesn't turn dangerous. I already told him I won't let him isolate you from your friends. You need more people in your life than only him."

"You know how it is. How often do you look to see what Veronica's doing? She's on TV all the time, and usually, it's live. You can't tell me you don't use your own website to keep tabs on her."

Shit. I'm never going to get anything past Emma. We've been friends for far too fucking long. "Got me, baby girl."

"Hmmm. Well, I need to get going. Jack and I are heading over to Mom's and after that, we're visiting Ron."

I sit back. "Now that's interesting. Is Claire back in town?"

"No, not yet. She said she's going to attend the fundraiser, though. Jack's a little afraid of what she's going to do once she finds out he and Ron are on speaking terms. I think if he had to choose between Ron and Claire, he'd choose his sister, but I don't want to put words in his mouth. He's still not used to talking to me about things like that."

"That you two are engaged and that he doesn't hate Ron is probably enough for him to deal with at the moment. Have fun at your mom's. Tell her I said hi."

"I will. Are you seeing Auntie Caro today? I miss her. You

should ask her to the fundraiser. Mom's all about seeing Veronica again, and I think she'd like to see Caro, too. We should all go."

I haven't fully switched over my Sundays to seeing Caroline since Jack asked Emma to marry him, but I've seen her more in the past few weeks than I have in a long time. Always content to simply be, Aunt Caro never gives me a hard time, reminiscent of the way she raised me. As long as I stayed out of trouble, she let me do my own thing.

"She's not into all that garbage, but I'll ask. Marti recognized Nic's lonely, and like she did for me, wants to take Nic under her wing. I don't think Nic realized it, but she's going to have an adoptive mom before long. Your engagement party was only the start. But if your mom's not up for that, I haven't hosted a dinner party in a while. We could do a family thing, something more casual at my place. Maybe invite Ron. He's not as grumpy as he used to be."

Emma laughs. "That's Mom. Nothing makes her happier than taking care of someone. A quiet night sounds fantastic and we should do it, whether Caro and my mom go to the fundraiser or not. Including Ron might be a little presumptuous, especially since we don't know how Claire is going to feel, but I appreciate the thought. I miss you, too, you know."

"I know. I miss you back. Stay out of trouble, baby girl."

"Now, there's no fun in that. Bye."

"Bye."

I disconnect the call slightly despondent, but the feeling grows weaker and weaker the more time that goes by. I had three years to prepare for it. I should have done a better job.

I field a few more emails before calling it a day. Damian thanked me again for the interview. They received a lot of good press from it, and with his handsome face all over the 'zine, I had more hits and subscriptions to the premium content than ever before. Going with my gut was a good choice. I email him a thank you in return, and after I click send, the open tab where I was reading about Blaise Barker catches my eye.

Nic didn't go anywhere last night, and it's unusual for her not to take advantage of a Saturday night. I should have asked her to go somewhere, but talk about her and Durand is slowly fading and going out doesn't seem as crucial as it used to be. The fundraiser will put an end to the gossip once and for all.

People are more excited to chatter about Emma, the richer, nastier socialites of Bridgeport declaring her an unsuitable match. Eventually, that will stop too, after real proof pops they're in love. Then the naysayers will twist it into a Cinderella story. No one can be happy with the truth, that Durand is just a man who fell in love with a woman who loves him back.

I bring up Nic's picture on my website's public feed. It's a random photo someone posted hoping for some likes—and getting them. She's standing on the corner waiting to cross, sunglasses shielding her eyes. The time stamp says it was taken sometime last week, but I don't care about that. I study her. The high-heeled sandals, the graceful curve of her calves. The skirt that stops right above her knees, the blouse, the bag that costs a small fortune. Her hair is a perfect curtain that shields one side of her face. Her posture is stiff, her lips not turned into a smile.

Can anyone really know someone?

"Who are you, dollface?" I ask Nic's photo.

I resist the urge to call her, and instead, shut my computer down and flip off the lights.

Standing on the sidewalk in the early afternoon sun, I debate going home or visiting Aunt Caro. All the old quotes run through my head about having to like your own company before being able to enjoy others', and misery follows you wherever you go if you're unhappy with the kind of person you are and what you're doing. It gives me pause. I've hated spending time alone since Emma crossed enemy lines, but it wasn't her job to prop me up.

I'm not unhappy with myself, and I do like my own company.

I'm dissatisfied with my family life. Reese rubbed my nose in it, announcing he's engaged to his pregnant girlfriend and his warning that Mom allowing me time to do what I like is drawing to a close, but I doubt my mother and I can reach a compromise.

I decide to visit Aunt Caro after all and hail a cab. She spends her Sundays at home like Emma's mother, and I find her lounging in the backyard reading. I flop into a chair next to her and let her finish the paragraph.

"Raff," she says, dog-earing the page. "You look tired."

"Not any more than I have been." I pause. "Why did you let Mom dump me on you?"

Her answer is immediate. "I wouldn't quite put it that way, but to answer your question, because you're family."

I shoot her a look. "I was a punk kid who couldn't stay in school. The last thing you needed was a twelve year old who could find trouble in the front yard."

"That's not true. Saul, bless him, had been gone for a couple of years by then. We never had children, and that had been my one wish when we were married. It never came to be, and it made me miss him more after he passed away. No one should die that young, and without leaving something good behind." Her fingers thrum against the hardcover, a killer's face leering at us from a novel based on a true crime. "When Barbie called and asked if you could live with me for a while, I said yes and thanked God for unanswered prayers. I don't think I would have had the emotional energy to help you find your way if I was already a single mother to my own children. I'll always remember you stepping into the baggage claim, a flight attendant fluttering right behind. You were such a scared little boy."

I was terrified that day, only having met Caro once or twice, and it built on the resentment the flight attendant couldn't let me find her on my own in the huge airport. A minor, I was to be handed off, my parents sent a receipt of delivery.

"Do you regret distancing yourself from the family?"

"Sometimes. You can't make an important decision like that without some regret. That Barbie considered me at all told me how desperate she was for a place to put you. She never approved of my simple life here, moving slow enough to smell the flowers and appreciate a sunny day. I love your mother, but she has a broom shoved so far up her ass the handle pokes out of her mouth."

I tamp down a laugh. Vulgar, but it describes my mother to a T.

"Even though she disapproved of it, disapproved of *me*, she realized a little distance could be a good thing. Not everyone craves the adrenaline high they get from working twenty hours a day. That we have people who do helps this country thrive, but the world wouldn't go around without different sorts of people, and you needed time. There's plenty of it here, and it gave you a chance to be a kid. You were at your happiest riding your bike around the neighborhood with Emma."

"Would you ever move back to Boston? Do you miss Grandma and Grandpa?"

She quirks her mouth and laughs. "I miss Barbie and Xavier, Reese's antics. My parents, not so much. When I was growing up, they were Barbie times ten, and my mental health couldn't tolerate it. They're still very much the same as they were the day I escaped. Your grandfather is going to die on the fourteenth hole of a heart attack, but he'll be proud because he'll have won a case that morning. The last thought going through his mind won't be me and Barbie, or his wife, or even a life well-lived, no, his last thought will be full of pride he convinced a jury his client was innocent, and it won't matter fuck-all if he was or not. Reese is growing up into the same, but I'm not surprised. Between the two of you, he was always your grandpa's favorite."

I never tried to relate to my mother's parents, and Aunt Caro's words don't hurt me. My father's parents are the same, attorneys and politicians, power-hungry, their eyes focused on the White House and the prizes inside.

She continues, "Not everyone is strong enough to live without family. You miss Reese, and you haven't seen your parents in a couple of years, but we create family with the people around us. Emma gave you more as a stand-in sister than I believe you would ever have gotten out of Reese if you'd stayed in Boston. The family you choose is sometimes more important, more powerful, than the family you're born into."

I sit back. That could very easily explain why I was never attracted to Emma. I considered her a sister, turned her into family the day we met.

"Reese is getting married. He called me the other day."

"To Belinda?"

"Melinda, yeah."

"They're a good fit. I hope they don't have children. They don't have time, and won't make time, to properly raise a child."

"Reese said she's pregnant, but I'm not supposed to tell anyone."

Caro *tsks* and flicks a glance at me, the lenses of her glasses reflecting the sun. "You may be taking in your own niece or nephew in a few years' time."

Laughing, I say, "I'd be a shitty role model."

"Don't be too sure about that. You know how to enjoy life,

and that has its own rewards. You also possess a good work ethic, something I'd like the credit for, if you don't mind. Your parents might not appreciate what you've built, but you give people a paycheck that helps them feed their families. You're doing what you love, what your mother should have let you go to school for in the first place. Don't be too quick to throw that away because of your mother's opinion or because Reese thinks you're wasting your time."

"Sometimes I feel like I should be doing more, but I don't know how."

"You are getting up there, have you thought of settling down?"

"I'm not that old."

"No, but I read the articles on your website, and one day you'll feel like Jack Durand, the world passing him by. Thirty-five, forty-five, there's not much difference. I saw the photos of you with Veronica Chapman and those two soap stars. You like her."

"Yeah, I do, but Mom and Dad would never go for it."

"My parents disliked Saul for the same reasons. A college professor wasn't enough for them, but he was a good man. We're not all meant to work nine to five, but your parents could never appreciate that a person needs more, needs to feed their creativity. You're an artist at heart, Raff, and so is Veronica Chapman. Now, no more talk. I can call your mother and tell her to lay off. I know how my family works. Reese, then your father, then your mother will rake you over the coals for not heeding the two warnings before her. Buy this old hag lunch, and we'll iron out a plan of attack."

I reach for her hand. "Thank you for always having my back."

"If you want to return the favor, then listen. Ten years from now, Reese will be caught up in a nasty divorce, their children pawns in a game no one will win, while you sleep in on Sundays with your wife and your kids munch cereal and watch cartoons at the foot of your bed. I want that life for you, and out of anything you can do for me for letting Barbie dump you on my doorstep, it's that."

I think about that for the rest of the day, and that evening, before Nic will go to bed for her early call time in the morning, I knock on her door.

She answers in her nightgown and robe, her face clean of makeup.

Without a word, I pull her into my arms and press my lips to the top of her head.

She stiffens for a moment and then wraps her arms around me too. We stand in her little entry way and I try to fight off a loneliness that I'll never be able to shake.

CHAPTER SEVEN

Rise and Shine,
Bridgeport!

Veronica

I don't know what to wear for an afternoon of shopping with the girls, and I choose a loose dress and flats. If I'm going to try on dresses, taking one off and putting it back on again would be easier than messing with slacks or a skirt.

The taxi driver drops me off in front of the huge store, the pristine glass doors sparkling in the sun, hurried pedestrians striding by. I walk into the gleaming lobby and instrumental music floats from the hidden speakers. I'm not a stranger to the store—I have my own personal shopper—but I've always browsed alone. I don't see Emma or anyone else, and I swallow a lump of disappointment.

They stood me up.

I turn to go. I don't feel like searching for a dress alone. I was looking forward to being included, to making friends, but they canceled without letting me know.

"I'm late, I'm late," Emma says, bursting through the front

doors, her hair streaming behind her, her cheeks pink. "Jack propositioned me in his office."

Surprised and relieved my ugly thoughts were unfounded, I blurt out, "Jack doesn't have sex in his office."

Laughing, she shoves her hair out of her face, her engagement ring glinting on her finger. "He does now."

Stunned, I laugh, too.

"Come on. Zoey texted me while I was in the car. They're upstairs in the dress section."

"Oh." I berate myself for thinking the worst of Emma and her friends.

Emma's a little shorter than I am, and I still have to trot to keep up with her. We ride the escalator to the second floor. "Did you just get here, too?"

"Yeah, but I thought . . ."

"We planned a different day and didn't tell you. We wouldn't do that."

"I'm sorry. I guess I don't understand this," I say, gesturing between us.

We step off the escalator, and my feet automatically know where to go.

She shrugs. "I think if you and Jack had been in a real relationship, he would have asked you to hang out with us. Well, not us, I mean, not *me*, but he's been friends with Heath and Zoey for years. You would have at least gone on doubles with them, and you never did."

"What does that have to do with anything?"

Tugging on my arm, she says, "You would already be friends with everyone, and it would be a non-issue."

"Yeah, but—"

Emma waves to Zoey, Mia, and Haisley who are already roaming from rack to rack.

"But what?"

"Don't you care I dated Jack for two years?"

She stops, finally, and meets my eyes. "Why did you want to marry him, Veronica? Everyone wants to know."

The real reason slips off my tongue. "Security."

"You needed him to be there for you."

Miserably, I nod.

"Is that why you're with Raff? Because you don't want to be alone?"

I press my lips together. "I'm not *with* Raff."

"Maybe not now, but I think he wants you to be. Are you using him, too?"

"No." I can barely speak.

Zoey, Haisley, and Mia catch the vibe from across the racks of dresses and they stop cooing over ballgowns to watch us.

"Are you in trouble?"

I avert my gaze and stare at the floor. Trust Emma to get to the bottom of it in five seconds. I don't answer.

Gripping my upper arm, she says, "If you need anything, Jack and Raff would be there for you in a heartbeat, you know that, don't you? All of us would do whatever you needed us to do. We care about you."

"I appreciate that, I really do, but there are some things you have to handle on your own."

"I understand, but sometimes when you feel alone, you think you *are* alone and that no one can help you. I don't want to wave Jack's money in front of you—you know better than me, probably, what his finances are like—but I have yet to come across anything money can't solve. He would help you, and I wouldn't say one fucking word."

My head snaps up. "You never swear."

"I know, but this is serious. I can't force you to accept our help, but please know that we would do whatever it took for you to be safe."

I'm tired of the conversation. She can't help me, and Jack's money is no solution. If it were, I would have asked instead of trying to trick him into marrying me. I'd have gotten better results. Jack has never cared about the billions behind his name, and chances are he would have given me as much as I needed. Contrary to popular belief, or what Emma wants to believe, money can't fix everything.

I stare at her, and she sighs. "Fine. I'll leave it there." Keeping her hand around my arm and leading me closer to to Zoey, Mia, and Haisley, she says, "Speaking of money, Jack said this afternoon is on him."

Haisley and Mia swoon, and I laugh. Zoey looks less than impressed, but she doesn't need the free shopping trip. Heath is wealthy in his own right. I don't need Jack's money, either. He didn't buy me dresses when we were dating, and I won't let him buy me a dress now. The salespeople here know my clothes go on the show's expense account, and it will be a moot point when we have our dresses boxed and we pay. I don't know what Haisley and Mia do for work, and come to think of it, I don't know how Emma paid for clothing before Jack asked her to marry him. She was always dressed in designer clothes whenever I would see her out with Raff. Maybe I'll find out later this afternoon if we head out for cocktails.

Emma and I haven't exactly set things straight, but I need to stop being suspicious of her motives. She's not out to get me. She wasn't that way before, and she's not that way now.

Besides, she has a point. Jack and I *didn't* double date with Heath and Zoey. In fact, they're little less than strangers and being included would have made Emma and me more than only the acquaintances that we are. Jack and I didn't follow the natural progression of a relationship because we weren't in a real one. I didn't lie, either. I care for Raff, and when he showed up on Sunday night and simply held me, the kind of future I could have with him flashed in front of my eyes. I want it, more than anything, but Raff doesn't have the power to get me out of my dad's mess. No one does.

I don't have an appointment with my personal assistant, and she's not working today. I'm a frequent enough shopper that the saleswomen know what I like, and one rushes to the back and comes out with a gorgeous black strapless tulle dress covered in silver-threaded flowers. "This will look divine with your hair," she gushes. "We unpacked it today."

I study the gown and run my fingers over the material. The fundraiser will be an important event for me. Showing up with Raff will cease the rumors about Jack and me once and for all. I'll be poked and prodded, weighed and measured. Nothing will go unnoticed, and I'll need to look perfect if I want the night to go exactly right. "Let's do it."

The other girls are in the fitting room, Emma trying on a deep blue dress that doesn't quite fit her correctly. Zoey's a bit luckier, trying on a gold sequined number with a slit up her leg. The saleswoman helps me into a fitting room, and without a thought, I slip off my dress. I won't be able to put the ballgown on alone and there's no point in being embarrassed.

The gown fits like the designer had me in mind, and I step out of the large stall and onto the dais in front of a three-way mirror.

"Holy God," Emma says from behind me wearing a black sparkly dress that's better suited for her. "You look great. Raff isn't going to be able to think about anything except sex."

"Emma," I say, blushing.

"What? Despite what everyone thinks, Raff and I never slept together. If he's getting some, I don't know where, and it wasn't from me. He's not going to be able to take his eyes off you."

"Thanks." It's nice she offered up that information without

me having to ask. I'm sure Jack has asked her several times—no one would believe that with as close as Raff and Emma seemed in the gossip blogs they weren't having sex—but her guileless expression holds no room for lies, lies of omission, or half-truths.

"Now that you have yours, can you help me? This is my first huge event with Jack, and I want to look perfect. I know everyone is going to say I'm not good enough for him, that I should have stayed his PA, but looking like I deserve to be on his arm will help."

Holding up my dress's hem, I step off the dais and grip her shoulders. "Jack is so in love with you, it doesn't matter what other people say. I have never seen him happier than at your engagement party. He bottled up a lot of pain for a long time, and you letting him release it and being there when he needs you is the only thing that matters."

She blows out a breath. "Thanks. I needed to hear that. Will you help me?"

"Sure. Let me change."

The other girls try dresses on forever, and three hours later, we spill out onto the sidewalk punchy from hunger and success. Mia and Haisley both took Emma up on Jack's offer, but in the end, Zoey paid for her own dress like I knew she would.

"Let's go drink, I need it after that," Emma says, hooking my arm with hers in an unfamiliar, but not an entirely uncomfortable, way.

We walk down the street to a little bistro done in stark white and dark wood. Emma orders bottles of wine and one of each of the appetizers off their menu. I melt onto the bench like a puddle and drain my first glass of wine in two gulps.

Emma pours more into mine and adds a little more to hers.

We all look at her.

She blinks. "What?"

"Aren't you pregnant yet?" Zoey asks.

"Not that I'm aware, though Jack's done his best," she says, blushing.

That turns us on to a conversation about babies, Zoey having the most to say on the subject.

"Will you and Haisley have children?" I ask Mia. It took me a long time to realize they were together and not merely friends.

"We've been trying to decide who should carry," Mia says, rubbing Haisley's arm. "Neither of us wants to miss the experience."

"You could take turns," Emma says, "or better yet, do it together."

Mia laughs. "What do you mean, together?"

"At the same time. I've heard about couples using the same sperm donor and then your babies can grow up together. We're old. It would have been helpful if Jack wouldn't have hidden how he felt about me. It's part of the reason we're not waiting. I don't want to be pregnant or taking care of a newborn after I turn forty."

"You'll have plenty of help, Emma," Zoey says, choosing from the appetizer platters and filling her little plate. "But I'm glad I had kids young. I don't know what my pregnancy with Paige would have been like if I'd been older. It was already difficult."

"She's adorable, and in a few years Gracie and Hil will be old enough to help babysit. We'll all do it for each other, right?" Emma asks, nudging me with her elbow. "After the babies are born?"

"Uh," I say, gripping my wineglass a little tighter. "I've never held a baby."

"Raff will be a wonderful father," Emma says. "He knows

what it's like to have it tough as a kid. He'll protect your children from that."

"Hey, now. How did we go from Mia and Haisley to me? I'm not having children." I say it stiffly, my lips frozen, but I can picture Raff as a dad, throwing a football to our son, or dancing with our daughter while she stands on the tops of his feet. He'll be an amazing father. I don't need Emma to tell me that.

She offers me a pained smile. "Sorry. Too soon?"

"Too at all."

"Oh. I'm sorry."

"It's fine."

An awkward silence falls over our table, and to break it, Zoey says, "Why don't you guys dress at my place on Saturday? The girls are coming with us, and they would be so excited if we put on our dresses and did our hair and makeup together."

"You're bringing Gracie, Hilary, and Paige?" Emma asks waving a hand at a server and circling a finger over our wine bottles indicating we need more. The server flashes her a thumbs up.

"It will be their first event. After Paige disappearing and Gracie asking if she could go since she's older . . . we thought it would be fun if we attended as a family. Besides, the subject matter is important. We need to support women's rights."

"That's terrific, and I think it's a great idea. Can we invite Claire? I would have asked her to shop with us, but she's not flying into Bridgeport until later tonight."

"Yeah, for sure. No problem."

"Thanks." Emma turns to me. "What do you think? Raff can pick you up at their place."

Zoey bounces on her chair, her cheeks rosy from the wine. "Let's do one better, while we dress, the guys can hang out and have a drink before we go."

"Oh," I say, flustered, not only from being included, but

Emma's acting like Raff and I are a couple, and I can't be, not with him, not now.

Emma sips her wine. "I'd ask him myself, but I have to stay on my side of the line. You two will work it out."

"What line?" I ask, pouring more into my glass. This conversation is a whirlwind of information.

"The line between you and Raff as a couple and me and Raff as friends. Jack would never say so, but he doesn't want me poking my nose into Raff's business anymore. What you and Raff do is up to you two, and I won't interfere. I promise."

I sag against the bench's cushion. "Emma, I don't want you to stop being friends with him. That would break his heart."

She smiles sadly. "Things change. I don't want to feel guilty I fell in love. You'll be there for him, won't you, Veronica?"

I tell her the absolute truth. "As much as I can be."

"Then that will have to be enough."

We finish dinner with more gossip, and to my utmost surprise, Zoey, Haisley, and Mia give me their numbers and ask for mine. They head out sooner than Emma and me, and Emma insists she pay the check even though I tell her I'm willing to split it with her.

"It's fine," she says, scrawling her name at the bottom of the slip. "But I should get home. Jack left the office at five and he's waiting."

I grab her arm on the way out the door. "Thank you for inviting me, seriously. I had a good time."

"And you found a drop-dead gorgeous dress. Tell me you don't imagine Raff peeling you out of—"

"Emma! Veronica! You two hanging out together?"

Flashes blind us, and my sight bursts from all the wine I drank while we munched and talked babies.

"Why wouldn't we?" Emma asks immediately, her footing

steadier than mine. "You don't work for Raff. What publication do you write for?"

"You remember me, Emma, from the play."

Her lip curls. "Bryce."

He grins. "You and Veronica, best buds? You don't care she was fucking your fiancé a little more than a month ago. What happened to, 'I'm nothing to Jack but his secretary?'" he asks in a false soprano.

I stiffen.

"Veronica is my friend. It's that simple. If you don't like it, stop following us around."

"You're not worried Durand is going to slip up? Old habits are hard to break."

Shocked and appalled, I can't get my mouth to move to defend Jack or myself. He would never cheat on Emma.

"I think," she murmurs, and the reporters lean in to pick up her voice on their phones, "that you better watch what you say. You don't want to make enemies, do you?"

Bryce smirks. "You think you can sic Clark on me?"

"I don't know about me, but with a remark like that, I know she can," Emma says, tilting her head at me. "Don't test it."

"You don't have anything to say, Veronica?"

I drudge up courage from somewhere. I never used to be scared. It was only after my father thought it was acceptable to trade my life for his that I retreated to a dark corner and never came out. "I've got plenty, but you know what? I'm not going to play your game by your rules, and I don't need you like you need me. Your mama should have taught you not to bite the hand that feeds you. Goodnight, *Bryce*."

Emma and I calmly walk away, and behind us, the other reporters taunt the humiliated blogger. "Burn!" "She told you, man." "I'm glad I didn't ask her that question." "See you in the unemployment line."

Around the corner, we lean against the building's wall laughing and trying to breathe.

"I'm sorry," I say, sucking in air. "That's all my fault."

"I don't know how it could be," she says, giggling. A black SUV glides to a stop in front of us. Someone is watching what we're doing. Raff, probably, but the truck belongs to Jack. I've ridden in one of his vehicles plenty of times. "People are nosy, and how we live our lives and who we're with will be put up for inspection forever. It will never be your fault. We can blame Jack."

I laugh.

The driver opens the back door for Emma, and she gestures for me to follow her. "Come on, we'll give you a lift home."

"I'll go if he drops you first. Jack's waiting for you."

I thought she would argue, but she says, "Deal," and I slip into the vehicle after her.

Settling into the backseat, I catch the driver's eye in the rearview mirror. "Hey, Brian."

"Miss Chapman."

Emma looks at me but doesn't say anything, only squeezes my hand.

Brian parks in front of Jack's building, and he's talking to the doorman, waiting for Emma to come home. It's sweet, and I like seeing this side of him. He always treated me with respect and kindness, but he never looked forward to seeing me.

Brian climbs from behind the wheel and rounds the hood to open the door for her.

"Text me later? And I'll see you Saturday at Heath and Zoey's," Emma says.

"I will. Thanks again."

"Not a problem. Thanks for coming along. Goodnight."

Brian helps her slide out of the SUV and doesn't let go until she's steady on her feet. She hurries across the sidewalk.

Jack opens the lobby's door himself and hauls Emma into his arms. She hides her face against the side of his neck, hugging him tightly. They're a beautiful couple, and I'm sincerely happy for them.

"To your building, Miss Chapman?" Brian asks, latching his seatbelt.

"Yes. Thank you."

Jack's drivers don't speak unless they're spoken to, but I've had enough talking to last me years. The silence is welcome.

Brian helps me out of the truck, the same as he did for Emma, and he watches me until I enter my building. I don't have a doorman. The security system used to be enough. I don't know how Blaise broke into my apartment, but there's nothing I can do to keep him from doing it again.

Thank God my apartment is empty, and the only other communication I receive from anyone are texts from Emma thanking me again for joining them and a goodnight text from Raff.

I wonder what he'll think of all the planning the girls did tonight. Will he still want to go to the fundraiser with me? Will he want to meet up at Heath and Zoey's for drinks?

All those worries fade when I wake up to a text from him he sent past midnight asking if I want to go out tomorrow night.

I do, and I say so.

I don't think of anything else all day.

———

During the two shows we film before the weekend, we do pieces on tuxes and ballgowns, the producers springing for fashion shows both days featuring an up and coming men's clothing designer who's set up shop in Bridgeport and a dress designer from Chicago who recently struck it rich with a new line during the fall fashion shows last year.

Filming is more upbeat than usual, and the live studio audience hoots, hollers, and sips on mimosas. Felix models the sleek tux he plans to wear to the fundraiser Saturday night, and he struts down the catwalk to the Bee Gees' "Stayin' Alive" like the ham he is, grinning and doing a quick-footed dance he learned only God knows where.

Still, my life wouldn't be my life if *Rise and Shine, Bridgeport!* didn't have an opinion on my social life and expect me to either a) defend myself or b) pile on to the gossip, and they run clips of me and Emma telling off Bryce from whatever publication he's reporting for. I never did care enough to find out, though Raff would have that information on the tip of his tongue.

To add insult to injury, Friday, after the makeshift runway show, the producers flash pictures of Jack and me when we attended both years. I'm expected to look over my shoulder at the huge screen behind me, smile like I'm not humiliated, and weigh in on my dresses and hairstyles, Jack's tuxes, and what I'm going to wear this year in comparison.

Emma helped me with that, and I write a mental note to thank her, otherwise I wouldn't have cared what I'm wearing and paid the price. I'm pleased I could tell the producers which ballgown I purchased while shopping with the girls, and they show a picture on screen they borrowed from the designer's label of a model posing in the black tulle and silver-flowered dress.

The audience murmurs appreciatively, one cocky gentleman yelling, "You'll be sexy AF, Veronica!" and I allow myself to sincerely laugh at his exuberance. I relax, and for the first time in many months of filming, I have fun.

When I was first hired to host the morning talk show, the

producers didn't always incorporate my social life into its programming. A nobody, I didn't make waves until the show made me popular. The attention was pleasant, and I was Bridgeport's sweetheart—everyone's friend. But then Jack didn't propose like I'd teased, and the gossip took an edge. It's only now fading with time, Raff spinning the situation, and Emma's friendship.

All of that was my fault, but I was desperate. The night my father called and told me he brokered the deal, I scrambled to find a solution that would keep me as far away from Blaise as I could possibly be. I was swept away in a tsunami of anger and despair that has subsided out of resignation.

I can put it off for only so long until Blaise becomes violent, and it would do me a helluva lot of good if the next time he showed up, I went with him and disappeared.

Cavern Lake isn't far, where Ma Barker and her husband put down their headquarters, and eventually photos of me and Blaise will surface. Raff would simply think I left him for another man, and he would be safe.

Melancholy, I wipe the stage makeup off my face and change.

"Good show," Felix says, doing the same.

"Yeah, it was. Thanks."

"See you tomorrow night," he says on his way out the door not waiting for me to respond.

Inevitably, we'll be expected to pose for pictures, popular hosts of the most-watched morning talk show in Bridgeport. I used to love my job, love when pedestrians would recognize me on the street and ask to take a selfie with me. I loved being the most sought-after guest for any charity event or luncheon, organizers paying me to go, not because I could donate a wad of cash, but because my appearance would prompt attendance by those who could.

I follow behind Felix, step into the sun, and linger on the sidewalk.

I dread going home. I never know what I'll find. Blaise sitting on my couch, waiting to torment me? My father, all too eager to threaten me now that his freedom is so easily within his reach, only my cooperation standing in his way?

Perhaps Raff, wanting to watch me dress for the evening?

Out of any of those possibilities, that's the least likely to happen, though it's the scenario I cling to in the taxi spiriting me away to my building. I unlock the door, thoughts of him and his touch grounding me, and I push it open and pause, gauging to see if I'm alone.

I am, and I sag in relief. I can't keep living this way.

Sooner or later Blaise will break me, it's only a matter of how, not when.

I sip on a glass of wine to take the edge off and text Raff. *Where are we going tonight?*

I wait for a response and imagine him thrumming his fingers against his desk, mentally sorting through all the places we could go, which would give us the maximum exposure, when really what I think he wants to do is keep me for himself, and that sounds even better.

He names a trendy restaurant on the corner of the busiest street in Bridgeport. I love him for thinking of my career and the damage Jack did to it, but I'm tired of living for the camera. I mention a little jazz club a block down from the restaurant that is so unlike me the paparazzi would never think to follow us.

Are you sure, dollface? You won't get any attention there.

I'm tired. I can do without it tonight.

He responds with, *Do you want a raincheck?*

No. I want to see you. What time?

I'll come for you at seven.

Okay.

He stops texting me, perhaps needing to rescind a few leads he put out earlier and tying up loose ends to his day.

Wearing a simple black dress and plain heels, I'm downstairs by seven exactly, not wanting to inconvenience him and force him to double park and come up. Unless he needs the elegance of a limo, he prefers to drive himself anywhere he needs to go and there's never a free parking space on my street.

"Dollface," he says, admonishing me and opening the passenger side door, "you should let me go upstairs like the gentleman I am."

"Raff," I say in return because I don't have a nickname for him but maybe I should think of one, "let me be the lady I am by making your life a little easier and meeting you downstairs. I just stepped out of the building."

I rub my lips over his, needing the connection.

He holds me in place with a hand to the back of my head and slips his tongue into my mouth, deepening the kiss.

I sigh.

Pulling away, he brushes his thumb over the apple of my cheek. Reluctantly, he releases me, and I slide into the cool interior of the truck.

"It's going to be a hot summer," I say.

He settles behind the wheel, clicks the buckle of his seatbelt in place, and merges into traffic. "Enjoy it while it lasts."

"Do you have plans to go anywhere?" Raff never goes on vacation. *Talk of the Town* never stops reporting news. I don't think Raff has ever gone anywhere in all the years we've boosted each other's careers. "Who would run your website?"

"Funny you should ask. My brother called not long ago and told me he's engaged. He wants me to fly home for drinks."

That sounds impossibly posh to me. Flying anywhere just to have drinks. "Can you leave like that?"

Winking, he says, "*Talk of the Town* is a well-oiled machine. I could get away for a few days without it rusting to a stop."

I push back a smile. "Right."

He parks in a public parking lot two blocks down from the Ivory Lounge, and holding my hand gently in his, we jaywalk across the street. He opens the door for me, the heavy notes of a sad song slithering to us before we even enter the bar.

Raff scans the seating area faster than I can through the hazy light, a dark-haired man on the stage crooning Frank Sinatra, and he tugs me toward a corner where he crowds me into a small U-shaped banquette.

"What are you having?"

"A chocolate martini."

A cocktail waitress spots Raff and hurries over, and he tells her our orders. We don't speak until she serves my martini and his beer. He pulls off his suit jacket and rolls up his sleeves. "Christ, what a week."

"It will only get worse this weekend."

He huffs a laugh and picks up his beer. "Looking forward to the fundraiser, are we?"

"I might have done a bad thing."

"Dollface, now there's a loaded statement."

I lower my head and sip my martini without picking it up. The bartender, bless him, filled it to the rim, and the waitress didn't spill a single drop.

"Do tell," he says, pressing the cold bottle of beer to my arm.

I shiver but don't lean away. "Zoey invited me to dress at her place tomorrow night and said I should invite you for drinks with the guys while we get ready."

"That's a bad thing?"

"I don't want to presume you'd do that."

"Hmm. Emma didn't say anything about it."

"She said she wouldn't." The reason why will stay between them.

"What do you want to do? It sounds like fun, yeah?"

I look up from my glass in surprise. "You'd do that?"

"I'm curious why you think I wouldn't."

"It all seems . . ." I don't know how to describe what I'm feeling.

"Couple-y," he supplies. "I don't think the question is if I want to do those things, the question is if you want me to do them with you. Do you want to dress at Zoey's? We don't have to go. You can say you prefer to dress alone." He studies me through the neon lights glowing in the bar.

"They were talking babies," I whisper, and I don't know if he can hear me over the music.

He drapes his arm over my shoulders and nudges me closer. "Of course they were. If Emma had her way, we'd be married and the parents of five kids. She's happy and wants everyone else to be, too. That's the way she is. Don't let her intimidate you. I'll text her and tell her we'll go to the fundraiser by ourselves."

I sip my martini, and the cocktail waitress stops by our table and asks if we want another round of drinks.

I nod, liking the quiet, liking the way Raff can listen to the music and appreciate and enjoy being alone with me.

"Will you go?"

He lifts an eyebrow.

"To Boston?" I clarify.

"I'm not in a rush, but I suppose I should show up. Would you like to go with me? Meet my parents and brother?"

"I'm having trouble processing a fundraiser, and you're inviting me to meet your family?"

Raff laughs and finishes off his first beer. "You're right. We should start smaller. One day soon I'll introduce you to my Aunt Caro. She lives here, and she would love to meet you."

"She's not attending the fundraiser?"

"No. She lives a simpler life."

"Sometimes I think I would like that, too."

"Then you can slow down and watch grass grow together."

I surprise myself by accepting. "Okay."

"This is nice," he says, slouching into the cushion and tipping his head back. "Thank you."

"I never used to like living my life on camera."

"What changed?"

"When thinking if my every movement was documented, nothing could hurt me."

"There will always be things outside the camera's view, the monsters just beyond the lens. What happens, dollface, when the camera stops filming?" He tilts my head, resting a finger under my chin.

I try to smile. "Then I do a slow fade into the credits."

"Why did you want to marry Durand?"

I sip my full martini, the sugar and alcohol creating a nice buzz in my blood. "I thought he could keep me safe, but no one can do that."

He begins to peel the label from the bottle. "What's going on, Nic? I thought you were acting differently because Durand didn't propose, but it's not that, is it?"

I can't tell him Blaise is after me, but I have to give him something or he'll know I'm lying. "Have you ever lived your life for someone else? I mean, made your choices based on what someone else wanted you to do?"

"Sure. I went to law school when I would have rather majored in journalism, but it was important to my parents so that's what I did. I don't think we can live our lives entirely without doing something for someone we don't want to do.

Having kids is a sure-fire way to test that theory. How many band concerts and dance recitals will you go to when you have children?"

I shake my head. "Those are harmless things. You have a law degree. What if your parents told you to drop *Talk of the Town* and open your own firm?"

He looks at me out of the corner of his eye. "That's something I'll eventually have to deal with. My parents dislike that I gossip for a living. They say it's crass and demeans our family's name."

"Okay, but then take it one step further. What if your mother's life depended on you opening your own firm?"

"I would do it in a heartbeat. Working as an attorney would be nothing compared to losing my mother, even if we don't get along in the best of times."

He didn't say anything I didn't expect him to say. Marrying Blaise is a small price to pay in exchange for keeping my father safe. "You're a good guy, Raff."

"Some would argue, but as long as you think so, dollface, that's all I care about." He pauses. "Is that what's going on? You have to do something for your family?"

"I can't get out of it, and the time I've been allowed to come to terms with it is slipping away. I want you to know that no matter what happens, it's nothing you did."

He frowns. "Why do I feel like you're saying goodbye?"

"We all do, in one way or another."

"That's true. In one way or another. Are you ready to go? You must be exhausted. I'll drop you home."

I down the rest of my martini, but instead of letting him nudge me off the bench and out of the banquette, I wrap my arms around his shoulders and nibble a trail from his jaw down his neck. I don't care if an inventive paparazzo caught sight of us and followed us here, I don't care if the cocktail waitress snaps pictures of us on her phone and posts them on social media.

Raff knows the truth now, as much as I can tell him, and I want to give myself time with him while I still can.

He moans, and his hand rests on my thigh, his fingertips digging into my skin. I do the same, my hand falling from his shoulder, down his abs, to his cock. He's stiff, and desire stirs in my belly. My nipples harden and my breasts ache.

When Jack and I would have sex, I gave him what I thought he wanted, what I thought I needed to keep him with me. He was a gentleman in bed, but having sex with someone you care about, making love, is different, and I don't only want to tell Raff how I feel, I want to show him.

He grabs my wrist, his grip a steel vise. "Let's go."

I slide off the bench and wait for Raff to pay our tab with the bartender.

The evening air is cool, but it does nothing to clear my head. His hand hovering near my waist, Raff walks with me to the truck. The sun hasn't quite gone down, the sunset lingering, drawing out the long summer day.

Pushing me against the passenger's side door, he brushes the hair out of my face. "You are so beautiful."

"Thank you." The words come out in a breathy gasp, and Raff leans in, smelling the chocolate and alcohol on my breath.

I refrain from kissing him again. We might not have had an audience in the lounge, but we will out here, and what we do from this second on is no one's business but ours.

Raff seems to realize this too, and he opens the truck's door, shutting it firmly once I'm inside. He starts the engine, and cool air pours from the vents.

"I want to go to your place." He'll drive me to my apartment if I don't tell him. I could invite him up, but that isn't where I want to have my first time with him.

He clenches the steering wheel so tightly his knuckles turn white. "If we go to my house, you know what I'll want to do. If you're not on the same page, let me bring you home."

"I want that too."

"If you're sure."

"I am and I'm not drunk."

He reaches for my hand and lifts it to his mouth. His lips brush my palm as he says, "Okay, but you can change your mind whenever you want."

"I'm not going to change my mind. I want this, Raff. With you."

Anticipation lays heavy in the truck, and I cross my legs hoping he doesn't see my thighs trembling.

I've never been to his house before, and I think he made a wrong turn when we cross railroad tracks and enter one of Bridgeport's industrial parks.

"Where are we going?" I ask, my heart fluttering. If I'd been with Blaise and he brought me out here, I'd think he wanted to kill me and cover up the crime.

"Home," Raff says pulling into a parking lot that butts against a huge stone building.

"You live in an old warehouse?" I blink.

"It's the best camouflage there is. I don't have anybody bothering me I don't want bothering me. Let me help you out."

I wait, and he kills the engine, climbs out of his seat, and rounds the hood. He opens my door, but before I can slide out, he twists his fingers in my hair. His eyes are sharp, searching for fear, hesitation, the pad of his thumb tugging down my lower lip in that sensual way that tells me he's thinking about sex.

I move some of his hair off his forehead, my fingernails skimming over his skin. "Why aren't you with anyone, Raff?"

"Never cared enough. Family issues, like Durand, maybe. Caught up in my friendship with Emma, *Talk of the Town.*

Haven't met anyone I connected with. Everyone is so superficial in our line of work. It's difficult to get to know the real person under the hairspray and the makeup."

"And you think you did with me?"

"I think, out of anyone I've met, that I'm willing to try with you. There's something about you that intrigues me, pulls me in. I want to explore where this could go."

I swallow around a lump in my throat. "I can't give you that much time."

"Then I'll take whatever time you *can* give me, Nic. What was so special about Durand's proposal? His money? I don't have as much as he does, but if all you need is a ring on your finger, marry me."

I love him so much and I want to say yes so terribly, my heart aches with it. "Jack did me a favor, and if he'd proposed, it would have done more harm than good. Sometimes, things really do happen for a reason." My father would have had shackles permanently attached to his ankles if I'd gotten engaged and that engagement had led to a legal marriage. I underestimated how dangerous the Barkers are, how far they're willing to go, and I can't make that mistake again.

Raff purses his lips and opens the door wider to let me out.

"Let's not talk like that anymore. It's hardly romantic, and now neither of us are in the mood." I step toward the old warehouse. "I want to see what you've done to the inside."

"Dollface, when I'm around you, I'm always in the mood," he says, tangling my fingers with his.

He leads me around the corner of the building to an alley and unlocks a door that would never be mistaken for a traditional home's front entrance. Flicking on a light, he steps to the side and gives me the first glimpse of an open floor plan that is so gorgeous it steals my breath.

"Jesus Christ, this is beautiful," I say, my eyes traveling

from the hardwood floor into the living room that's scattered with rugs, huge couches, a fireplace, and bookshelves that hold not only books, but trinkets and figurines. A large wet bar sits next to a portion of wall made of reflective glass, letting in the sun but hiding what would be a view of abandoned train tracks overgrown with weeds. The living area melts into a spacious kitchen complete with an island, copper pots hanging above it from large hooks to a dining table that seats at least ten, but I don't stop to count the chairs. Above my head, exposed metal beams create a cavernous feel, and a second floor seems to hang suspended in the air. Without walls to obstruct my view, I can see two sleeping areas and a study sectioned off by more bookcases.

On his way to the bar, he drops his keys into a bowl that's sitting on a side table near one of the couches and he pulls his suit jacket off and tosses it onto an armrest.

Pouring from a crystal decanter, he says, "I bought the building and refurbished it when *Talk of the Town* started making money and I could live off the income. I had to do a little here and a little there as the money trickled in, but this is the end result. That was a few years ago now, and the e-zine's success far outweighs anything I ever thought possible. People love gossip."

He offers me the glass but doesn't move, forcing me to walk across the living room to accept the drink.

"Yes, they do," I agree. If they didn't, I wouldn't have a job, either. "Do you have people over a lot?" I don't ask because I'm hurt he's never invited me here. Until recently, I wouldn't have considered Raff a friend. A business partner maybe, a coworker. If I needed to speak to him about an event I wanted coverage for, I always went to his office. When he was helping me after Jack's party, he would come to my apartment, but we never went farther than my kitchen table.

"I'll host a dinner party every once in a while, but I'm rarely home. I don't like to be alone."

"Then we're a lot alike." I sip the whiskey he poured me.

"I think maybe we are."

I amble through his living room, trailing my fingers over the back of one of the couches, admire the paintings hanging from the brick walls. He has a fondness for true crime books and dragon statues.

He watches me walk around . . . I can feel his eyes on me. "Will you show me upstairs?" I finally ask, circling back to him. He lounges against the bar, his ankles crossed.

Pulling me close with an arm around my waist, he tilts his head and nuzzles my lips with his. "There are beds up there."

I lean away, a smile playing with my mouth. If someone had told me how chivalrous Raff was going to be, I would have been surprised. He seems the type to take what he wants, maybe not in such a straightforward way as Jack, but I doubt whenever Raff wants something, he walks away empty-handed. "Yes, I can see them, but maybe I want a closer look?"

Setting my glass on the bar, he says, "If you're sure."

"I've never been surer about anything in my life."

He tangles our fingers together in a way he wants to feel casual, but to me, it's anything but. Before we take the stairs, I pull my heels off and leave them on the floor. I like how they look, and I'll remember the picture and how I feel. Like I had a chance to belong somewhere.

Raff tugs my hand and I follow him, the stairs stopping at a second floor that's as wide open as the bottom.

"You don't like feeling closed in," I guess, my gaze sweeping over the study and two bedrooms, only squat bookshelves, plants, and rugs turning the areas into "rooms."

His eyes widen. "I never thought of it like that, but I

suppose you could be right. My family life can be stifling at times."

I don't explore here like I did downstairs, instead walking with him toward a huge king bed flanked by two nightstands. A steamer trunk used as a hope chest sits at the end of the bed. Because there aren't any closets, his suits hang from bars attached to the walls, and his dress shoes are arranged meticulously underneath them.

"Where are the rest of your things? Don't you have bathrooms?"

"There's a bathroom here," he says, pointing to a door the same color as the brick, and he pushes it open revealing a large room containing a shower, hot tub, sink, and a vanity and stool. "I treat the entire upstairs as my bedroom, and I have armoires and dressers over there, where I keep my socks, pajamas, like that. I have another bathroom downstairs, between the kitchen and living room. Why? Do you need a minute?"

I laugh. "No, but thank you. You're used to what a woman needs from spending so much time with Emma." I don't say it in a bitter way. It's actually nice to have a man considerate enough to ask if I need to pee before we have sex.

He chuckles. "She does have to go a lot if she's drinking. If Mia and Haisley were with us wherever we happened to go, and they all went, I could count on losing them for a good twenty minutes. But," he says, pulling me close, "that's not romantic, either, and I've been looking forward to this for a very long time."

"Have you now?" I murmur, resting my arms on his shoulders and pushing my fingers through his hair. I lost a couple of inches when I pulled my heels off, and he bends down a little to brush his lips over mine.

"Hmmm. I see you all the time—when your show is on, or if someone catches you walking home and they upload their clip to the site. It's hard enough to get you out of my head without the constant reminders," he says, but he slips his tongue into my mouth and there are no more words.

He growls low in the back of his throat. This is more than a kiss, it's an introduction to what's to come, and I shiver.

His lips move from my mouth, across my jaw, and to the sensitive skin of my neck. He he reaches the low neckline of my dress and stops, but only for a moment, pausing to yank the straps over my shoulders and past my breasts. He tugs the material over my hips and thighs, and I lift one foot and then the other.

"I hope you weren't attached to that dress," he says, balling it up and tossing it aside.

"You didn't ruin it, it's how I put it on before you picked me up."

"Good," he says, but he's not thinking about the dress. He's swallowing and staring at my black lace bra and panty set.

I didn't choose my lingerie with this in mind, but I'm glad I did. "Like?"

"More than you'll ever know," he says, kneeling at my feet. He kisses up my thigh and nudges my cleft with his nose, inhaling the scent of my arousal. "I want to kiss you here. Do you like oral sex?"

This is the time for all the birth control talk, and I say, "I do, and I haven't been with anyone since Jack. That's been quite a while now, actually, and I don't have anything, I mean, an STD. I'm on birth control, so you don't need a condom unless you'll be more comfortable wearing one."

His hand cups the back of my calf. "I don't want to, and if you're giving me permission to go without, I will. I trust you. I hope as much as you trust me."

"When was the last time you had sex?" I ask, wrapping his

hand around his tie and urging him to his feet. I don't want to be the only one naked.

"Right before Durand's party. I met her at a dinner and let her bring me home. I wore a condom when I was with her, Nic."

I unknot his tie and let it hang from his neck. I love how it looks. Sexy. I unbutton his shirt. He's not wearing a tank under it, and I splay my hands over his chest lightly speckled with hair.

"Then it's been a little while for you, too." I don't question him about the whos or the whys. Raff didn't have anything going on with Emma, and I don't expect him to be a monk. I trust him to tell me the truth, and if he says he's okay to go without protection, I believe him.

He tips his head up and looks at the ceiling. "You have no idea."

I pull the hem of his shirt from his pants. "Then we should both have a good time."

"I think it will be more than that," he says wryly, not waiting for me to unbuckle his belt. He does it on his own and shucks his pants next to my dress.

"You still have more clothes on than me," I point out.

"Can't have that. You do me, and I'll do you."

"Okay." I slide his shirt from his shoulders, and once it's on the floor, he unclasps my bra. I'm a little self-conscious since I've been told my breasts are less than a handful, but Raff doesn't seem to mind, filling his palms and rubbing his thumbs over my nipples. They harden under his touch.

We're both standing in our underwear, and I push my hands under the waistband of his boxer briefs. His cock is silken smooth, the tip already wet. He's rock hard and he throbs in anticipation.

"Okay, this has gone on long enough. I need you under me,

right now." He's naked before I can blink, and he gently slides my panties off. That's the last of his patience. Advancing, he crowds me until the backs of my legs meet the mattress and he pushes me backward, crawling on top of me.

Instinctively, my hips lift, searching.

His mouth covers mine. "Not yet," he mumbles against my lips. "I said I wanted to taste you."

I blow out a breath. "Okay."

But he lingers, giving my jaw, collarbone, and cleavage attention first, his stubble scraping my skin.

I like foreplay as much as the next girl, but I'm going to be burning up by the time I come.

"Raff," I say, begging.

"We have all night." He roughly pulling one of my nipples into his mouth.

I gasp, the pleasured pain shooting straight to my core.

"You're not going to make me wait all night, are you?" My fingers twist in his hair.

"No. I plan to have you many times. Now, shh." Wiggling farther down the bed, he whispers kisses over my stomach. "You weren't lying when you said you were a blonde. Widen your legs for me, dollface. I want to see you."

I do, and he spreads me open, my heels digging into the comforter. There's still light coming in from the windows, and I know he can see all of me: the taupe color of my skin, my arousal leaking out of me, how huge my clit is.

"You're beautiful, Nic," he says and he covers me entirely with his hot mouth.

I cry out even as I lift my hips, adding to the pressure.

His tongue finds my clit, and he pushes two fingers into me.

"Raff," I whimper. I need this, I need him.

He raises his head quickly to say, "I want you to come like this," and he sucks my clit between his lips, ramming his fingers into me in such a painfully delicious way there's not one thought left in my head.

"I'm coming," I gasp, though unnecessarily which is just as well because I barely understood what I said. I'm sure he can feel my pussy clenching at his fingers, my clit quivering under his tongue. I buck in time with his fingers' thrusts, and when I start to orgasm, he shoves a third finger into me and holds them there, his knuckles bruising my bone, the pain heightening and rushing my release.

I tilt my hips, my butt lifting completely off the bed and push his head into my pussy. The climax explodes through my body. I don't come down for what feels like forever, and tears drip from my eyes in satisfied exhaustion.

He raises his head and wipes his chin and lips with the back of his hand. "Did I hurt you? Not every woman likes three fingers."

Letting out a shuddery sigh, I tell him the truth. "It hurt, but it was good. I haven't come that hard in a very long time."

"Just as long as I don't hurt you in a bad way," he says, a hand to my hip. "Will you turn over for me?"

I prop myself onto my elbows. "You like a woman from behind?"

"I like a woman in all ways, but it's what I feel like right now, if you don't mind."

"Okay."

Rolling over, I crawl onto all fours and arch my back. I'm not a stranger to this position, men preferring it because it allows them to go deep, and deep Raff does, not giving me a second to prepare.

"Jesus Christ," he mutters gliding into me with one, smooth stroke. "You're so wet."

"You did that to me," I say, sucking in a breath.

"You okay?"

"Yeah. You're big."

"I'll take that as a compliment."

"It was supposed to be one."

He rubs his hands over my ass and spreads my cheeks open. "Do you like being touched here?" he asks, massaging the tight muscle with his fingertip.

"I've never done anal," I say, though I guess with the right man, a patient man, I would be willing to give it a try.

"I'm not interested in that at the moment, but I like to play while I fuck."

I turn my head, but I can't see much besides his foot near the edge of the mattress. "I like you touching me anywhere."

He pulls his cock out and pushes back in, and once he's deep, his tip touching my center, he gently slides his finger into my ass. I like how it feels, the pressure, the fullness of it, and I press backward.

That's all he needs to take the hint, and his cock fills me, his finger adding to the deliciousness.

"I'm going to fuck you hard, Nic, and I'll only need a second. I'm warning you now."

"As hard as you want to," I say, bracing for the impact of his cock.

He keeps his finger in my ass, and grabs my butt cheek with his other hand. He pulls out and slams into me, his balls slapping against my skin. He doesn't hold back, grunting with every thrust.

I feel another orgasm coming, and I rub my clit, the added pressure of his finger in my ass turning me on.

We come together, and I press my face into his comforter. His cock surges, filling me with cum, and my pussy desperately clutches at him, using him for my own release.

Minutes tick by and we drift down from our high.

"I want to watch you do that someday," he says, brushing my hip with his free hand.

"Do what?" My voice is muffled. I'm too drained to turn my head.

"Play with yourself. I find it so sexy when a woman is confident enough to do that with a man."

I laugh. "I wanted to come again, but your hands were busy."

"So they were. I'm going to pull my finger out, and it might hurt a little."

"Yeah."

He does, so slowly, and it does hurt a bit, my pussy swollen, his cock still inside me.

"Doing okay?" he asks.

"Yeah, thanks."

"I love looking at you," he says, slicking his fingertip up my spine. "You're so elegant."

"I don't feel elegant with my ass in the air."

"Not elegant then. Fucking sexy."

"Was it good for you?" I ask, needing to know.

"Any better and I'd be dead. I'm gonna pull out. I went at you pretty hard, and I'm sorry if you're sore."

I know men. "No, you're not. You all have that masculine pride if a woman can't walk after a vicious bout of sex."

"Well, it wasn't all for me," he points out and gently, his cock slips out of me in a warm gush. "You happened to have benefitted from it as well."

"I can't argue. I wouldn't win."

Raff pulls his comforter and sheet back and settles onto a pillow. "Come here. I'm not letting you leave."

I blink in surprise. "You want me to spend the night?"

"If you want to. I can drive you home if you don't, but I would like you to."

"I'd like that, too, but I'm not used to sex being an all-night thing."

"Durand never stayed?"

Sore and sticky, I crawl into bed with him and curl into his side. "Do you really want to talk about Jack now?"

He thinks for a moment. "I'm curious."

"About what?" I shift and rest my knee on his thigh. His cum is trickling out of me, dripping onto the sheet.

"What you felt for each other. Two years is a long time to invest in a relationship you don't care about."

"We were nothing more than friends with benefits. A little less serious than if you and Emma had been sleeping together because I know you love her as a friend, but I can't claim Jack loved me in any way. We got along, obviously, used each other for dates and I think, for the most part, we enjoyed each other's company. You know why I wanted to marry him, and it didn't hurt when he dumped me. The aftermath damaged my reputation, and it was totally my fault. I deserved everything I got—"

He opens his mouth to defend me.

"No, it's true. He had every right to be angry. Besides, he told me he wouldn't have faced up to his feelings for Emma if I hadn't done what I did, and if that's true, then some good came out of it, and I'm happy for him."

Raff frowns.

"I'm not jealous he treats Emma better than he treated me. That's how it should be. He loves her. He never loved me, I never loved him, and we never pretended we did." I pause, a realization popping into my head and exploding as painfully as wrapping your hand around a firecracker, and I recoil emotionally and physically. "You think I'm using you the same way I used Jack."

It hurts, but I should have expected it. If I wouldn't have been so wrapped up in the making-friends part of shopping the other night, I would have listened when Emma asked me the same thing. Hell, he and Emma might have even talked about it behind my back. You can't use someone for two years and not think other people will believe the same. Especially since, well, I have been using Raff to help me turn my public persona around online after Jack's party. There's no way I could have swayed the public's opinion of me without his e-zine and quick thinking.

"It's not that—"

"Right." I can't keep the bitterness out of my voice. I should never have slept with him.

"It's not. When I was putting out your fires, I promised myself I wouldn't accept Durand's . . ."

At least he has the tact not to continue, but I fill in the blanks. "Leftovers? Nice. You're no better than all the city gossips. I thought you reported the truth."

"No one knew the whole story, and to be fair, I still don't."

I sit up and wrap the sheet around my boobs. He might have had his dick inside me ten minutes ago, but I still have some integrity. "Does anyone when you start dating someone new? That's what a relationship is for, to learn about each other and all their dirty secrets. No one forced you to ask me out, and I thought I was in your bed because you wanted me to be. My mistake, but this one I can fix on my own."

I twist to slide out of bed, find my dress, and go. I'll need to walk a few blocks before I'll be able to find a taxi, but I'm not staying here a second longer.

He grips my arm, and before I can utter a single objection, I'm under him, the tip of his cock nudging my pussy faster than a juicy piece of gossip travels from the north side of Bridgeport to the south. He has his entire weight on top of me, and he brushes the hair out of my eyes. "I needed to know," he starts, his voice low and rough, "because I'm falling in love with you, and Jesus Christ, tell me now if it's a mistake."

I look away and try to swallow the tears burning my throat. No one's told me they love me before. Not my mother who despised me the second the doctor pulled me out of her. My father says the words, but God, if actions don't prove the words to be true, what are they? Lies. The look in Raff's icy blue eyes is the only proof I need to know he means every word he says.

"I can't." It *is* a mistake. It's the biggest mistake he'll ever make.

He slides his cock into me, and I angle my hips, encouraging him to take all of me.

"Then tell me you won't break my heart," he murmurs against my ear.

I wrap my arms around him and press my face into his neck. "I can't tell you that either, all I can promise is I'll love you while I do."

———

My stomach growls.

We lie panting, covered in sweat. He was ferocious, and come morning, I'll have bruises everywhere, but I stretch, sated. No one has made love to me like Raff, and maybe that's the secret. He devours me like he wants to consume every cell in my body, like he'll love me for the rest of his life no matter what happens.

His mouth covers my nipple, his teeth scraping my already sensitive skin. "Raff," I say on a sigh. "I need a break."

"Let me do this," he says, pushing three fingers inside me and rubbing his thumb against my clit. This will be my fifth orgasm in three hours, but I come quickly, my cum mixed with his as it oozes out of me. "I'm going to have you many more times before the sun rises," he says over the buzz in my ears, "but I agree. We need fuel since we didn't eat dinner earlier."

Raff doesn't remove his fingers, flexing them inside me, brushing the exact spot that sends shivers over my skin. I'm trying to recover from the aftershocks of my orgasm, and he's not helping.

I look at him through hooded eyes. I'm not going to get any sleep tonight. "We can't eat like this."

"*You* can't," he says, chuckling, delicately pulling his fingers out of me, my pussy sore and aching.

"I never would have thought you were a sexaholic."

He rests his forehead against mine. "Only with you, doll-face. You're a good lay."

"That's . . . sweet." I hide my face with his pillow.

Laughing, he sits up, moves the pillow aside and brushes my cheek with his sticky fingers. "I will never get tired of your body. Let's go downstairs. I'll figure out something."

I sit up, wincing. "You cook, too?"

"I can scramble eggs without burning them, if that's what you mean. When I said I throw dinner parties, I didn't tell you where the food comes from." He slides out of bed and bends over to pick up the slacks he wore to the bar.

"Then maybe I should be in charge of the toast." His shirt's laying in a crumpled heap near my dress, and I slide my arms through the sleeves, the cuffs flapping around my wrists.

"I like that. After we eat, I want to have you while you're wearing it."

"It would be nice if we got a little sleep. We'll be up late tomorrow night, too."

He pulls me into his arms. "Let's skip it and stay in bed all night."

I want to say this is supposed to put a nail in the proverbial coffin that was Jack's and my relationship, but the subject is touchy, and bringing up *Talk of the Town* and *Rise and Shine, Bridgeport!* may not be the best idea. I could look at it as simply a date with Raff, something we'd attend because we're a couple and we both support the cause, and I like that more. Who cares what nasty things people will think, or if they'll call me a whore because I jumped from Jack's bed to Raff's.

"We can, but I think the next morning you'd regret not seeing your friends."

"*My* friends? Heath and Zoey are Durand's friends. The only friends I have in the group are Emma, Mia, and Haisley, and Mia and Haisley couldn't afford to go to something like this if Emma didn't drag them along."

"You're closer to them than I am. Besides, I already bought a dress. I'd have to reimburse the show if I don't go. That's not a big deal, but skipping causes more problems than simply going for an hour, saying hi to everyone, and leaving before things get dull."

"Will you come home with me afterward? Spend the night? On Sunday I'll introduce you to my aunt."

Raff might be falling in love with me, but he doesn't like it, and I don't feel comfortable meeting his family. I drop my arms from around his neck and back away. "I don't think that's a good idea after the conversation we just had."

He sighs and rubs a hand over his face. "I'm sorry. I'm sorry I'm jealous that son of a bitch had two years of your life and he didn't appreciate it. I'm sorry I'm pissed off you gave him those years as if they meant so little to you. *I* want your time, Nic. Every second you can give me, I want. If I'm an asshole for that, so be it."

"It's not that simple."

"I'm not asking for simple. I'm asking for a chance."

There's not a sound in his apartment. Not the blare of horns and the grumble of engines from the traffic outside, not the ticking of a clock. There's only silence, and I have nothing to say to fill it.

Blaise will come for me, and when he does, I have to go. No two weeks' notice at the show, no goodbyes to friends. I'll disappear, and when Blaise deems enough time has gone by, I'll resurface as Mrs. Blaise Barker, and the life I know here, right now, will be like it never existed.

I know how it will work. I was researching what happened to his other wives, and that's the pattern I discovered. They vanish without a trace only to pop in the news when a pedestrian happens to catch them walking down a busy street, takes a photo, and plasters it all over social media. What people don't realize is the two men wearing suits walking behind them are armed handlers, working for Barker to ensure what little freedom he gives his wives won't be misinterpreted as a means to escape.

I will be, forever and always, a captive of the Barker family, a knife to my throat to keep my father silent as he lives out the rest of his life, free.

That is what my father offered the Barkers, that is what Blaise accepted, and if I don't go along with it, my father will disappear like Blaise's wives. I'll never see him again.

Maybe someone else could do that, but even if I don't love my father in the way a daughter loves her daddy, my father's death would eat at me until I eventually went crazy with guilt.

Sagging, I step into his arms and rest my head on his bare shoulder. "I will give you all my seconds, all my minutes, all my hours, until I can't anymore. If that's not enough for you, break it off with me now because with the situation I've found myself in, that's all I have to give."

He rubs his hands up and down my back. "I wish you'd tell me what's going on. I could help you."

I look up and meet his eyes. "I have family obligations. You must know what that's like."

He nods slightly. "Yes, I do."

"Then you know sometimes there's nothing you can do but do it."

"Yeah. I know that too." Framing my face with his hands he says, "I'm going to lose you, aren't I?"

"I'm sorry."

"Don't be. I'll enjoy you while you're mine."

I shouldn't have started this with him. I shouldn't be here, but I couldn't stop myself from needing it, this little piece of happiness I've managed to find in the most unlikeliest of places. The love in his touch will keep me warm during my coldest nights, and that's nothing I can regret, no matter how much it hurts him.

"I need the minute you were going to give me earlier."

"Okay. I'll meet you downstairs."

I turn toward his bathroom, but he says my full name, "Veronica," the sound of the syllables skipping smoothly from his mouth like a flat stone jumping over the calm surface of a pond.

"Yeah?"

"Don't leave without saying goodbye. Ever."

"I promise."

He holds my gaze, unwavering, until he shuffles out of the room, his pants sitting low on his hips, unbuttoned. He trudges down the stairs, his footfalls are silent.

In the bathroom, I do my business, wiping gently. I am so sore, everywhere, but I wouldn't ever tell him no. I need him touching me. The shocks make me feel alive, the pain reminding me I'm more than a pawn in a deal.

I put my panties on before I go downstairs, and I find him

in the kitchen, melting butter in the bottom of a frying pan. "You were serious about the eggs."

He looks at me over his shoulder and quirks his lip. "I'll never lie."

"Is there coffee?" I ask, wiggling onto a stool at the island, the marble cool under my arms.

"Now? It's one in the morning."

I try to keep it fun. We've already had a month's worth of serious talk, and I don't want the rest of the time I have with him to be sad. "Someone told me I won't get any sleep tonight. Might as well add a little caffeine."

He laughs. "Sure, but can you get it going? The eggs really will need all my concentration if they're going to come out right."

"Tell me where everything is."

His coffeemaker isn't complicated, and he points out where he keeps the grounds and new filters. The second I'm finished and the coffee is brewing, I settle onto the stool again. I feel like a guest and I'm not comfortable helping him with anything else, but is it wrong to daydream about living here with him, doing this in the middle of the night after making love?

"You said you have family obligations, too. Is Rafferty a family name?" I ask his back.

He whisks eggs in a shallow bowl. "It is. It's my grandfather's first name, my dad's dad. Reese, my younger brother, is named after a grandfather, too, our mother's father. They're both hotshot attorneys in DC, fending off retirement, though they should have years ago."

The scent of coffee fills the air, and the atmosphere is cozy, Raff and I talking alone with no public expectations.

"Is that what your brother does?"

"Hmmm." He pours the eggs into the warmed pan, and they sizzle in the melted butter.

"It's not hard to guess that's what they want you to do, too."

Dumping the bowl into the sink, he says, "I'm on a time limit." He flicks a glance at me. "Same as you. Mine doesn't sound as devastating as yours, but it's there, nonetheless. Boston. A place in the family firm."

"Oh," I say, both relieved and disappointed. "You're not going to stay in Bridgeport."

"Not if my mother has anything to say about it. Now that Emma's settled, she says there's nothing keeping me here. She was hoping we'd get married, gave me the space she thought I needed for it to happen. I told her it wouldn't, but she never believed it for as long as we've been friends. Now she's pressuring me to get my professional life figured out since my personal life is such a dismal disaster."

"I wouldn't call it a disaster," I say.

He motions to me over the island. "Either you're going to have to pour the coffee or stir the eggs."

I slide off the stool and pad over to the stove. "It would help if you turned the heat down." I pull the wooden spoon from his hand and lower the heat under the pan myself. "Eggs are delicate. Too hot, and you'll burn them."

"You're delicate too, but you like the heat," he says, his lips close to mine.

I reach up the millimeter I need to kiss him. "Being burned is worth it."

He tugs my lip down with the pad of his thumb. "Maybe it is. Anyway," he continues, sliding two large *Talk of the Town* mugs out of the cabinet, "my parents don't consider the 'zine a professional triumph."

"I'm sorry. I know how difficult it is to be considered a failure. What are you going to do?"

Raff fills the mugs with steaming hot coffee and adds the milk and sugar he knows I prefer to one of them. Setting it by my elbow, he says, "Fight them on it. My Aunt Caro told them to fuck off and married the man she loved. I can do the same."

I scrape the pan. "What did your family do to her?"

"She's my mother's sister, and they disowned her. No access to the billions," he says in mock sadness.

"Billions?" I ask, blinking.

"Old family money. Generations old. I don't consider it mine, not like Jack considers Ron's his. They can threaten me all they like, but there's nothing they can do that would persuade me to do what they want."

"It's nice you have options to hold your ground." I'm not bitter. Different lives, different circumstances. Raff worked hard to get *Talk of the Town* up and going, though he would deny it and say it was people like me who did the real work. Maybe to a small extent, but he has a reputation celebrities, personalities, and influencers trust, and for as long as *Talk of the Town* has been reporting entertainment news and gossip, it's all been true.

"It is, but I don't know how bad the war is going to be. I don't want to lose my family, but they don't understand I need my freedom."

"Freedom isn't free," I say, turning the burner off.

"It sure as hell isn't. Shit. I forgot toast. If we spread the slices with peanut butter, we can call it dessert."

"Okay." I smother a laugh and dish up the eggs. Hungrily, I sit at the island with our plates, ready to dig in. I should have suggested we melt cheese over the eggs. I'm starving, and this won't fill me up for long.

He turns from the toaster and walks toward me. "I like you like this," he says, sliding a piece of toast slathered in butter and peanut butter onto my plate.

"Like what?" I ask, my fork poised above my small pile of fluffy eggs.

"You, in my shirt, in my kitchen." His eyes gleam and he grins like a shark.

I straighten. "We're supposed to be eating."

"It's not my fault you're so sexy sitting there. Let me touch you," he says, dropping his hand from my collarbone to the inside of his shirt. He pauses when I don't say yes. "Nic."

I sigh his name. "Raff." I love how he touches me, how his fingers slick over my skin.

He captures my breast in his hand, his fingers immediately squeezing my nipple.

Heat floods my panties, and I tip my head back.

His other hand skims up my thigh and eases my legs apart.

I acquiesce, my heart racing.

He lowers his pants and his cock springs free, the tip glistening in the light over the stove. "You are the perfect height for me to do this," he says, moving the material in the crotch of my panties over giving him access to push into me. "Scoot forward a little, dollface."

I do, perching on the edge of the stool, and his cock fills me to the brim. I adjust, pressing my lips to his chest and sucking in a breath.

Sex turns into an embrace, and he wraps his arms around me. "I love you, Nic," he murmurs, his face buried in my hair.

I don't want to be maudlin, and I could turn quickly. I flick his nipples with my tongue. "Show me."

With his hands under my butt, he rams into me, and he comes, growling my name.

———

He lowers me to the stool. I didn't come, but I don't know if I can. Tired, worn out, and hungry now, I want to eat, drink a glass of water, and fall asleep.

Raff has other plans.

He pulls out, adjusts his pants, and drops to his knees.

I press my thighs together. "What are you going to do?"

"Get you off," he says, like it shouldn't be a mystery what he wants to do kneeling in front of me.

"You don't have to. I've had more orgasms tonight than I have in the past six months."

"Good. I want you to have one more. Watch me play with you."

"What do you mean?"

He moves the black lace aside, and through the dim light, my pussy oozes his cum. "Do you see that? How that turns me on? I've been inside you, left something behind. That means you're mine now."

Without waiting for me to respond, he pushes two fingers inside me, and it is a bit surreal, sexy, to watch his fingers disappear and to feel where they went. He moves them in and out, his hand resting on my knee.

I widen my legs.

"Unbutton my shirt, dollface. I wanna see your breasts."

I do what he says and let the shirt hang open.

"Pinch your nipples, Nic."

"Raff."

"Do it. I want to watch you, feel what it does to you."

My nipples are sensitive from all the sucking he's done on them since the bar, and I don't need to squeeze them very hard for my core to tighten around his fingers.

"Christ," he mutters. "You're going to kill me."

Closing my eyes, I do it again, and bear down on his hand.

"That's right," he says, adding another finger.

I whimper. Three of his elegant fingers is almost more than I can handle.

He uses the hand that was sitting on my knee to rub my clit, and to find a more comfortable position, I prop one of my feet on his shoulder.

"Raff."

"Open your eyes. Look between your legs. Look at what I'm doing to you."

My eyes flutter open, and I do look, my legs spread, his fingers inside me, my panties obstructing my view in a sexy, sleazy way.

"I want you to come on my hand. I want to feel how much I excite you."

"I'm close." The words are more of a moan.

"Yes, you are. I can feel how close you are. Pinch your nipples harder. Make it hurt for me."

I move my hips the best I can, thankful the stool has a back-rest. His thumb rubs my clit in frantic circles, and his fingers are so deep inside me he's bruising me again.

The orgasm comes out of nowhere, and I pinch my nipples as hard as I dare without hurting myself. Raff doesn't let up on my clit until I start to cry.

Tenderly, he pulls his fingers out of me and adjusts my panties. He picks me up with an arm under my knees and one braced against my back and walks into the living room where he sinks onto a couch, cradling me in his lap. "Was I too rough?"

Wiping my cheeks, I shake my head, my hair grazing his skin. "No. I'm only a little overwhelmed. I didn't think we'd have . . . this."

"You didn't think we'd find this, and then lose it so quickly," he clarifies, tilting my face with a finger under my chin.

"Yeah, something like that."

"Can you tell me, please?"

"I have to help my dad. He's found himself in some trouble and I'm the only one who can get him out. It might not be forever, but I'm going to need to leave the city, *Rise and Shine, Bridgeport!*, you. Maybe I'll come back, but by the time I'm able, maybe it won't matter anymore."

He tightens his hold on me and swallows. "Okay. I'll stop asking because if it's something I could help you with, you'd tell me, and you haven't."

I rub my nose against his jaw. "Emma said I could ask her or Jack. She said our whole group of friends would do whatever they could. Trust me, Raff. Please. No one can do anything but me."

"Sometimes, dollface, that's the way it is. My parents won't be happy with anything but getting what they want. Believe me, I understand. You'll have to forgive me. I can feel us slipping away, but being rough with you will only hurt you, not keep us together. I'll lighten up."

I tip my head up and when I move, his shirt falls open, revealing my breast. His eyes rake my body greedily, but he only lowers his head and kisses me, holding me tight.

We end up reheating the eggs, and we're so famished it doesn't matter they taste like glue and have the same consistency. Even cold, the peanut butter toast is better, and I'm feeling more like myself after another slice and two more cups of coffee. By then it's close to three in the morning, and I insist I need sleep. Monday morning is going to suck shit. I can't keep weekend hours and expect to look decent on Monday, but snuggled in the crook of Raff's arm as we drift off, I wouldn't have changed a thing.

I sleep until almost twelve, which feels like heaven but also hell. By noon I'm already done taping for the day. Yep, Monday morning is going to suck shit.

Drowsily, I reach for my phone, Raff lying next to me, his arm secured around my stomach. His dick is soft, which is a relief. He might want to make love after the fundraiser tonight, and I think that's going to be the earliest I'll be up for it, though I'm sure he will be long before I am.

I scan my notifications with gritty eyes, and Emma's name pops out at me. *I've been trying to reach Raff. Do you know where he is?*

Christ. Emma's lucky I'm not some psycho bitch. A text like that to a jealous girlfriend could land Emma in a world of hurt.

I turn over and poke Raff's shoulder. "Hey."

"Two more minutes," he mumbles, burrowing into his pillow.

"You're the sex fiend. You deserve to be tired," I say, shaking him awake. "Emma's been trying to get a hold of you."

"Hmmm," he mutters. "Didn't tell her I was busy."

I scowl. "Were you out past curfew?"

Though his eyes are closed, his lips find my cheek, and he falls back asleep.

"For goodness' sake." I call Emma. It *is* late on a Saturday morning. By now, Raff has usually put in a few hours looking over blog posts and videos taken on Friday night.

"Hi. You didn't have to call me back. I wanted to let you know we're meeting at Heath and Zoey's at five, and Jack ordered the limo to pick us up about seven."

I groan. That's only five hours from now. I still need to shower and run to my apartment to see if Saks delivered my dress and if some kind soul brought it up from the vestibule and set it by my door. If my dress is MIA I'll need to run to the store to find out where it is, and I still have to pack my makeup and hair product.

"Did Saks deliver your dress?" If Emma has hers, then hopefully mine will be at my place.

"I had everything sent to Zoey's, remember? She said they were delivered yesterday, and her girls went ballistic. She let them open the boxes and they're hanging in her sitting room to let the wrinkles fall out. They can't wait to meet you and see how you look in your dress. They know who you are, from the show, and they can't believe their mom knows a real-life celebrity."

I did forget we had the dresses shipped to Zoey's, and I'm glad I called Emma after all. I would have rushed home and then to Saks in a tizzy. "Thanks. My brain is a little fuzzy."

"Hot sex will do that. When Jack . . ." she fades off, well aware I know what Jack can do, but I'm not thinking about it with Raff's arm tightening around me. He didn't fall back asleep after all and he's listening to every word we say, Emma's voice carrying from my cell crystal clear.

I fill in the awkward silence. I'm sure there will be many more. "I should get going. I have a lot to do before five."

"See you later!" she says, relieved I saved her and anxious to get off the phone.

"Bye," I say to empty air and toss my cell onto the nightstand.

"She didn't mean anything by it."

"I know. God," I moan, stretching, in no mood to get out of bed, "it would have been so much easier on all of us if you'd been sleeping with her."

"If we'd been sleeping together, I wouldn't be here with you. We'd be married with two point five kids and a house with a picket fence."

"Is that what you want?" I peer at him with one eye, my other hidden by my pillow.

Raff grabs his own phone, scrolls through his notifications. He has several more than me. "That's what she wants. Wait and see. The second Durand knocks her up, they'll be building a house in the suburbs."

"It's what Jack wants, too, but he never let himself believe he could have it." I sigh. "I better go. We'll need the entire two hours to get ready—I can't be late."

"You decided to go over there after all?" he asks, setting his cell aside.

"I have no choice if I want to wear that dress. She had it shipped to Zoey's. Besides," I say, scooting over and resting my head on his chest, "our relationship is a little different than it was last night at the bar."

He rubs his fingers up and down my back, but he doesn't say anything.

"Unless you didn't mean what you said." I prop myself up and meet his eyes. I know he meant what he said. He didn't need to say he loves me. He showed me all night long in the desperation of his touch, in the urgency of his lips as he ravaged me.

But just because he said it doesn't mean he wants it to be true.

The saddest look fills his eyes, and he smooths his hand over my hair. "There's a lot going against us, dollface. Does it matter if I didn't mean it?"

"It matters to me."

"Then yeah, I meant every fucking word."

He rolls me onto my back, and we make slow, gentle love. He knows he hurt me last night, and I'm still sore this morning, but I don't ask him to stop. I need this. I need him. I don't bother to wish that I can keep what I found with him.

One night in late summer when I was a little girl, my dad found me in the yard wishing on the brightest star in the sky. He laughed and said, "No wonder your wishes don't come true. You're not wishing on a star. That's a fucking satellite."

Devastated, I ran off, and from that day on, I never made another wish.

I've made my own dreams come true.

CHAPTER EIGHT

Rafferty

Over a fresh pot of coffee, we linger. *I* linger. Not because of what's to come—I'm an adult and I've made peace with that—but because I like her here, in my house. I like watching her move carefully, gingerly, testing every movement before following through. I did that and she's right. I *do* take male pride in the fact I claimed her so completely her entire body aches. I can still feel how soft her pussy was clenched around my fingers, rubbing her swollen clit until she came. She's beautiful, sensual, sexy as sin, and getting her off as she cries my name gives me more satisfaction than all the millions *Talk of the Town* brings in every year.

Even thinking about it hardens my cock to an uncomfortable level, and she knows it, stiffening in response to my unspoken thoughts. "I can't, Raff," she says, knowing what would be in store for her if she let me have my way. Wall sex, right here by the door before the car I ordered arrives, her panties in shreds on the floor. I imagine her wrapping her legs around my waist, moaning into my ear, and letting me do what I need to find my release.

I will never get enough. She created a man obsessed with her body and the tremors that run through her when I tell her I love her.

"I didn't say anything," I say, trapping her against the wall, my hands braced above her shoulders.

The car pulls into the lot and idles.

"You didn't have to. Do you still want me to spend the night tonight?"

"Do you have to ask?" I suck her bottom lip into my mouth. She's wearing her dress from last night, her panties in a ball in her little purse. She's barefoot, her heels dangling from her hand, and her mascara is smeared under her eyes. There's nothing I want more than to push my face between her legs and make her come.

"Just checking. I better go. I don't want him to wait too long."

"I'll pick you up at quarter to. Pack a bag, and I'll have it delivered to the house."

"Okay. Thank you, for last night." She cups my cock in her hand, and feeling how hard I am for her, a soft moan rumbles from the back of her throat. Maybe tonight I'll ask her for a blowjob. I want to watch her suck me off.

"It will always be my pleasure. Get out of here now, or I'll have you under me one last time."

She presses a hard kiss to my lips and hurries out the door, not taking any chances that I won't do as I say. I didn't hurt her this morning, going slow and easy, but I didn't let her rest, and that's what she needs between now and tonight when I go at her again.

Christ, I have it bad, and there will be no way I can disguise it tonight. Emma will be happy, but Durand, maybe a little less so. I don't think he has any residual feelings for Nic, but he never liked me, still doesn't even though he and Emma came out the other side of his shit engaged, and I don't need him telling her to stay away from me. She wouldn't listen to an ex, but our relationship is already a dead end. We don't need to add anymore roadblocks.

I clean up the kitchen before I shower, reliving last night. Unable to keep my hands off her, I licked peanut butter off Nic's lips, making her laugh. I love the sound. She doesn't do it nearly enough.

That's it.

It's not so much the sex, the orgasms, that I need. It's our connection. Her soul glimmering in her eyes as she stares at me. The emotions radiating from her when she kisses me. What I feel when I'm deep inside her, the tip of my cock touching the deepest part of her. It's more than saying we're soulmates, but maybe that's what it is. The utter, all-consuming need to know that she's mine, and the only proof I'll accept is if I'm inside her in some way. My fingers, my tongue, my dick, my cum. My heart. Something that tells her she will always belong to me.

I'm rock hard again, but it's not sex I need. It's her clothes in my dressers, her toothbrush in the holder next to mine. It's sharing a car to work. It's sleeping in on Sundays, like the vision Aunt Caro planted in my head, but maybe without the kids. I don't need any like Durand, and I think, if I asked her, Nic would prefer not to have them, too. We would be happy, the two of us.

I want to marry her, but what I know of her family, she would say no and she would be correct to do so because with my own family shit, I have no right to ask.

I shower, but I don't take care of myself like I would have in the past. It's only physical gratification, and after spending the night with Nic, I need more.

There's still time to hit the office, and half my bloggers are there, writing up news reports about the things that went on last night. Mini interviews with Bridgeport's elite, soundbites, and clips of them coming and going, who they're wearing, what they're doing. Every blogger I hire signs a thousand forms legally swearing they would never submit a lie for me to print. I hold the legal authority to sue the ass off anyone who dares to make shit up or stretch the truth, and they all know with my law degree I would have no qualms doing it.

Not that it's something I worry about. For some reason, I attract good people, and everyone who works for me possesses the same set of twisted ethics that keeps me out of trouble.

I walk through the bullpen to my office, and they all grin and wave.

I don't have anything to do unless I want to report on myself and my relationship with Nic. I couldn't care less if people know we're dating or not and I'll let the rival bloggers who work for the *Bridgeport Beat* write up something tonight. They'll see Nic and I attended the fundraiser together, and that will be good enough.

Because I was offline last night and this morning, I scan my own e-zine. There's an interesting reaction article one of my guys wrote up in regard to CNBC's piece about Durand and the state Variant will fall into once he marries Emma. I like it, and I write a mental note to tell him so. Thought-provoking and meticulously researched, sprinkled liberally with quotes from both Ron and Jack, my guy defended Jack's engagement and told anyone who thinks Jack is going soft to take a hike.

Maybe I *am* slacking—it's a piece I should have written myself (considering I have the connections) if Nic hadn't crawled under my skin and turned into an itch I can't scratch.

There are a few more pieces I appreciate having on my 'zine: the history of the Bridgeport's Women's Reproductive

Health and Resources Center, the work it does, and why it needs the donations that will be raised tonight, an interview with an opera singer who will be visiting Bridgeport for a performance at the beginning of July and who will sing the national anthem at the baseball game that Sunday afternoon, and a scandalicious piece about the president of a local bank leaving his wife for his mistress. I appreciate the business article and the opera singer's interview—they give *Talk of the Town* the class our reputation needs to stay on top, but it's pieces like the banker cheating on his wife that pay my bills.

The content is hot, fresh, and strong. Everyone deserves an extra bonus at Christmas.

I push away from my desk, ready to leave for home to change into my tux, but my cell rings, and I pause. It's my dad, and I'm tempted not to answer it. Reese warned me this was coming, but the war strategies Aunt Caro and I talked about at lunch last weekend did little to prepare me for what the real downfall will feel like. I'll do anything to keep my freedom, keep my e-zine, and more than that, *not* turn into a walking robot posing as an attorney spewing case verdicts and the damning, last piece of crucial evidence in my sleep to prove I'm the best of the best, but I may not be so resigned to losing my family as Caro was. What little there is of it.

"Hey, Dad," I say, leaning back in my chair. My father will know if I try to multitask and accuse me of not giving a damn about what he has to say. If I give him my full attention, he'll get off the phone a lot faster. I don't want to be the reason we're late. We're on an unstable enough path that if I'm running behind, Nic will think I changed my mind and stood her up.

"Rafferty," he says, his voice smooth and holding a bit of humor. Like the saying goes, I am my father's son. Reese is all Mom. "You know why I'm calling."

"It's not to catch up," I say, trying to keep the bitterness out of my voice. He does call on occasion because he misses me, and the first time he admitted that, I choked up. Christ, I was what, fourteen, maybe. Not long at Aunt Caro's but long enough she and Emma had made a significant impact on my life.

"Yes and no," he says easily. "Reese said he called and told you the good news. I'm wondering if you've made any progress on that front now that Emma's off the market."

When it came to Emma, she was never in my market, but I let the comment slide. Everyone thought we'd get married, and I can't fault my parents for doing the same.

"Maybe."

"Good, good. Why don't you bring her out for the Fourth? Let us take a look at her."

I wince. "Mom would like her job about as well as she likes mine."

"What is she, a stripper?"

Barking out a laugh, I say, "No, but with a body like hers, she could be."

"Then I think your mom would be okay. She's hard on you, but in her own way, she's proud of you."

That's news to me, and probably a lie. Dad wants me to move to Boston as much as Mom but for entirely different reasons. He would expect me to join the family firm because what else would I do, but he wants me to be near family first and foremost, something that is significantly lower on Mom's list.

"Right."

"There's no reason why you can't do what you're doing there up here."

No, there's no reason at all, except I would have to start from scratch and the news I report on would take a sharp turn into a territory I don't want to go. I don't care about politics and politicians behaving badly. I don't care about lobbyists and bills passed and vetoed. And I really don't care about what happens in the White House.

I don't answer.

"I wish you'd work with us," he says. "When we sent you to Caroline's, we didn't think you'd stay in Bridgeport."

"What did you think I'd do? Aunt Caro let me do as I pleased, and it was because of that freedom I straightened out. Mom was constantly breathing down my neck. Do this, do that. And I would try, and I could never get it right. 'Not that way,' she'd say. Aunt Caro taught me how to use the washer and dryer, take out the trash, and she expected me to clean the kitchen after she cooked. If I did that and got good grades, she left me alone. Emma picked up the rest. You probably *are* lucky we didn't get married. She was born in Bridgeport, you know. Her mother lives here, and she'd never leave. You can hound me because I haven't met anyone I'd stay here for."

I'd stay for Nic if she liked Bridgeport and didn't want to live anywhere else, but she already told me she's not in it for the long haul and it's easier for me to accept it than fight her on it.

Dad sighs.

"I don't know why you can't let me be. I like it here and despite Mom hating what I do, I employ some good people doing what I love. Why can't she be happy for me?"

"She feels guilty, Raff."

"*Excuse me?*" I can't believe what I just heard.

"She feels guilty we sent you to live with Caroline in the first place. Believe me, it's not what your mother wanted, but we didn't know what else to do and your happiness was a priority. You were supposed to come home after high school graduation, but Emma talked her into letting you go to college with her. She thought maybe after you'd done some growing up, you'd see things our way. You went to Harvard like we wanted, but then you went back to Bridgeport. She underestimated your ties to Emma."

"It wasn't only Emma. I love Aunt Caro, Dad, something I don't think anyone has considered, not that anyone has bothered to ask. She's getting up in age, not so much she needs help, but I'm not leaving her alone. She's family. More family than Mom ever was. I was only a burden who didn't fall in line."

Dad sucks in a breath. "That is not true."

"Sure it is, but I stopped caring because she did me a favor sending me here. I miss you too, but I can't put up with Mom. She should be happy Reese found a wife who will have so much in common with her. Belinda's the perfect addition to the family."

"Melinda."

"I don't care. Love me for who I am or not at all. Mom made that choice when she packed me up instead of sitting me down and asking me what I needed, and you didn't stop her. I found that with Aunt Caro. It's past the time for you to regret it."

"I told her that sending you to live in Minnesota would do more harm than good."

"By whose standards? Thanks to Aunt Caro and Emma, I had the resources and support I needed to build . . . what did *People* call it? A media empire? By reporting the truth, the whole truth, and nothing but the truth, so help me God. A phrase you should be well acquainted with. I'm a self-made millionaire, and to anyone else that would be something to be proud of. But Jesus Christ, for the kind of life Mom thinks I'm living, Nic might as well be a stripper. According to Mom, that's all I'm good enough for. Now, you'll have to excuse me. I'm due for a fundraiser for women's reproductive rights, something Mom would probably also find fault in, because I could never, and will never, be good enough. Enjoy the rest of your weekend," I say, ending the call as I would any other business associate.

I resist the urge to fling my phone across the room. I'll need it to document my time at the fundraiser. I'm Nic's date, but I'd still go alone if only to cover the event for the 'zine myself. My personal life is tangling with my professional life. It always has, to some extent, but now that Nic and I are together, reporting her comings and goings may not feel as comfortable anymore.

Emma texts while I'm standing on the sidewalk waiting for my car, and I'll grab another to pick up Nic. There's no point in driving to Heath and Zoey's. We're riding in a limo to the event, and I scheduled a limo to bring us back to my place when it's done.

Sorry about this morning, I read, the text accompanied by a grimacing emoji.

Not a big deal. If we can talk about Durand knocking you up, you can talk to Nic while she's in my bed.

I don't want her to be uncomfortable.

Are YOU uncomfortable? I ask.

The three dots appear, and I wait. With as friendly and as open as Emma is, I never gave it a thought she wouldn't want to be Veronica's friend, but maybe that's not true. She puts my mind at ease right away, like I should have known she would.

Maybe if she would have loved Jack, but she said she didn't, so, no, I'm not uncomfortable.

Thanks, baby girl, I type, the endearment difficult to let go of.

It's okay. After last night, are you a couple?

I pause, consider the implications of what I'm about to tell her. I never loved Emma Cox. As a friend, as a sister, but never as a potential lover. If I'd had those kinds of feelings about her, I would have told her to see where it led, to see if she felt the same. But I didn't, and she didn't, and telling her the truth should be easy, but somehow, it's not. *I'm in love with her, Em.*

I'm happy for you. I really, really am. She ends the sentence with a red heart.

Thanks. We'll see how it turns out, yeah?

Yeah. See you in a little bit.

Sounds good.

She doesn't respond, and I slip my phone into my pocket. I want to text Nic and see what she's doing. Has she showered? Is she taking a nap? Popping some ibuprofen? I was rough with her, her body not sating my hunger even for a second. I need more, and I won't be embarrassed finding a dark stairwell and letting her give it to me.

I've already proven her panties are an inconvenient obstacle and easily remedied. A poufy skirt might be another obstruction I'll need to conquer, but I think I would very much like to fuck her while she's wearing heels.

Whenever Emma and I dressed for something like this, we would do it at her apartment. We'd sip wine, listen to music, and gossip about who would be there. The change in routine is strange, and it feels disconcerting to partially dress at my place alone. I leave my vest and suitcoat for last, hanging them on a padded hanger, and I shove my bowtie into a pocket. I haven't mastered tying it, but Emma will know how if Nic doesn't. Maybe I shouldn't ask Emma to do things like that anymore. Zoey will know how. She'll be a safer bet if I don't want to ruin the evening with hard feelings before things even start.

Maybe Nic's right. Maybe swapping partners would have been easier if Emma and I had been sleeping together. Things couldn't feel any worse. Actually, they could. I should shut the fuck up.

Wearing a sundress in mint green, Nic's waiting for me on the sidewalk the way she always does, right on time, two blush pink duffle bags hanging from her hands, sunglasses hiding her eyes.

I climb out of the car and pull her to me, pedestrians eyeing us as they walk by.

"Kiss me," I demand, and she does, slanting her lips over mine, dropping her bags to rest her hands on the nape of my neck, her painted nails scraping my skin. "Do that to my back tonight."

She leans away and lifts her sunglasses, her eyes wide. "You like it rough."

"I don't get carried away—"

She quirks an eyebrow in disbelief.

"—very often. But yeah. You don't? I can tone it down. It's not a dealbreaker."

"I've never needed a safe word," she says.

I pick up her bags and nod my head toward the car. "You won't need one with me," I say, tossing her bags into the front passenger's seat. The driver doesn't pay us any attention. "Telling me to stop or that you need a break will be enough."

She bites her lip. "I'll need to explore first, before I can decide what I like and what I'll need."

I sit next to her and close the door.

The driver merges into traffic, and I drag her into my lap and nibble on her neck. "That sounds good to me. Explore away." I tilt my hips, letting her feel how hard I am.

She laughs and rests her palms on the sides of my face. "I'm not ignoring what you said last night. I love you, too. I want you to know that."

Searching her eyes, I look for regret or maybe remorse she can't follow through with the words, but her eyes are clear, and there's nothing on her face but truth. "I was going to give you time, but I'm a very happy man you can tell me now. I'll enjoy fucking your brains out that much more."

She giggles against my lips, and we kiss the entire way to Heath and Zoey's.

———

The driver lets us out in front of their brownstone, and from the sidewalk we hear Graciela's, Hilary's, and Paige's shrieks.

Nic steps back, her lips parted. "What's happening?"

I chuckle. "Children. Are you good?"

She puts on a brave face. "I have to be. My dress is being held captive in there."

"Zoey will have some liquid courage."

"I hope so."

Cracking the front passenger door, I ask, "I assume one of these is for here, and the other for my place?"

"Yeah. You'll have to look inside them. The one with the hairspray is for here."

I find the one she needs easily enough, yank my coat and vest off the garment hook, and tuck the hanger under my arm. I instruct the driver to drop Nic's sleepover tote at my place. I don't want her worried about her things.

Holding her bag, the dry-cleaning plastic covering my tux fluttering in the light breeze, I stop her on the steps. "Nic."

She looks at me, one step above mine, eye-level. "What?"

"Thank you." I don't have to explain what I'm thanking her for.

She drags her thumb over my lower lip the way I like to do to hers. "Emma and the others make it easy. You don't have to thank me for anything. You want me to be a part of your group, and I would like to be. Very much."

I open my mouth to respond, but Zoey flings the door open. "Are you kissing? There's no time for that. The girls are dying to meet Veronica."

"Don't let my love life get in their way," I mumble.

"What did you say?" Zoey asks, Paige peeking curiously around her leg.

"I'm excited for tonight," I lie.

She laughs. "That's exactly what you said. Come inside. I'll hang up your tux. You can leave Veronica's bag by the stairs."

"Thanks."

I wrap my arm firmly around Nic's shoulders in case she gets the bright idea to cut and run, and we follow Zoey into the living room. Durand is sitting in a recliner sipping something that looks damned good, and Heath is perched on the edge of the couch cushion. Our arrival might have interrupted some business talk—talk I may want in on later. Now that I'm getting to know Heath, maybe I should let him steer me in the direction of a little investing.

Footfalls thunder down the hall, and Graciela and Hilary start shrieking as if the world caught on fire.

"Your hair is really silver!" Hilary yells, jumping up and down, her own blonde hair the color of Zoey's bouncing around her shoulders.

"Let me see!" Paige demands, and confused, bemused, and not used to being around children, Nic drops to the floor giving the little girl easier access. Paige immediately takes up residence in her lap, Hilary sits on the floor next to her, and Graciela has the courtesy to ask, "Can I touch it?"

"Uh, sure," Nic says.

"Oh, my God, it is so soft! What do you use in it?"

Nic answers, but I can't hear what she says.

Zoey offers me a drink and watches her girls fawn over Nic. "She dated Durand for two years and your girls have never met her before?" I ask, disapproval heavy in my voice.

She lifts a shoulder. "If we hadn't gone out, I wouldn't have met her either. Jack didn't do things like this with her."

"Why?"

"You'd have to ask them. Jack never acted like his relationship with her was . . . personal."

I scowl, Durand sinking a few more notches. I try not to let it bother me, and I know what Emma would say. Nic condoned him treating her like that, maybe even wanted him to. If I'm being honest, I wouldn't be here either, except it makes Emma happy, and this will be the only way I'll get to see her anymore.

"Mom! Can I do this to my hair?" Hilary asks, twisting a strand of Nic's around her finger.

"Me too!" Paige says, her head resting on Nic's shoulder.

"Is that what you want, Gracie?" Zoey asks.

From the couch, Heath raises his eyebrows. In response, Zoey lifts her hands in an exaggerated gesture that says, *What are we gonna do? Say no?*

"Maybe some highlights?" Graciela says, older, wiser, and more practical than her sisters. "I don't know. Is it a lot of work, Miss Chapman?"

"Oh, call me Veronica, please. The first time lasts a couple of hours, but after that part is done, it's not so bad."

Zoey pauses, no doubt wondering how much of a pain in the ass it would be and if the outcome will be worth it. Finally, she says, "I'll call for appointments if Veronica says she'll come with us. I wouldn't have any idea what to ask for."

In alarm, Nic's gaze flies to mine, and I chuckle. "That's up to you, dollface. I want no part in it."

She bites her lip. "I'm free during the week after one o'clock, or the weekends are pretty open. Does that work?"

"Yep. I'll book my stylist and let you know when she'll have time for all this," Zoey says, waving her hands around, but I can't hear her over the girls' piercing exclaims of delight.

Nic winces.

Zoey laughs, the light sound just between us. "We're going to pull her in kicking and screaming, aren't we?"

Thinking of my promise of liquid courage, I say, "She might go a little more willingly if she had wine."

"You're right, I'm being a poor hostess, but the girls were so excited when I told them they would get to meet her. Girls," she says, raising her voice, "let's go upstairs. Veronica needs to dress and do her hair and makeup with the rest of us."

High on anticipation and the tantalizing adult night ahead, the girls run for the stairs, Paige scrambling out of Nic's lap as quickly as she can to keep up with her older sisters.

I drain the whiskey Zoey gave me, set the glass on the kitchen table, and hold out a hand to Nic. I haul her to her feet and cover her mouth with mine, my palm to the back of her neck holding her still. I don't care if Durand's watching. If he'd wanted her, she'd been willing, but he let her go. There's nothing he can say about our relationship or how fast we fell into it.

Zoey waits until I release her, and they disappear up the steps. Nic snags her bag from the hallway where I dropped it when we came in.

"There's wine upstairs with Emma, Mia, and Haisley," I hear Zoey say, but they're too far away for me to hear Nic probably reply, "Thank God."

Christ, I love that woman.

Durand eyes me from across the living room wearing black tuxedo pants like mine, his shirt undone in a similar fashion.

I don't want to deal with him now, and I know it's rude, but I retreat to the kitchen without thanking Heath for the invite. This was mostly Zoey's doing anyway, and I need more to drink before I face Durand. Because he and Nic parted as friends, he'll want to know where my thoughts are headed. If we're going to stay a part of the group, as Nic called us, I'll need to tell him she's mine and assure him I have only good intentions toward her.

Claire's in the kitchen, leaning against the sink, a glass of wine in her hand. She's not dressed yet, perhaps waiting for some of the chaos upstairs to abate.

"Hey, kid," I say, hooking my arm around her neck and kissing her temple. I was never close to Claire Durand until she asked me to check into what Ron told her and Jack. After a couple of late nights snooping and a box of tissues, I feel the brotherly warmth Jack feels. Plus, she's spunky. I like her abrasiveness despite her using it to keep people at bay.

"Fuck off, I'm six years older than you," she says, but she's smiling.

I shrug good-naturedly. "Would you prefer Claire Bear?"

She rubs the top of her nose with her middle finger.

Chuckling, I ask, "What are you doing in here all by yourself? Why aren't you with the others?"

"Catching a minute to breathe. Tonight's going to suck, and it will start the second I go upstairs."

"You don't like Emma and her friends?"

"It's not that. I like her and think she's a better match for my brother than Veronica, no offense."

"None taken. If she were with your brother, she wouldn't be with me."

Claire tips her head. "It's all the . . . happy."

"Not everything is the way it seems," I say. Nic's family shit is hanging over my head like an anvil in an old cartoon. My family is no better, but if I didn't have Nic's father to worry about and what he needs that will eventually steal her from me, my mother wouldn't be the stressor she is. I can only handle one thing at a time.

Claire snorts in that inelegant way she's adopted. "Really? Watch this."

She pulls her cell out of the pocket of her slacks, brings up Emma's contact information, and sends a text: *Jack has a question for you. Can you come down here?*

"He's talking with Heath," I say uselessly. Claire knows this.

Nudging me to the side and giving us a clear view of the living room, she says, "Dummy. I know that. Watch."

A minute later we hear footfalls on the stairs, and Emma pads barefoot into the living area from the hallway. She's wearing a robe over a bra and panties, but her hair is done, a massive number of curls cascading down her back. Durand looks up, and Jesus Christ. I see what Claire means. He's like a different person. His eyes turn gooey, and there is nothing on his face but utter, complete, and undiluted love and devotion.

I am so glad Emma found what she was looking for.

She settles in his lap, and he lowers his head to kiss her.

Heath smiles and rolls his eyes in amusement, but it's clear he's happy for his friend. It was a rocky month for Durand and Emma, and it was only Emma's persistence and forgiveness that guided him through it.

"I can't deal with it," Claire whispers.

"Are you angry your brother found happiness despite what Ron told you about your mother?"

"That's a big part of it," she admits, "yet, how can I resent him what he found with Emma? She's so generous and kind. I wouldn't even be here if she hadn't insisted I come. I'd be the shittiest person alive if I didn't want him to be with her."

"It's not shitty. Misery loves company. That's natural. But you don't have to be miserable, kid. Now that you know the truth, find your own happy."

"When did you become so naïve? I divorced the one man I could have been happy with. He put up with my shit, thinking if he hung in there long enough he could melt the Ice Queen of Bridgeport."

"Hot sex wasn't enough?" I ask, teasing her.

"I needed him to set my heart on fire, not my body."

"A real man can do both—"

She frowns.

"Okay, okay, but I hate seeing you like this. Roman did that, didn't he? Your heart? Don't tell me about the sex."

She glares at me and downs the rest of the wine in her glass.

"It wasn't him, it was you. If that time's passed, then find someone else. Zeke was an asshole and you married him hoping Roman would trot to your rescue on a gleaming white steed and he didn't. Put all that crap behind you and start dating, for real. Not just for show or something to do. Better yet, forget about romance for a minute and figure out what the fuck you want to do with your life. A little direction couldn't hurt."

"I'm a fisherman."

I've heard Durand equate Claire's social life with trolling a lake for walleye. I didn't care for it then, and I don't care for it now. "Then that's why you're fucked. The nearest body of water is hours from here."

"I guess you have a point."

"I know I do. You have the money, and you have the brains. You have connections. Figure your shit out, Claire."

She meets my eyes. "You know what, you're right. I've been wallowing."

"You think?"

Emma slides off Jack's lap. He tangles his hand in her robe, not letting her go, and if they'd been alone, she would have been under him in five seconds.

"We can see you," I call across the living room.

Durand loosens his hand, and Emma looks over her

shoulder at us, the pure joy emanating from her lighting the entire room.

"That's what I mean," Claire mumbles.

"Emma worked hard for what she has, and you know that," I mumble in reply as Emma walks toward us. "She deserves it."

"Hey," Emma says, stepping close to me and it's that habit I have to wrap my arms around her, and it's her habit to rest her head against my chest. "Jack didn't want anything."

Claire sighs. "Sorry. I must have misunderstood."

"That's okay." She peers up at me, her eyes luminous and accented with a glittered eyeliner. "Veronica's having a good time up there. We had to stop Paige from painting her fingernails, and Paige demanded she sign a raincheck agreement."

"Jesus." It's not like Veronica hates kids, not that I'm aware of, but she hasn't had much experience with the whole friends and family discount plan.

"She's definitely a hit. Are you coming up?" she asks Claire. "If you wanted to use the hot curlers, they're free."

"Sure. Do we need more wine?"

"Probably by now. Come on."

Emma steps out of my embrace but doesn't move to go upstairs. Claire knows she's trapped, and she grabs a full bottle of rosé off the counter by the neck. "I'm coming."

I wink at Claire, and finally, she lets herself smile. We all want to have a good time tonight, and Claire has habits of her own.

She'll be fishing all night.

———

"Can't keep your hands off my woman," Durand grouses.

I knew arriving at the same time as Veronica would drag me into unwanted conversation with Heath and Durand for at least an hour, but to ease the pain, I help myself to Heath's stash of whiskey at the bar, adding to the empty glass Zoey gave me. The only booze in the kitchen was wine, and that's definitely not strong enough.

"We don't need to talk about what you did with mine," I say mildly, "so I think if I want to hug Emma I can and you need to let it go."

"The first aid kit is upstairs. Knock it off," Heath says, holding out his glass to me.

"We'll get it out of our systems eventually," I say, trickling whiskey into his glass from the half-empty decanter. "No one here's tapped Zoey, or you'd know how we feel."

He blanches at the thought of his wife being with anyone but him.

"You two getting serious?" Durand asks, shooting Heath an amused glance and hitching an ankle to his knee, making himself comfortable.

"You didn't mention the wall is six feet thick, twenty feet high, topped with barbed wire and I'd have to cross a moat first, but I'm trying my best."

"Emma mentioned after they went shopping for dresses that she might be in some kind of trouble."

I rub my forehead. "All she's told me when I've been ballsy enough to pry is that her father got mixed up in some shit. Did she ever talk about her family?"

"No, nothing, but we've already determined I'm a son of a bitch, and I didn't ask. She wouldn't have told me if I had, but I didn't. You look her up?"

"I was hoping she'd tell me on her own."

"You haven't been together long. Give her time."

"I don't think that's something we have."

"I feel that," Durand says. "You might have to push if you want to get anywhere."

"Yeah." I sit on the armrest of the couch.

Durand and Heath resume their conversation, and I scribble mental notes of stocks and to ask Heath to get a hold of me for an appointment at his office.

Forty-five minutes later and more booze than I should have consumed before the event, the staircase shakes with three little girls thundering down to the first floor. They stand in front of Heath, and even my heart tugs when his eyes water.

"You look beautiful," he says and clears his throat. "I want each of you to promise me a dance."

Paige giggles and begins to twirl, her dress's skirt flying around her waist. Hilary and Graciela try to rein in their excitement, but their flushed cheeks give them away. They're cute, and their characteristics are all Zoey's.

She steps into the room, and Heath, Durand, and I stand to our feet. I never thought of Zoey as beautiful, not in a classic way, but pretty, in an easy-breezy hippy kind of way, with clear skin and freckles, delicate features, and blonde hair that today she's braided into a fishtail, the long plait resting over her bare shoulder. She reminds me of someone, and I can't place who until she says, "The girls wanted me to do my hair like this—it looks like Elsa's in *Frozen*."

"You're gorgeous," Heath says. "You're going to knock 'em dead tonight."

"Thank you," she murmurs against his lips.

Emma, Claire, Nic, and Haisley and Mia come down together, and if I had to guess, Emma orchestrated that on purpose not wanting Claire to feel left out without her own date.

Durand and I join them, and though I knew what Nic was going to wear, she still knocks the breath out of my lungs. I've never seen her hair done in the curls she's wearing now, and all

I want to do is tangle my fingers in them while I fuck her from behind.

She reads my face, and her lips pull into a smile. "Behave."

I chuckle. "For a little while."

I put on my vest and suitcoat and Nic expertly ties my bowtie, relieving me of the uncomfortable task of asking.

We're the last to climb into the enormous limo, and I nuzzle her lips with mine, my fingers brushing the bare skin of one of her shoulders. "You're beautiful. I love you so much."

She sighs, her hand resting against my side under my jacket. "I love you too. Don't be sad tonight, okay?"

Already reading me well, I force a smile. I don't want her to worry. "Sure, dollface. I'll be fine."

"Good."

We squeeze into the limo with the others, and Durand pops a bottle of champagne.

The driver navigates through the traffic to the most anticipated event of the year.

———

The red carpet in front of the Bridgeport Hotel is crowded, reporters and photographers jostling for position and our attention. I know them all, from the sleazebag at the end to the professional journalists covering the event for their papers' entertainment sections.

Though Nic is my date, my *real* date, I can't forget the part I have to play, and when it's our turn, walking behind Heath, Zoey, and their children, I'm prepared with answers that will not only claim Nic as mine, but also bump up her standing in Bridgeport society. She never said anything about what this evening means to her career, not after the conversation we had when I accused her of using me.

"Are you and Veronica dating?" a reporter asks. The photographer with him snaps our picture. No one asks who she's wearing—*Rise and Shine, Bridgeport!* already broadcasted that information.

"Yes," I say, holding her close, and she stiffens. "It was hard and fast for me, and I hope she feels the same."

"And do you, Veronica?" he asks, his phone poised in front of us, capturing her answer.

"Yes, I do."

"What about Jack Durand? It wasn't that long ago you wanted him to propose."

I open my mouth to defend her, but she says, "Jack and I were a mistake, and he did something about it. He's with the person he should be with now, and so am I." She turns her face toward me, inviting me to kiss her, and I do, a hand to her cheek.

We gave the paparazzi what they wanted, and we walk the rest of the red carpet without stopping. In the lobby, I pull her off to the side to wait for Durand, Emma, and Claire. The paparazzi aren't going as easy on them. Someone at his attorney's office leaked the surrogacy contract, and they're talking babies with the reporters while Claire answers questions about their father's involvement with the Bridgeport's Women's Reproductive Health and Resources Center.

"You did good," I tell Nic, and she blows out a breath.

"I told the truth. I'm with who I'm supposed to be."

"One day, Nic, I'm going to ask you to marry me, and I hope you say yes." I don't know why I said it. Yearning, perhaps, when I look into her eyes, or the glimpse of a future I caught standing in Zoey and Heath's entryway, waiting for the limo. Maybe it was thinking about going home with her after an event like this and needing it for the rest of my life. All those things and more, but one day, I will ask, and one day, she'll say yes.

She looks away, and I tamp down my temper. I'm not like Durand. I will figure this out.

"Come on. We can't forget you're at work, and so am I," I say, tugging gently on her hand. The other guests swirl around us in a cloud of elation, delight, and champagne. From down the corridor, I hear Paige squeal, and I wonder what she saw that would elicit such a response.

"I thought you didn't want to talk about that?" she asks, walking by my side, waving at people and pretending that four weeks ago they weren't talking shit about her whenever and however they could.

I slam to a stop, and the couple walking behind us veers away before plowing into our backs. "Do you love me?"

She blinks. "You know I do."

"Do you have a problem with what I do for a living?"

Her eyes widen. "No. That would be a bit hypocritical, wouldn't it? Being that I've benefitted from it?"

"Do you think I'm using you to boost subscribers to the e-zine?"

"I think we've used each other. Raff, what's wrong?"

"Nothing. It's nothing. There's no point in pretending we're here because we want to be."

"I'm here because I want to be with you. You're here because you want to be with me. That both our careers benefit from it isn't something to be ashamed of. You and Emma used to come to stuff like this all the time because you needed to. It's not different."

"Do you wish I did something more respectable?" I grip her arm, my fingertips sinking into her soft skin.

"We both gossip for a living, but we do it in different ways.

Do you wish I did something else?" she whispers, brushing her lips over the shell of my ear.

"Sometimes," I admit, though the thought didn't occur to me until just now. "I hate other men looking at you."

"That's sweet. Let's go have fun. We have to be here, so let's make the most of it."

"All right," I say, though fun is going to be the last thing I have tonight.

"Hey, are you guys okay?" Emma approaches us, her short train dragging on the floor behind her.

The paparazzi finally let them go and Durand looks pissed. I wonder what they asked him.

"Yeah. Grabbing the last second we can to ourselves."

"It's over. Let's go." Claire grins at me.

I resist trapping her in a headlock. "Brat." We step into the ballroom, and I ask Nic, "Will you be okay if I go do a couple of things?" Normally, I would have already had all my cameras in place for the live stream the board of the Center granted me permission to use, but I've been so caught up with Nic that I'm hours behind.

"Yeah. I'll see you for dinner?"

"We should be seated next to each other, but I'll find you before that."

"Okay." She whispers a kiss over my cheek and walks away with Emma and Durand. They head in Heath and Zoey's direction who are standing at the bar, the girls flitting from table to table exploring and exclaiming over the elegant place settings and centerpieces.

Are you around here somewhere? I text Justin. He's covering the event with me and should have brought our streaming equipment ahead of time.

All done, boss. Don't worry about a thing.

It's not that I don't trust him, but before I respond, I bring up *Talk of the Town*'s app on my phone and navigate to the live stream. Justin set up one camera in the back, above my head, and if I stepped a few hundred feet forward, the camera would catch me. This one will stream the speakers when the program begins. The other he set up at the front behind the dais—giving people who watch a full view of the ballroom—and I do see myself in the very back, hidden by shadows, since I haven't stepped deeper into the party yet.

He did good. *Thanks. Where are you?*

In the hallway. Going to try to get some soundbites. They asked if we would share for the promotional materials for next year, and I said you wouldn't mind.

No, that's great, thanks. Bump into you later.

I don't care if we give the center's board some of the interview content for next year's event. It's a worthwhile partnership, and I'm pleased Justin didn't put them off.

At the bar, I ask for a tonic water and lemon. With the amount of booze I drank at Heath's and the champagne we chugged in the limo, if I don't stop drinking, I'll be trashed before the evening ends. I want to be sober enough to enjoy peeling Nic's dress off her delectable body, having my way with her, and making her cry my name.

"There's a man who knows when to stop."

"Here's a man who wants to be able to get it up later." Some would say that's no way to talk to Dennis Iverson, but he chuckles, tipping his head in acknowledgement. "Mayor. Nice to see you," I say, holding out my hand. Bridgeport's mayor shakes it firmly.

"Clark. You're in fine form."

"A person needs stamina if they're going to party for a living."

"You're not kidding. I read the piece you wrote about that

soap star. My wife gobbles up anything that has to do with *Shattered Yesterdays*. He really didn't cheat, huh?"

I lift a shoulder. "Did he nail a chick who wasn't his wife in a dark closet where prying eyes couldn't find him? I don't think anyone will have a true answer to that except him. There are good liars and there are bad ones, but if he was lying, he's good enough I believed him, and I'm not duped often."

"No, you wouldn't be. It's a skill, telling the truth and learning how to sniff out the shit."

I sip my water. "Telling the truth isn't a skill, Mayor, in a naturally honest person, it's ingrained. Now, if we're talking shades of grey and lies of omission, I would think pulling that off would require a bit more talent, and trust from the person who's asked to swallow the poison with the sugar. I've built *Talk of the Town* on truth, and I doubt I would be where I am today if I hadn't."

"Yes, I agree. My question to you is, where are you?"

I shoot him a look, puzzled. "What do you mean?"

"You hold this town by the balls—"

"I don't think that's an apt description of my position in this city. That's more your thing."

Mayor Iverson shakes his head. "I'm getting tired, Clark. I've been Bridgeport's mayor for the past ten years trying to steer her in the right direction. Growth, opportunity, keeping the gangs under control and drugs off my streets."

"You've done a good job."

"I have two more years to finish out this term. I'm not going to run again."

"That will be a blow to the city."

"Thank you. You're dating Veronica Chapman now, is that right? You're a nice looking couple."

"We're fumbling in the dark. I don't know the kinds of bugs that will scurry away if I turn on the lights."

Iverson cuts me a sharp glance. "You think she's hiding something? She's been co-host of *Rise and Shine, Bridgeport!* for years. Nothing's ever popped."

I search for her in the crowd and find her in front of an enormous ice replica of the Variant building in honor of all the money the Durands contribute to the resource center. Hollowed out and lit up with lights, the colors represent Variant's logo—black and deep shades of purple. Paige is in her arms, her skinny legs wrapped around Nic's waist. They're touching the ice, then pulling away, laughing.

"Or no one's cared enough to look," I murmur.

"Do you think a background check would go south?"

I frown. "With all due respect, Mayor, I don't know what you're getting at."

"I'm not running for another term."

"I heard you."

"I want you to take my place."

I sputter, and a server walking by hands me a cocktail napkin. Gratefully, I dab at my lips. "Are you fucking crazy?"

Iverson twists his mouth. "No, actually, I think I'm quite sane."

"I'm not qualified to be mayor."

"You're as qualified as I was when I first ran—a law degree and a few million bucks. Elections are nothing but popularity contests, and like I said, you already hold this city by the balls. The second you announce your intentions, you'd trounce anyone who had a thought of running."

"Why me? I sling mud for a living."

"You don't. You report the truth on your terms, and that's made you a favorite in this town. You know as well as I do people need to trust any politician on the ballot. If you don't have their trust, you have nothing. With my endorsement, you'll be a shoo-in."

I scowl. "You don't have *anybody* else?"

"I don't want anybody else. Look, we've tested the waters—"

"You've *what?*"

"I wouldn't have approached you if I hadn't done my own research. What kind of mayor would I be? We've done some social media surveys, a few phone calls, canvassed some of the poorer parts of the city, see if you connected with them, too. There's no one we spoke with who had one bad word against you."

Agitated, I run a hand through my hair. How the fuck did I miss that? "I can't believe this. What would I do with my 'zine? I couldn't run it anymore. There are days you don't have time to shit, so don't insult me by telling me I could do both."

Iverson has the grace to laugh. "Classy, but you're right. I'm asking a lot."

"Damned straight you are."

"And you'd have to marry Veronica as quickly as possible. No one votes in a single guy."

"I don't hear what I'm getting out of this." I should have had a real drink after all.

"What every civil servant gets in return, the satisfaction of a job well done."

"Christ. You'll need to come up with something better than that."

Iverson's shoulders hunch. "Unfortunately, I don't have anything better besides my admiration which doesn't mean a goddamned thing to you. I won't endorse just anybody, and you're the first person I've approached. You're likely the only person, and when I go public with my retirement, you'll know where those bugs are. They're quick to come out of the wood-work if they think there's food."

"You're not kidding." I sigh. "When do you need a real answer?"

"Friday at the latest. You'll need to start laying your campaign foundation, figure out what you'd do with your e-zine. Marrying Veronica. If that's not in the cards, tell me now."

"I want to, but I don't know if she'd pass your background check. That's going to require a conversation we haven't had yet."

"If you can't, you can't. There are some things you can't control, but I'd be in your debt if you took this seriously. Bridgeport's in a good place. I worked hard and I would like to keep her there."

I hold out my hand. "It's an honor you think I'm the man for the job."

He shakes it, glancing over his shoulder at an attractive woman slightly older than me gliding across the room toward us. I could see Nic as a mayor's wife. She's elegant, sophisticated. Well liked.

Without another word to me, Iverson drifts from my side as if he didn't put my whole life into a tailspin. A mayor's position isn't a long-term life plan. Iverson might have served three full terms, but he's not retiring. He's got bigger fish to fry he didn't tell me about and securing a reliable replacement will only help his own approval rating when he runs for whatever it is he's got his eye on.

I don't want to give up *Talk of the Town,* and I don't want to marry Veronica because I have to. I don't want to do something my parents would be proud of me for. There would be nothing that would please my mother more than if I told her I was running for mayor and won the fucking election. I don't doubt Iverson's findings. I know people admire me and my integrity, they think I'm handsome, and in a game like that, with Nic by my side, yeah. I'd win.

Fuck.

I'm pissed and need to get it sorted out or the rest of the night will turn to shit.

Nic's talking to a woman I don't know, and I grab her arm and drag her away, not giving her a second to wrap up her conversation.

"What's the matter?" she cries, scrambling to keep up with me, her heels tangling in her dress's skirt.

"I need you," I say between gritted teeth, and I don't stop. I pull her through the ballroom—I don't care who's watching us—down a long carpeted corridor, and through a set of glass doors that lead to the garden where Durand and Emma held their engagement party.

"What happened?" she asks, clinging to my arm.

I don't answer. I'm painfully hard, Nic's panicked little puffs exciting me like no woman has before. There's a side of me that comes out around her, and I let him free, dragging her down the cobblestone pathway to the back of the garden where no one will be able to see us.

There's a bench in the corner, hidden by shadows, and I push her down onto it. I sit next to her and cover her mouth with mine, forcing my tongue into her mouth, not giving her even a moment to suck in a breath.

There's so much of her dress, but somehow I find the hem, my fingers searching for skin.

"Raff," she moans, submitting to me, wrapping her arms around my neck.

"Open your legs," I order, moving the silky material of her panties aside. "I need to touch you."

She does as I command, and without waiting one more second, I slide two fingers inside her. Her wet heat envelopes me, and I spurt in my briefs. I'm angry and for some stupid reason, hurting, and I want to hurt her too. I do, my fingers viciously ramming in and out of her, my knuckles bruising her.

I rub her clit with my thumb, and I devour her mouth, swallowing her mewling. She's close to coming. I know her every movement, and her clit quivers with an orgasm.

She whimpers against my lips.

"Pull your breast out of your dress. I want to suck on your nipple."

"Raff, no."

"Do it."

She releases my neck and does what I say. Her dress is strapless, the bodice tight, but she has no problem revealing her left breast and offering it to me.

I suck her nipple into my mouth and bite.

With the pain and a sob that echoes over the garden, she comes under my hand.

I release her breast and stop moving my fingers. She drifts down from her high, tears on her cheeks, her breath watery with release and lingering pain.

My balls hurt, and her cries almost made me come, but I don't forget what she needs first. I lick at her nipple, soothing the delicate skin, and she shudders, her hands still holding her breast in place up to my mouth.

Trying to be gentle now, I pull my fingers from her in a gush, but the friction still makes her shiver. I tuck her breast into her dress and cuddle her to me, praising her with little kisses over her face, thanking her for allowing me to have what I needed. I felt out of control speaking with the mayor, talking so casually about giving up close to what all my life consists of, and I needed to take it back in Nic's arms.

But I'm not done. "Nic, I need you on your knees."

She pulls away and I grab her hand, forcing her to feel how hard my cock is. She swallows.

"You w-want—I mean, can't we go upstairs? I'm sure there's a room—"

"I'll wait until I get you home to fuck you. I want you to suck me off. Can you, dollface? I need that."

"Oh," she breathes, and the surprise and her wide, startled eyes almost do me in.

"Please?"

"All right."

Wincing, she slides off the bench and arranges the dress under her knees. I let her do everything, and she unbuckles my belt and unbuttons my pants.

She pulls my briefs down, and my cock springs free, the tip wet. The scents of semen and sweat waft into the air, and I tangle my fingers in her curls the way I imagined when I first saw her dressed for tonight. I tug her head toward my cock.

She resists.

"How often did you give Durand blowjobs?" I ask. Not out of some sick curiosity, but I want to know how experienced she is. Most of the women I've been with haven't enjoyed giving them, and one woman had a gag reflex so sensitive all she had to do was think about a cock in her mouth and she'd throw up.

Nic looks at me, her blue eyes watery, shimmering in the twilight. "Never. We weren't that . . . close."

"Then when was the last time?"

"I've . . . Raff, I've never . . ."

I let out a breath. Christ. I am so fucking glad she's never given a blowjob before, but my blood is boiling and her inexperience is not something I want to tolerate right now. Still, I'm going to have to face it at some point, and we're alone and have time.

"Do you want to? I'll never ask you to do something you don't want to do. I love you, and I know I was rough with you just now, but you were on board with that or you would have said something, yes?"

"Yeah."

"Okay. Tell me what you want."

Instead of answering me, she lowers her head and licks at my cock.

I hiss out a breath. My balls draw up, and I am so hard I can't think of anything else except exploding in her mouth.

"Is that bad?" she asks, looking at me, her skin pale.

It kills me, you know, to see this confident woman kneeling at my feet, scared of, fuck, I don't know. She hasn't been the same since Durand fucked her over the night of his party, a little mouse frightened of her own shadow. Now she's on her knees, saliva and my semen shining on her lips, and I want nothing more than to keep her locked in that tower where nothing can hurt her ever again.

"It's good, Nic. Hurry. I'm gonna come hard, and you need to swallow it. We can't get messy, do you understand me?"

She nods and without another word, covers my cock with her mouth. Any other time my hands would be gripping her hair, but she needs space to do this her own way, and God knows, I'm going to shoot off like a geyser.

Her hand is fisted at the base of my cock and her mouth claims the rest. It's all I need, just a couple seconds of suction, her tongue pressed against the side of my dick. I come with a groan, pulsing beneath her hand. Nic struggles at first, my cum filling her mouth faster than she can swallow, but I wind down and she catches up. I finish and sit in a sweaty puddle, my hands aching from clenching the edge of the bench. Tipping my head back, I let loose a shuddery sigh, but the tension Iverson planted at the base of my skull is still there.

She licks at me, cleaning me off, but like her clit after an orgasm, I can't handle it, and I jerk away.

Laughing now that my temper has faded, she tucks me into my briefs and buttons my pants. I don't give her time to buckle me up, instead, wrapping my hands around her ribcage and lifting her onto my lap.

I kiss her, tasting myself on her lips. Leaning away, I rub her cheek with my thumb. "Are you okay? You make me wild, but if it's too much, you have to tell me, okay, dollface?"

"If I don't—"

Furiously, I cut her off. "I love you, Veronica. That means meeting in the middle. If I do something you don't like, you need to tell me, always. There will never be fallout because I'm mad. There is nothing you could ever say to me that would make me angry with you."

"There will be, one day."

"Maybe one day," I concede, "but it will never be about sex."

She scrapes her nails over my jaw, and I swear to God, I get hard all over again. "I like what we do."

"Good. I like what we do too. I never want you to not like it. We better go inside. Thanks for the blowjob. You do good work."

She presses her face into my neck and her hug turns into a kiss, and her kiss could have turned into another round of lovemaking if we weren't technically in public.

"We better go inside. Everyone is probably looking for us by now."

She looks into my eyes. "I love you, Raff."

I sigh. "Dollface, we need to talk."

"Tomorrow?"

"I guess that will have to do. Now isn't the time. Come on." I nudge her to her feet. I stand too and buckle my belt.

Outside the ballroom doors, I press a hard kiss to her mouth. I try to tell her all the shit I can't say, all the stupid feelings I have for her that I can't possibly put into words because I don't have them. I don't have the future mapped out—if I did, we'd be at the courthouse. My parents are breathing down my neck, Aunt Caro tells me to go my own way even if it will hurt because doing what my parents want me to do will hurt more, and here's Nic, running from something that is gaining on her by the second.

Something is going to explode in our faces, and it won't end as happily as my blowjob.

What we're doing is going to end in fire and ash, and it won't be so kind as to give us a warning, not like the smoke that creeps around the corners and under the doors before the flames burst and eat at the walls devouring us with them.

CHAPTER NINE

Veronica

I'm sore, but I'm beginning to realize that unless I ask Raff to lighten up, he won't. I need to tell him he can't actually eat me, though the thought of him trying sends delicious shivers up and down my skin. My nipple still tingles, but that was a turn on, holding my boob out for him to suck. Sex with Raff will never be boring.

I don't know what got into him that would cause him to yank me out of the fundraiser like that, I'm only glad I was there to absorb his anger. I know what it's like to be angry and have nowhere to put it. Every time I speak to my father, I want to punch a hole in my apartment's wall. I think some of Raff's fury has to do with me. What little I told him about my situation gnaws at him, but I don't know what else I can do. He can't save me. I should end it, tonight. Then maybe when I have to leave with Blaise it won't hurt so badly.

Zoey's girls crowd me the second I step into the ballroom.

Raff squeezes my hand and hurries off, maybe to get a drink. I need one, too. The wine I drank at Zoey's wore off.

Paige wants me to pick her up, and I do, my back protesting. I like holding her, her legs wrapped around me keeping her from sliding down my hip.

We'll be seated for dinner soon, but my rendezvous with Raff set me back and I should network. If Felix and I didn't do our photo ops to promote the show, the producers would never let me live it down. I catch Raff across the room, and that's what he's doing, standing in a small group, someone gabbing in his ear. He pretends to listen, nodding. I envy him the glass of whiskey he's downing.

"Leave Veronica alone," Zoey says, rescuing me. "Your daddy wants to show you around the hotel, okay?"

"Okay!" Paige agrees, releasing her locked ankles and dropping to her feet. My back relaxes in relief. She hurries toward Heath who's a few feet away doing some networking of his own.

"Sorry about that." She grins sheepishly. "The girls can be a handful, and Paige has had your attention all night."

"That's okay. It's nice she likes me."

"She definitely does. I think you need to visit the ladies'," Zoey suggests, tamping down a smile.

"Why, what's wrong?"

"You've got . . ." she fades, circling a finger around her lips.

"Shit." I never would have suspected giving Raff a blowjob would leave evidence on my face.

"Umm, that's not what it is, but go look and fix your lipstick. It's not frosting you've been eating."

I cover my mouth with the back of my hand, mumble, "Thanks," and rush in the direction of the restrooms.

Emma tries to stop me, but I wave her off. Let Zoey explain what the hell I'm doing. Raff will never hear the end of this.

My heart plummets. Losing him will hurt me more than my mother leaving. More than my father accepting the Barker's offer of employment. More than Jack jilting me in front of the entire city. I've had a shitty life, and it's not going to get better.

All I can do in the bathroom is clean my face with a wet napkin and dry the tears clinging to my eyelashes. I didn't bring a purse with me—the keys to get into my apartment are in my bag at Raff's. I thought with Raff as my date, if I needed anything, he would be here. I don't have my phone with me all the time. Social media is already my life. But a lip gloss would have come in handy about now, or a mint. God knows what my breath smells like.

I rinse my mouth with water from the faucet and pat my face with a hand towel. Some of my makeup has worn off, but I don't look bad. Tired, but then, when haven't I lately?

Using the opportunity, I go to the bathroom and clean up down there, too. I'm tender, and resting my cheek against the cool metal of the stall, I relive what he did to me in the garden. I don't want him to go easy on me. I'll always want him to attack me like he's never going to see me again. Tonight, I'll let him do whatever he wants, and I'll carry the pain and love with me for the rest of my life.

I linger, arranging my dress, adjusting my cleavage. Pinch my cheeks and practice a smile. Then I step out of the safety of the women's restroom.

"Miss Chapman?"

"Yes?" I say, twirling in the direction of the speaker.

A hotel employee smiles apologetically and says, "There's a gentleman waiting in the lounge area near the garden exit. He says he'd like to speak with you. Do you know where that is?"

"Yes, I do. Thank you," I say, a smile flitting over my mouth. Raff can't get enough, but I can't let him have his way again.

They'll serve dinner soon, and with the cost per plate, it's nothing we'll want to miss.

"You're welcome. Goodnight."

"Goodnight."

I follow the carpeted corridor to the rear of the hotel, and I pass by the decorative mirrors hanging on the wall. They offer me brief glimpses of my pale face and naked lips. My curls are slowly dying too, more from Raff not being able to keep his hands off me than from failing hairspray.

The air is cool and the sweat on my skin dries. I hope my deodorant is stronger than my resolve.

I turn the corner fully expecting Raff to yank me into the elevator and have his way with me against the wall, but a hand clamps over my mouth.

Instantly, I sag. I would know the strength of his arms, the smoky scent of his skin, and his ominous presence anywhere. Everywhere. They haunt my darkest nightmares.

Blaise's low voice growls, his lips grazing my earlobe. "I'm done fucking around. I want what was promised to me. Do you understand?"

I nod under his grip.

"I don't think you do. I've been patient, hoping you'd do this the easy way and come to me on your own. I'll give you one last chance, or you'll wish you never heard my name."

"I will. I'll do whatever you say. Please don't hurt my friends." Tears drip from my eyes.

Blaise laughs. "I don't give a fuck about your shitty little so-called friends. I want you, and only you. Monday night, I *will* come for you. I have business in Fairfax early that morning, but I'm clearing my schedule for the rest of the week so we can get to know each other. Make your phone calls, pack your things. Quit your fucking stupid job because my wife won't work. Your only job will be to see to my happiness. Do you understand?" he asks again.

"Yes," I whisper under his palm.

He loosens his grip, and his hand slides up my side and caresses the breast Raff was sucking on a few moments ago. "This is mine." He lowers his hand and grabs my crotch through the layers of tulle. "This is mine. I know what you were doing earlier, you think I haven't been watching you? How hard he went at you, making you moan. You like pain? That will be nothing compared to what I'll want when you're in my bed. Your father gave you to me. Remember that. Look at me."

Blaise drops his arms, knowing I would never run. It won't mean anything to him, but it means everything to me. I turn and look him straight in the eyes. If he were kind, maybe this wouldn't be so bad. Blaise Barker is gorgeous in the dark and dangerous, bad boy kind of way most women fall for. Dressed in a well-cut suit, his hair combed away from his face, his jaw covered in stubble, he looks like he's attending the fundraiser. It's his eyes that are scary—hooded, like he's stoned, but hard and flinty. There's not an ounce of compassion in Blaise's entire body, and he won't show me any when he touches me. I'm nothing but a possession, one he'll do with as he pleases until he grows bored and I disappear like his other wives.

He reaches out to touch my cheek, and I need every ounce of willpower I have not to flinch. "Work with me, and I'll work with you. This doesn't have to be hard . . . Nic. That's what he calls you. Do you like that? Do you want me to call you that too?"

If Blaise started calling me by Raff's nickname, I would never recover, and so I lie. "I hate it."

"Then maybe you like Annie better."

"Call me whatever you want."

"All I need to call you is mine, and if you do what I say,

things will go a lot more pleasantly for you. Finish your evening, Annie. Say goodbye to the friends you care about so much. If they get out of here alive."

"W-what do you mean?"

He grabs a hold of me again, his hands grasping my upper arms, his fingertips digging into the muscle until he reaches bone. "Don't you smell that?" He deeply inhales, his eyes closed in elation. "It's been so long since I've held a match to that sweet, sweet gasoline."

I don't know what he's talking about until I smell the faint hint of smoke. "I don't—why aren't the alarms going off?"

"Things don't work when they're disabled. Something you might remember for future reference."

My mind goes blank. Absolutely blank. I'm frozen in place but there's nowhere to run. Where did Blaise start the fire? How far has it spread since he distracted me, taunting me with a future I can't escape from? Who's helping him? The Bridge-port Hotel is huge. He couldn't be working alone.

Finally, the warning breaks through the horror.

Blaise knows the moment I comprehend what he said. "Don't be stupid." He traps me with his arm secured around my waist and drags me out the door and into the garden. The night is cool, and the trees and flowers are bathed in sunset. The summer days are long, and it's not quite nine o'clock. There isn't anyone out here—everyone is inside anticipating dinner and the guests of honor who will be giving their speeches, Jack's father among them.

"This would look much more satisfying at night," Blaise murmurs into my ear. Trapping my chin in his hand, he forces me to watch the flames licking at the windows. The fire is spreading through the first floor and up to the second.

I close my eyes, and tears run down my face and over his fingers. Did Raff and the others get out? Are the girls okay? I didn't listen, and this is all my fault. The night I found Blaise on my couch, I should have gone with him then. All of this would have been avoided. I wanted time with Raff, and now I have to pay.

"They give you so much freedom if you're wearing the right uniform," he muses thoughtfully.

"The man who said you wanted to speak to me—"

"Yes, he's one of mine. It's amazing what a little gasoline sprinkled here and there will do. You wouldn't think a building made of stone could go up in flames, but everything on the inside is so flammable. So delicate. So fragile. Don't worry, Annie. I could have made it a lot worse than it is. This was a little warning. Something between you and me." He brushes his lips across my cheek.

Sirens wail from down the street, and I want to cry in relief.

"That's my cue," he says, letting me go, and I crumple to the cobblestone, my legs too weak to hold me up. "Monday evening, Annie. We'll start our lives together." He backs away from me until the trees swallow him.

I could stay here, in the garden, safe, until the Bridgeport's fire department extinguishes the fire, but I can't. I've already taken the easy way out and this is what happened. I put my friends at risk. Emma. Raff. Zoey and Heath's daughters. They're going to find out this is all my fault and they'll never forgive me.

I do the only thing I can—the only thing I have left.

I love Raff with my entire heart and soul, and I can't sit here for hours waiting to find out if he's okay. I need to see for myself.

Slowly, I approach the hotel, heat radiating from the doors.

The glass is warm under my touch.

I push through and step into the back of the hotel.

Smoke and regret consume me.

Fire licks above my head, eating at the wall, and heavy grey smoke hangs in the air. I'm alone in the lounge area where Blaise cornered me, a decorative tree burning, flames eating at the leaves turning the vibrant green to black ash.

Sweat runs down my back, and my lungs struggle to find oxygen in the dirty air.

When I last saw Raff, he was in the ballroom, and that's the direction I go, though there's no chance of him still being there. He would have gotten out with everyone else, maybe helping people into the street, Paige safe in his arms to keep the panicked crowd from trampling her.

Unless he stayed behind to look for me.

The hotel's fire alarm remains eerily quiet, the sprinkler system dry. Whatever Blaise did worked, and fire will eat as much as it's able before the firefighters drown it with water and courage.

Through the smoke, I think I see someone dart into the restroom I used to wash my face. My eyes are burning, tears of fear turning into a defense mechanism against the fumes. Maybe I imagined it, but I push the door open to check before I resume my futile attempt to reach the ballroom.

The air is clearer in here, the door an effective shield, but it's hot, so hot, and the heat chokes me. I drop to the floor and try to inhale a ragged breath. I crawl past the leather loveseat and the small table decorated with a floral arrangement toward the stalls. The tiles are warm under my hands. There isn't anyone here, and I back away.

A thin, faint sob trembles through the crackling.

Quickly, on all fours, my dress snagging on the heels of my stilettos, I peer under every stall door. There's nothing until in the last stall she slips off the toilet's seat, and her little French kitten heel touches the tile.

Graciela.

Zoey said she was old enough to wear heels tonight, and she was so proud.

"Gracie," I sputter, gripping the bottom of the door and rattling the lock.

The door swings open, hitting me on the forehead, and stunned, I rear backward. She scrabbles out of the stall, sobbing hysterically, and flings herself into my lap. The momentum knocks me over and my elbow slams onto the tile sending painful vibrations up and down my arm. We lie in a crumpled heap, surrounded by fire.

"We need to get out of here," I mumble, my hand numb, trying to push myself up, Gracie's face pressed against my neck. "We have to go, honey."

I try to stand.

"Don't leave me alone!"

The smoke is thickening, and I'm scared of what we'll find in the corridor. There's no way we can reach the ballroom now. I would have tried if I hadn't found Gracie, but there's nothing I can do except get her outside to safety.

I hold my hands to her cheeks. Tears are streaming from her eyes, terror mixed with smoke. "Look at me!" I demand. She's going into shock. "I won't leave you, but we can't stay here. Do you understand me?"

She nods, but I doubt what I said penetrated the horror. She doesn't know where her mom is, her dad, or her sisters. And she won't know for hours.

I don't know where Raff is, if Emma and Jack made it out. If Mia and Haisley are okay. But I have to hold it together because right now, I'm all Gracie has.

Clutching her hand, we scramble to our feet. In any movie

I've seen that featured a fire, they always held damp cloths to their faces. Maybe it helps, maybe it doesn't, but there has to be a reason they do this, and I do it now. I wet a handful of paper towels, the water blessedly cool. "Cover your nose and mouth."

She seems to understand what I said and holds on to the dripping napkins, but despite the heat and the sweat beading along her forehead, her teeth are chattering and her skin is a pasty white. She's not going to last much longer before she's a quivering mess on the floor and I'm not strong enough to carry her out of here.

I wet a paper towel for myself and leave the water trickling into the sink.

We drop to our knees, and it's slow going, holding the wet towels to our faces, our dresses tangling around our legs. I nudge the door open with my shoulder. The wall opposite the restroom is on fire, and a billow of smoke drops on top of us.

Gracie gags into her paper towel.

I can't see down the corridor in either direction—the smoke is too thick.

She grapples for my hand and links fingers with mine, and I tug, urging her to follow me out of the restroom.

We have to get to our feet. We have no choice. She won't let me go, and we can't move fast enough on our knees.

A piece of the ceiling drops a few feet away from us, and it crashes to the floor, spitting sparks. Gracie screams, her shrieks barely audible over the growling of the fire. I guide her toward the rear of the hotel, the only way to escape from where we are. I can't see anything, leading the little girl by instinct alone. I'm fortunate I've been to this hotel so many times. I'm fortunate Raff wanted to have his way with me in the garden, refreshing my memory of the hotel's exit, and it wasn't a half an hour ago that's where Blaise wanted to meet me.

My skin burns, and in my heels, my feet ache. Mere inconveniences at a time like this, though my mind has decided to let me know.

I trip over something, and Gracie, clinging to my waist, loses her balance and tumbles with me. I drop to my knees onto the floor, my hands breaking my fall. Nothing should be in the hallway, and the only thing that would have been in our way is another person.

I skim my fingers over a shoulder covered in the smooth material of a tux jacket, and my heart stops. Please God, I pray, hoping Raff didn't come after me.

I find his jaw and his cheek, but his facial features don't feel similar. I know the planes of Raff's face, and I let out a sob of relief.

Unexpectedly, he grabs my wrist, and in reflex, I try to pull away. "Help me," he rasps.

"You have to get up," I shout, fighting against his grasp. "There's a door not far from here."

I don't know if he heard me over the roar of the fire.

Gracie wails into my ear adding to my fear and urgency, and frantically, I try to free my wrist from his hold. I'm just about to attack him to force him to release me, but he staggers to his feet, and gratefully, I follow, tightly linking Gracie's fingers with mine. If I can't feel her, I'll lose her, and I suspect that's what this gentleman thinks too. He doesn't release my arm.

Both of my hands are occupied, and I can't shield my face. My eyes sting with smoke.

He knows the hotel as well as I do, and it's only seconds later he's pushing the door to the garden open. He lets me go and drops to his knees, his hands braced in front of him against the stone steps. He struggles to breathe, wheezing and coughing.

I trip over my skirt and stagger down the steps and away from the hotel, Gracie holding onto me as desperately as she was inside, and my shaking legs carry me a good thirty feet away before they can't hold me up any longer.

Gracie falls onto the soft grass next to me and cries into my chest.

There are several more people in the garden than when Blaise dragged me out here. One man searching for a connection sits beside me and explains he twisted an ankle running down the stairwell from the third floor. Another was at the fundraiser, and he covers Graciela with his tuxedo jacket.

I tuck it tighter around her trembling body.

At that moment, the hotel's interior collapses, the second floor sinking into the first. The impact shakes the ground, and several people who were watching the fire lurch onto the grass, falling on their asses, stunned. The hotel shrieks and screams in agony, the fire eating away at its insides.

My throat is raw from smoke inhalation, my eyes burning.

I did this.

I tested him, made him wait too long.

He wanted me to know, without a shadow of a doubt, that he can kill me. He can kill anyone I'm close to.

I need to see that Raff is okay. That Emma and Jack, and Ron and Claire, and Mia and Haisley, Heath and Zoey and their two other girls are okay, and then I'll disappear.

My father promised me to Blaise Barker.

I belong to him now.

CHAPTER TEN

Rafferty

My hands shake like a recovering alcoholic's and I try to hide it from anyone who steps too close to me.

Chaos broke loose the second someone smelled smoke, but by then it was already too late. Dependent on smoke alarms and the sprinkler systems, we partied unaware until the fire boxed us in.

Closed off by flames, no one could reach the lobby, and smoke filled the corridor Nic and I used to go outside to the garden. We were trapped, like fish in a bowl, until a waitress who didn't understand what was happening entered the ballroom from a service hallway carrying a full tray of champagne. She unwittingly revealed an exit, and it was every man for himself. Not even the mayor could force people to walk single file through the kitchen to the alley that runs parallel to the west side of the garden.

Jack herded Emma and Claire ahead of him, keeping an eye on his father who assisted long-time friends of their family.

Mia and Haisley spread word through the kitchen and laundry staff. The chef and his assistants had been too caught up in the frenzy as they prepared the meal for the fundraiser to realize what was going on. The housekeeping staff were busy at work washing and folding sheets and towels, located too deep in the guts of the hotel to hear warnings about the nightmare happening in front.

I looked for Nic, I tried, but there were so many people running and screaming, and Heath and Zoey . . . they couldn't find Graciela, and I will never forget the sheer terror that covered their faces.

Hours later, Emma and her friends are sitting on the curb across the street. They're watching Bridgeport's fire department try to unsuccessfully douse the flames. There's nothing they can do but delay the inevitable. The fire won't stop until it eats everything in its path.

The only thing keeping me together is that I know how smart Nic is. She's a survivor. And the fact that Emma saw her head in the direction of the ladies' restroom gives me hope that away from the crowd in the ballroom, she somehow managed to make it outside.

Somehow.

The BFD tried like hell to suppress the fire and contain it to the second and third floors, but the alarms had been disabled and the fire was already out of control by the time they arrived. They'll fight it for the rest of the night, and firefighters are still searching for guests, evacuating the sleeping rooms on the highest floors. Accounting for everyone is crucial. I look for Nic with every fresh wave of people who are escorted away from the building by police officers, and every time I don't see her, my stomach heaves.

I've already thrown up twice.

I lean wearily against a building diagonally across the street from the hotel. I have a clear view of the firetrucks and the firefighters spraying down the building, the lobby charred and hollowed out. The fire knocked out the electricity and the Bridgeport Hotel is nothing but a glowing orange spear slicing at the sky scattered with stars.

Durand's sitting with Heath, Zoey, Hilary, and Paige, desperately jabbing at his cell trying to do whatever he can to organize a search party to look for Graciela. I constantly look at mine, but the phone lines are jammed, cell service bowing under the weight of so many eager to touch base with their loved ones.

I frequently catch sight of Mayor Iverson who called in the cavalry. Medics are on scene treating injuries, dispensing water bottles, coffee, pain relievers, and ice packs, but what people really want—and what they can't have—is clearance to search the hotel's grounds. I tried to look for Nic, but the second I stepped foot onto the property, I was ordered off the premises, and I listened. I don't need to be the reason their jobs are any harder than they already are. I don't want to be stupid, either. The only reason I'm forced to stay out here is the only reason I desperately want to go inside: the building isn't safe, and Nic could be in there.

Pressing the heels of my hands to my eyes, I try to block out the flames still flickering from the hotel's shattered windows, but to no avail. It will be a long time before I can close my eyes and not see fire. Longer still for Heath and Zoey. What a nightmare this must be for them.

I don't have to open my eyes to feel her, and Emma steps into my arms, offering me a Styrofoam cup of coffee. "She's going to be okay," she says, holding me close and resting her head on my shoulder. I relieve her of the brew that waters my mouth but churns my stomach.

I sip gratefully, hoping I can keep it down. "I want that to be true, baby girl."

"It has to be. It's all Zoey has right now. Heath let Graciela go to the bathroom by herself, and they never saw her again. I saw Veronica walk that way too, and we're hoping that they're together."

"We'll be waiting for a while. Go back to your friends, Em. I'm not fit to be around."

"You *are* my friend, and I'm not letting you stand here by yourself."

There's no use arguing with her. "How are Ron and Claire?"

"Claire's shook up, and I saw her give Ron a hug. They have a lot of healing to do, but I'm glad Claire isn't completely closed off." She pauses. "You're right. I should go sit with Zoey. Come with me. You shouldn't be alone."

I don't want her to worry, and I agree. She links her fingers with mine, and I let her lead me toward Durand and the rest of our friends who are sitting near the tire of a firetruck parked sideways in the street. Someone wrapped an aluminum emergency blanket around Zoey's shoulders. She's keeping it together better this time, maybe because when Paige disappeared, she didn't have her other two girls with her. Now Hilary and Paige need her, and Zoey's face is blank and dry.

Mia and Haisley are sitting on a cop car's trunk farther down the block, both scrolling on their phones. Mia senses someone looking at her, and she meets my gaze and shakes her head.

No news.

In the opposite direction, Mayor Iverson is strategizing with the Bridgeport's police chief and an architect. The Bridgeport

Hotel's blueprints are laid out on a table anchored by useless cell phones outside a large white tent set up for medics who are treating the injured as they're evacuated from the hotel.

Though the sun has set, there's plenty of light to see by, the swirling lights of the police cruisers tinting the scene in blues and reds and spotlights set up along the tents and street, their glow cutting through what normally would have been a city avenue bright with traffic.

I squeeze Emma's hand and nod at Durand. "I'm going to search the tents again," I tell her, and take a step in that direction. Every fifteen minutes I walk through, looking for Nic or Graciela, hoping someone escorted them there without us knowing.

I'm halfway to Iverson, and I catch Justin out of the corner of my eye, weaving around people to rush up to me. His tux jacket and bow tie are missing, and his shirt's rumpled and untucked. He's holding his cell phone to his ear, listening intently to whoever is on the other end.

"How do you have cell service?" I ask, irritated.

He waves his hand into the air and angles his phone away from his mouth. "Satellite. Don't you?"

"No."

He scowls. "No word on Veronica?"

"Nothing."

Justin nods in sympathy. "I'm on the phone with WVBP. A contact there is saying this is suspected arson."

I freeze. "Why do they think that?"

"They found traces of accelerant on the ground floor outside the ballroom and inside the conference rooms located down the adjoining hallway. The ballroom's a total loss, along with the hallway near the garden entrance and the lavatories. They're looking for the point of origin. Whoever did this targeted the fundraiser."

"You mean an activist?" I say, struggling. I can't think past Nic and Graciela.

"Possibly. Someone who didn't like what the funds would be used for. But that's only a theory. Some very high-profile people were in attendance."

"Okay." I bite back a sob and focus. "Okay. Got anything else?"

"Is that coffee?" he asks eyeing the cup Emma gave me that I forgot about.

"It's cold."

"Better than nothing."

I pass him the cup. "Is the website up?"

"Nope. Crashed along with our server. Too much traffic and too many people trying to upload their shit to the feed. Everyone knew you'd be here, so a lot of the talk online is about if you're okay. The bigger sites are still going strong, and the hits are off the charts. Jez is interviewing Felix Rivera over there somewhere," he says, gesturing with the Styrofoam cup in the direction of the tents. "She'll post it to the exclusive content as quickly as she can."

"No. This information should be free for everyone. Do they know how many guests are still unaccounted for?"

"The fire took out the hotel's computer system. They're trying to retrieve the information from the cloud. The center's director supplied a list of guests, but that's only a partial list of everyone who was in the building."

"I should be working with them, but I can't—" I don't know how much longer I'm going to be able to go on without breaking down. Every second they don't find Nic is another second that confirms my worst fear. She didn't survive.

Justin rests a hand on my shoulder. "We all know she's missing, Raff. It's okay not to think about anything else for a few hours. No one is going to blame you. Go look in the tents. Maybe she's there and you didn't see her."

"Yeah, I was going to—" I'm interrupted by a scream so full of joy my heart shatters. I whip toward the shriek, and Heath and Zoey stand shakily to their feet, knowing their little girl's voice.

Graciela races toward us, and Heath scoops her up, his shoulders shaking with sobs.

Distraught, I search the crowd hoping Emma was right and Gracie and Nic had been together. A bulky firefighter wearing his gear moves to the side, and I see her stumbling toward our group, her face smeared with soot and tears.

She spots me, and gripping her torn dress in her hands, she runs.

I meet her halfway.

Crushing her to my chest, I pick her up, and she clings to me, her feet dangling. I bury my face in her hair and cry.

———

I don't keep track of how much time passes. She's patient, letting me hold her, but eventually she wiggles to her feet and pats me down, all the while searching my eyes looking for a sign that I didn't escape unharmed.

I'd forgotten, in all my worry about her, that she didn't have news about me, either.

"Are you okay?" she keeps demanding, tears choking her throat, her hands fluttering over my chest and shoulders in agitation.

Gripping her wrists until her eyes widen and she stills, I say gently, "I'm okay. I want to know if *you're* okay. What the hell happened?"

Before she can answer, Heath pushes me aside and hugs

her as tightly as I did when I first saw her. "Thank you," he keeps mumbling, tears streaming down his face in unabashed gratitude and relief. "Thank you."

She meets my eyes over his shoulder and doesn't say one word the entire time he holds her.

———

We're all strung out on relief that those closest to us are uninjured, and I'm torn between bringing Nic to my place and hiding and helping those in need.

She makes it easy to decide, and I love her so much for it.

"Let's go to your place and change and then come back. We'll be of no use to anyone hungry and dressed like this," she says, sliding her hand into mine.

"We can't," Zoey says, holding Gracie so tightly her knuckles are white. "We just can't."

"We understand," I say, running my hand over her hair like I've done so many times to Emma. "It's been a rough night. Go home and get some rest."

"I don't know how I'll ever repay you," Zoey says to Nic around a mouthful of tears.

She pulls Zoey into her arms, including Gracie in the embrace. "You never have to think that way. I'm only glad I was there."

The closest a car can pick us up is three blocks away, and we slide into the cool back, Nic looking dead on her feet. The description running through my head roils my already acrid stomach, and needing desperately to be close to her, I encourage her to sit in my lap. She immediately rests her head against my shoulder.

"I didn't ask if you need a doctor," I say, rubbing my hand up and down her arm. "Do you need to go to the ER?"

She tilts her head and rubs her nose along my jaw. "No, thank you, though. I'm thirsty, hungry, and tired. I'm so glad you're okay." She starts to cry, and I hold her as she keens against my chest.

It took me a long time to find a woman I could love for the rest of my life. In my kitchen, I watch her sip coffee and poke at a sandwich wearing her ripped and stained dress, dirt and tear tracks covering her face, and I promise right then and there, I will do whatever I have to do so I never lose her again.

———

We go where we're needed. Everyone knows who we are, and they're both grateful for the help and awed we came back. Felix stayed, and dressed in his slacks and tuxedo shirt, hugs Nic so hard and so long, I think I'm going to have to break it up. She laughs, and as co-hosts and friends, head toward the emergency tents.

I write up press releases and match people's names to the hotel's reservation list and the fundraiser's guest list. In bits and pieces, I listen to the story of Nic checking the ladies' bathroom and finding Gracie standing on top of a toilet seat trying to hide from the fire and Nic's selfless bravery helping Heath and Zoey's daughter to safety.

The story winds its way from group to group and I'm humbled and not a little choked up hearing that Nic had already been outside in the garden talking to a friend. She saw the smoke and ran back inside for me. She didn't tell me that when we were changing at the house, knowing if she had I would have spanked her for being stupid. But, as the obstinate female she is, she would have pointed out she'd been able to save Gracie and the president of Bridgeport State Bank who had gotten disoriented in the smoke and I would have had no argument.

Standing across the street at a table and borrowed laptop, I catch her eye every now and then. She's been moving non-stop, distributing water bottles from plastic-wrapped pallets, filling coffee cups, and feeding children, helping worn-out mothers who need a reprieve. She's exhausted, and I'm not letting her out of bed until Monday morning.

Mia and Haisley are around somewhere ensuring people have rides home or waiting with hotel guests who are alone until they hear word of friends and family who can take them in. Claire and Ron are here, as well, handing out blankets or finding alternate places for people to stay—the hotel will be uninhabitable for months. Like Heath and his family, Emma and Jack didn't return. Emma's late and Jack wanted her to rest. When he told me that, he couldn't keep the light out of his eyes, though he did a good job tamping it back. I shook his hand, and unbelievably, he hugged me. Maybe he doesn't hate me after all.

The Bridgeport Hotel isn't completely evacuated to the satisfaction of the fire department until close to four in the morning, every room checked and rechecked. The fire is out, smoke curling into a sky lightening with the sunrise.

Nic's helping break down the tents that were used to administer emergency medical services, and despite her protests, I lead her away to the sound of tired and grateful thank yous from the other volunteers.

We ride across the city, and I ask, whispering into her ear, "Will you stay with me?"

"Yeah, I will." She snuggles into my side.

"Good."

She falls asleep and I carry her into the house, kicking the door shut behind me. I've never taken the stairs with a woman in my arms, and I move slowly, my hip grazing the handrail to steady myself. The bedding is still messy from the night before, and I lay her on the sheet and undress her. I free her legs of her jeans and her eyes flutter open, but I cover her with the comforter and they drift shut again.

I undress too and slide in next to her curling my body around hers.

Her breathing deepens. I rest my hand on her stomach and try to relax and let go of the tension. A headache starts at the base of my neck, but I drift off without getting up for ibuprofen.

My dreams are full of fire and smoke. I wake up, my eyes gritty with tears and fear, and I know it will be a long time before I'm free of the demons that chase me when I'm sleeping as well as when I'm awake.

———

I wake up close to noon, and Nic's still sleeping, lying in the same position she fell asleep in. I brush a kiss over her cheek and roll out of bed. I didn't get nearly the sleep I need to function with all pistons, but I can't stop thinking about how fucking scared I was while she was missing, the garden the last place firefighters looked for survivors. It will be a long time before that will fade to a dark shadow in the back of my mind.

I make a pot of coffee and snag the paper from outside. I slump against the doorframe, and the heat of the early afternoon's sun warming my skin goes unnoticed. Nic and I are featured on the front page. Someone took our picture the second I lifted her off the ground and into my arms. The headline reads *Lost and Found*, and the photo is captioned with a scant, *Talk of the Town's Rafferty Clark and Rise and Shine, Bridgeport!'s co-host, Veronica Chapman, reunited after the Bridgeport Hotel fire Saturday night.*

In the background, the fire is still smoldering, the building's brick charred and streaked with soot. Firefighters pop in their bright yellow gear.

I scoff.

Compared to the photo of Jack holding Emma outside this very hotel the night of his birthday party, the picture of Nic and me is the most romantic thing I've seen in a long time.

People are going to eat it up.

It's ironic that the evening was supposed to end rumors of Jack and Nic once and for all, and it will, but not in the way we expected. It's horrific that gossip mongers need this much grief and tragedy to forget something as shallow as a rejected almost-fiancée.

I tuck the paper under my arm and carry two mugs of coffee upstairs. Nic's lying on her side. Her eyes are open, and tears are running over the bridge of her nose.

"Hey, what's this?" I ask, dropping the paper onto the bed and setting the mugs on the nightstand. I crawl into bed and rub the tears off her face. "Tough night?"

"A little emotional," she says, sniffling. "I can't stop thinking about what would have happened to Gracie if she hadn't slipped off the toilet seat. I almost left her there."

"But she did, and you didn't, so that's all that matters. You can't think about the what ifs. If I had done that all night . . . I was pretty fucking scared waiting for word about you. I don't know how I would be right now if you hadn't made it out." I clear my throat. "How about I give you a little something. Would that help?"

A smile quirks her mouth. "Like what? A Xanax?"

"I've got something better."

I peel the comforter from her body. She's still wearing the black strapless bra and panties she wore under her dress.

"Oh, Raff, I don't have the energy—"

"I'll take it easy."

"*You* take it easy?" she asks, glowering, but she's smiling.

I pretend to be affronted, but really, I'm glad I can turn her thoughts in a different direction than the fire. It will be on everyone's minds for months, maybe even years, but if I can give Nic five minutes of something else to think about, I'll be happy.

"Do you trust me?"

I meant it as kind of a joke, but her serious reply humbles me.

"With my life."

"Then lie back and enjoy." I unhook her bra, freeing her breasts from the lace, and skim my lips over a sensitive pink nipple. Goosebumps cover her skin, and a shiver runs through her body. I chuckle and meet her eyes.

The absolute love and devotion shining in them would have brought me to my knees if I hadn't already been there.

She brushes my hair with her fingers, her touch gentle, and it's what I need to forget my own nightmares of last night.

My lips play with the waistband of her panties, and she laughs. "I love you."

"Ah, dollface. Don't ever stop." Hooking my fingers over the elastic in her panties, I pull the scrap of lace and silk over her thighs and throw them onto the floor. "Open yourself up to me. Let me look at you."

Sunlight slices over the floor and across the comforter. She can't hide here, and she pauses. I wait, patiently, a hand resting on her knee, and she reaches between her legs and spreads her pussy open with her fingers. She's wet, the delicate skin glistening.

"You're beautiful, Nic. You truly are. Be still, now. Just like this," I say, lying on my belly. I cover her with my mouth. She tastes sweet, like biting into a peach that has ripened to perfection. She moans. I push my tongue inside her, but I know that can't give her the satisfaction she's craving, the connection she needs after last night. I replace my tongue with two fingers. I said I would go easy, and I will. I focus on her clit, and lazily, I lap at her, her muscles clenching around my fingers.

She's quiet, but I know when she's about to come. I don't give her a last minute shock of pain, don't add a third finger when I suspect it would get her off a little harder. I let her come on her own terms, tilting her hips, riding my hand. I gently nuzzle her clit with my tongue, and gasping quietly, she finds the release she was looking for.

She relaxes and I whisper kisses over the insides of her thighs and pull my fingers out, discretely wiping them off on the comforter.

I undress quickly, having thrown on a pair of sweats to make coffee, and I cover her body with mine. "Is this okay?" I ask.

"Yes," she breathes. That's all the invitation I need, and I glide inside her.

I want to let go of the tension from last night just as much as she did, and I thrust three times, quick and hard. I brace my body over her and fill her with cum, my arms trembling. She's so beautiful, her hands on my shoulders, her fingers digging into my skin, encouraging me to take whatever I need to find what the fire stole from me, from us.

I want this, but if I asked her to marry me, she would say no. I haven't broken down her wall, and I'm not sure if I'm strong enough.

Blowing out a breath, I lower onto her, our bodies slicked with sweat.

"Do you like that?" she whispers.

"Like what, dollface? There are so many things."

"Looking between a woman's legs like that. I've always felt so ugly down there."

I reach between her legs now—my cum trickling out of her is a turn-on that will never get old. "I love looking at you." Gently, I push a finger inside her. "This is where families are made. Two people creating something more. I never understood it before I fell in love with you. The need to have children. What Heath feels with Zoey when they're in bed, or what Jack feels with Emma trying for a baby. There's something humbling when a woman lets a man this close to her. Of course I love looking at you."

"Do you want kids?" she asks, her hips rising and falling in rhythm to my tender strokes.

"I don't know. What Heath and Zoey went through last night when Gracie was missing—not even missing, they thought she was dead. I don't think I want to subject myself to something like that, but then, if the woman I marry really wants a couple, I could be persuaded. I'm not against having them, but I think, once Jack and Emma have theirs, I would be content to be an honorary uncle and leave it at that." I kiss her belly and say, "But watching you grow with my baby would possibly change my mind. How about you?"

The light in her eyes dies and blinks out. "I never thought I'd have the chance. I've been on my own for a long time and there are days I feel like I can't take care of myself much less want to put myself in a position where I need to take care of someone else."

"Raising children is easier with help. Emma made that pretty clear to Jack."

Nic scoffs. "Jack didn't want babies, he wanted Emma. Now he has both."

"Are you happy for him, dollface?"

"Yeah, I am, but," she says, rolling me onto my back, "I'm happier for me because I'm here with you."

She lets me have her again, but this time she's on top, and like Aunt Caro's vision of the kind of future she wants me to have with my wife, Nic and I while the day away in bed, sipping coffee and dozing between bits of conversation.

What I didn't realize was that this was Nic's way of saying goodbye, and I don't know how much I would have changed had I known.

———

"I really, really hate to do this," I say, stretching, my joints popping. It's dinnertime and I'm starving, but even at five o'clock on a Sunday evening, for people in professions like ours, life doesn't stop. I wanted to hide until tomorrow morning, but my sense of responsibility toward my e-zine and my employees is pressing on me. "But I need to go into the office for a couple of hours. The website crashed last night and I have guys working to get it up, but I should be there. I haven't been online all day, and I'm sure people are talking about this." I toss her the paper that's crumpled now, an innocent bystander of the love we made all day.

"Holy fucking shit," she says, covering her mouth with a hand. She traces our picture with a finger. "That's what we looked like."

I laugh. "That's what we looked like."

"Jesus. I don't want to see my phone. We've been offline all day."

"We have, and I'm scared too. Tomorrow morning will be a rude awakening if we don't poke our heads out of this tiny piece of heaven we made here in my bed." I cuddle her to me and ask,

"Are you going to stay here? Will you spend the night with me again?"

She rubs the tip of my nose with hers. "I can't. While you're at your office, I need to go to mine. I have to talk with the producers. I don't know if I feel like taping tomorrow, but that depends a lot on how Felix is doing after last night, and if they can find replacements. Half the phone calls I missed today are probably from them, but I left my cell at home."

I blow out a breath. I should have expected that. "Okay. I guess it will be a few days before we can meet up."

"Yeah, I'm sorry."

"Nothing to be sorry for. We both have jobs and that didn't change because of last night. Let me grab a quick shower and I'll drop you at your place."

"Thanks."

I move to slide off the bed, but she grabs my arm. A chuckle and a warning that we don't have time for more sex are on my lips, but she meets my eyes and my laughter and amusement dies. There's something sad about her, somber, and she says, "I want you to know that today was the best day of my life."

I tug on her lower lip with the pad of my thumb. "Me, too, dollface. Wanna shower?"

She smiles. "I shouldn't, but what the hell."

We end up having more sex anyway.

———

I drop her off with a sick feeling in my gut. I watch her walk up the concrete stairs, her arms full of ruined ballgown, and I don't pull away from the curb until she's inside.

For once, there isn't paparazzi loitering on her stoop—everyone knows she's been with me, and no one would dare camp outside my door.

I expect the office to be quiet, maybe Justin and a couple of others writing up pieces, but every one of my bloggers is sitting at their desks, their fingers frantically flying across their keyboards. One by one, they notice I'm there, and the clicking fades. They stand, and one young girl, my newest hire, bursts into tears. "You're okay!"

This cuts through the heavy atmosphere, and everyone laughs, some of them sniffling into tissues.

"Jesus Christ," I say to break the last of the tension. "I didn't know you all liked me that much. You're here on a Sunday. That doesn't mean you get tomorrow off. Get back to work."

I walk through the bullpen, rubbing my bloggers and streamers on their backs, shaking hands, thanking people when they say they're glad I'm not hurt. They all want to know about Nic, the picture on the front page of the paper causing waves I'll have to surf for days, maybe weeks, to come.

Justin's made himself comfortable behind my desk, and I scowl. He's not my second in command, though he might as well be. I help myself to a drink at the bar, staring out the window at the city below me.

When Nic told me goodbye, she searched my eyes, her breath coming out in panicked gasps. She wanted to say something, but all she did was brush her lips over mine and hurry out of the truck, not giving me time to open the door for her.

"Five people died last night," Justin says to my back.

Everything he'll tell me will be news. I didn't care about anything but Nic.

I don't answer. I need a moment to shift gears.

"One of the fundraiser's guests, and four people who were in a different area of the hotel," he says over the silence.

Pushing thoughts of Nic aside, I ask, "Who were they?"

"The guest at the fundraiser, her name was Maisie Rutherford. She had a heart attack outside in the street. Paramedics performed CPR for a half an hour before they called it. Ronald Durand actually helped her to safety, but the excitement got to her."

I turn. "How old was she?"

"Ninety. I guess the good Lord called her home."

"It's in poor taste to make jokes," I say, though the booze is hitting me and I tamp back my own smile.

"Not a joke, Raff," he says, scowling. "I'm a God-fearing man."

"Sure you are. That's why you work for me. Who are the other four?"

"Zeke Kavanaugh and his mint julep of the moment, a Lacey Lawton, and a couple from out of town. They were in the bar."

I raise my eyebrows. "Claire's ex-husband?"

"The one and the same."

"What happened to them?"

"Drinking. Didn't know what was going on until it was too late. According to a couple of witnesses, Zeke and Lacey were necking like teenagers in a dark corner, and they were distracted. Along with the other two, the smoke turned them around and they couldn't find an exit. Asphyxiation."

"Were the couples together?"

"Not that I'm aware of, but I don't think anyone cares at this point."

I sigh. "That's too bad. I don't think Claire liked the guy very much, but it will still upset her."

Justin shrugs.

"I take it with everyone out there working overtime that I'm not going to pay, the website's up?"

"Yeah. They got it up this morning. I texted you, but I didn't figure you would see it. The feed's going crazy. So much footage from last night. Are you going to interview Veronica about saving that kid? No one can shut up about it, and the banker, what's his name? He keeps saying he wouldn't be alive if it weren't for her."

"With the way Kavanaugh died, he could be right." I sip my drink and resist adding more. If I'm going to be working all night, I should do it sober. "I wasn't going to interview her. Our relationship is going to cause a conflict of interest. I'll get Todd to do it. He wrote that piece on Variant and we got a lot of good feedback. I'll ask her the next time I see her."

"You're not seeing her later?"

"No. She needs to speak with the producers of her show. I don't think she's totally shaken off last night and she was talking about not filming tomorrow if they'd let her out of it. That's a big if. They'll want her stories."

"She might not have shaken off the fire, but she shook off Durand. There won't be one person in Bridgeport saying their names in the same sentence ever again."

"Can't say I'm sad about it."

Justin hems and haws, and I've worked with him long enough to know he's got something to say that I'm not going to like.

"What? You're making me nervous." I pour another drink after all. "Do you want one? For your nerves instead of mine?"

I've never offered him a drink in my office before, and he doesn't know if he should accept or not. I'm not a hardass with my employees, but I don't turn them into friends. That's why I won't do any reporting on Nic now that we're together. We benefited from each other professionally and now we'll benefit from each other on a personal level. I won't mix the two. Durand tried with Emma, contract and all, and he's lucky he could talk his way out of the shit he jumped into.

"Yeah, sure," he says, and turns to my computer. "Do you

remember last night?"

I pour and set the glass on the corner of the desk. "Which part?"

Tentatively, he tastes my whiskey, but he won't have trouble choking it down. "The part where I said they thought this was arson?"

"Vaguely. Nic was still missing, yeah?"

"Yeah. Okay. So I spoke with a little cutie at the fire department—"

"Firefighter?"

"Ah, no. I think she does their paperwork, I don't know, anyway, she was saying that they *did* find traces of gasoline on the site, and they passed the case to the arson investigator who pulled the security footage from the hotel."

"Great. Wait. The security cameras were working?"

"Yeah, right up until the fire. It's all stored digitally online."

"They catch the guy?"

"Yeah, kind of."

"How did they 'kind of' catch the guy?"

Justin taps a couple of keys on my keyboard and brings up the corridor outside the ballroom where the restrooms are located. It's empty until a man, maybe in his late twenties and wearing a hotel uniform, steps into the frame and lurks outside the women's restroom. I don't like that, and my good whiskey curdles in my stomach.

Nic steps out, her expression drawn. That was right after I had my way with her outside. Maybe I was too hard on her . . . she doesn't look well.

The guy stops her, and her eyes brighten. I can't read his lips—the angle of the camera only gives us a shot of the back of his head.

She nods and turns in the opposite direction of the ballroom.

Okay, I know this part. She met a friend outside, but I never did ask to whom she was speaking. Nic's a well-known personality in Bridgeport. She could have been chatting with anyone.

The guy steps out of view, and there's no one else in the corridor.

Justin stops the video.

"Is that it?" I ask, irritated. "What does that prove? That Nic had a message and someone on the hotel staff was sent to relay it?"

"He's not hotel staff."

I stiffen. "How do you know that?"

"When the arson investigator watched it, the hotel manager watched it with her, and he didn't identify him as an employee. He didn't know who the fuck this guy is," Justin says, jabbing this thumb toward my monitor.

"Do you think Nic did?" I ask.

"It doesn't look like it."

"No, but she trusted him, and she knew who he sent her to meet. How does this tie in with the fire?"

"He's a suspect and they're trying to find him because a different camera picked him up later."

"Do you know who Nic met?"

Justin downs the rest of his drink. "No. If she went all the way to the rear of the hotel, there's a lounge area near a door that opens to the garden and there aren't any cameras there. The only reason there's one near the restrooms is to deter creepers from ambushing people using the lavatories."

"If the cameras were working, they recorded the asshole who dumped gasoline all over the fucking place," I point out, leaning a leg against my desk. I don't care Justin's sitting there, and after spending the day in bed, I can't complain about having to stand.

"The guy knew what he was doing," Justin says, turning

toward the computer again. "He's not dressed in a hotel uniform, but he blends in with the fundraiser crowd. I know an expensive suit when I see one." He taps a couple of keys and a different shot of the hotel pops up, this one of the corridor where the meeting rooms are located. Were located. A man wearing a nice Ralph Lauren walks into the frame, his head down. He knows the angle of the cameras and how to avoid them catching his face.

"When was this?" There's no timestamp on the video.

"Earlier in the day. He doused the hotel all afternoon."

"They're looking for him then."

"Yeah."

"Why did you show me Nic first if this is the guy they're looking for?"

"For one thing, this." He presses a button on my keyboard and fast-forwards the video. The guy in the suit is having a grand fucking time dumping gas all over the place and fucking hell if I don't know how anyone didn't smell that shit. Justin slows it down when the guy Nic was talking to enters the picture, dressed in his hotel uniform, pushing a cart full of cleaning supplies. There's some kind of swapping going on between them, but I can't tell what it is from the angle of the cart. Ralph Lauren is very careful not to show his face, but I can see the other guy clearly now, tanned skin and blond curls. He looks like he should be surfing in Hawaii, not here setting things on fire.

"They knew each other."

"Yeah. I was watching this guy, the suit, and it hit funny. The posture, something, and then he did this." Justin fast-forwards again and slows it in time for us to watch Mr. Suit light up a cigarette. Pretty ballsy for just drowning the hallway in flammable liquid. "So then I pulled up the footage from when I was filming Nic—Veronica," he stutters, unsure if he can get away with calling Nic by the pet name I've given her. Nic, yes, but if I ever hear anyone call her dollface, there will be hell to pay.

On a different monitor, he cues up the footage from the day I called Nic's cell and watched her talk to me. A lot has changed since then, but my heart still trips when I see her. On the monitor, she looks over her shoulder and stumbles, and after she hangs up with me and disappears inside, Justin moved the camera off her stoop and zoomed in on the guy.

I lean closer. "What did you say his name is again?"

"Blaise Barker."

His name clicks. "The teenaged arsonist. Looks like he didn't give up his hobby. You sure it's the same guy?"

He leans back in his (my) chair. "Not a hundred percent. The way they both hold a smoke is exactly the same, though."

"You report this?"

"No. I was waiting for you. I thought maybe you'd want to talk to Veronica. See what she knows."

I frown. "Why would she know anything?"

"Why wouldn't she? The guy posing as hotel staff spoke to her and he's working with the suit. It's not a coincidence, Raff, and you should connect the dots before the police do."

I press my lips together. He's right, and I hate it. I already knew Nic had secrets, things she doesn't want to share with me. Reasons she wanted Durand to marry her that she still hasn't told me.

Emma thinks Nic's in trouble and consorting with an arsonist can't land you in a bigger pile of shit.

"Okay. Keep quiet about this for now. I'll handle it."

"You got eyes on her?"

I sigh. "No. She's at her place." I pause. "Go."

Justin is up and out the door.

I pour another drink.

Thanks to a handful of good people, my 'zine is doing okay and I can focus on something else. I navigate to a search bar and reluctantly, I type in Nic's name. I know so little about her, I don't even know if she has a middle name.

I scroll through the results, and as a public figure, and a popular one at that, there are hundreds of pages of results. I try to refine my search and enter Veronica Chapman + hometown. Like everyone on this planet, Nic's name isn't unique, and I find several results for people who aren't her. I try again, Veronica Chapman + high school, and I get the same results about people who aren't my Nic. My Nic. My leg bounces under my desk. Is she mine? She hasn't felt like it from the moment my heart decided I was in love with her.

I search for hours, digging deep into the results and all that pops about her are items about *Rise and Shine, Bridgeport!*, her audition footage on a social media sharing site that I stop and watch, fundraiser appearances, and lots of shit about her dating Durand. But the deeper I search, the less I find, the oldest hit seven years ago when she first appeared in the newspaper's *Movers and Shakers* section. A short writeup announced her as the new host of a crummy little morning show that's been canceled for years. That would have put her at twenty-four, maybe, but I don't know Nic's birthday. I look for that too, a birth announcement, something, but I can't find anything on her.

Groaning in frustration, I run a search for Blaise Barker again, but nothing new comes up. Business articles about his importing and exporting business near Cavern Lake, a mention of some lakeside property he purchased last year. I get a good look at his face, his attendance featured at a ribbon-cutting ceremony for a factory he renovated, and he could definitely be the guy at the Bridgeport Hotel. He has a penchant for a well-cut black Ralph Lauren. He's slick, and on him, the pinstripes make him out to be a gangster in a mobster movie, complete with the cig hanging from his lips. All he needs is a nine millimeter gun in his hand, and I wouldn't put it past him to own one.

What would Nic have in common with him?

Do I want to find out?

Nic's dealing with her own business right now, or I would call her. I bring up the digital edition of the paper, and Nic and I are front and center, clinging to each other without a thought to anyone else.

Fuck.

I close out of the window and open the backend of *Talk of the Town*. I write up my own experience with the fire and what I can remember of the fundraiser before all hell broke loose. I schedule that to post in the morning and watch the videos my cameras filmed of the ballroom until the fire took them out. I gloss over me talking to Mayor Iverson, though the anger I felt after that conversation is nothing compared to the anguish the fire caused. Heath and Zoey's girls were so excited to be there. Paige looks so comfortable in Nic's arms, and it tugs at me a bit. Maybe I wouldn't mind if she said she wanted a kid. Just one, the best of both of us.

I scoff. I guess I gotta marry her first, and with her wall up all the fucking time, I'm surprised she admitted she loves me. It seems the sort of thing she'd keep close to the vest, unless she thought there wasn't a chance I could do something about it.

That's probably closer to the truth than I want to admit.

I work until close to midnight, sorting through my bloggers' posts and double checking everything is on the up and up. People will talk about the fire for a long time, but eventually other news will replace it. If Emma's pregnant, gossip will focus on that. Claire slipped out of the spotlight for a while, but people will start talking about her again once they find out her ex-husband was one of the people who lost their lives last night. It's curious who his date was and if they were with the other couple, but I'm too tired to dig into that now.

Before I leave, I spend a few minutes cleaning out my phone and my email inbox. Monday is a fresh start to a new week, and I might as well do it on a clean slate.

I don't have any texts or phone calls from Nic buried under all the bullshit, and I already miss her.

If Emma wasn't with Durand, I would call for a pity-party talk, but she's probably sleeping and I don't want to bother her. For a little bit there, I thought things were changing, shifting to a life with Nic and our friends. Now I feel as alone as I did when Durand proposed to Emma and I hadn't started seeing Nic yet.

Aunt Caro called once, let me know she knew I was all right, and to call her when I got the chance. She's a night owl, and despite the late hour, I return her call. She hears how despondent I am and invites me over. I accept, not wanting to sleep in the bed where I messed around with Nic all day.

We chat over wine and I stay up later than I should. She passes on a message of concern from my mother (her voicemail was one I deleted without listening to) which surprised me considering I haven't heard from any of my family members since hanging up on Dad. I figured it was only a matter of time before she called and said her piece, but maybe the fire will hold her off.

Talking with Caro is nice, soothing, and it brings me back to my childhood when things were simple if I took out the trash and Emma was always my friend. Those things haven't changed, but other things have. Some things you lose, some things you find only to lose them again.

I'll talk to Nic tomorrow and have it out with her. I want to marry her, and it's time she knows how serious I am.

CHAPTER ELEVEN

Rise and Shine,
Bridgeport!

Veronica

The first thing I do is check my phone. I have no choice, though it's the last thing I want to do. I know what I'll find, and I do. Threatening messages from Blaise, not-so-politely reminding me to be ready to go tomorrow night. I can pack two suitcases and he would graciously pay my rent until he can arrange to have my things moved.

I'm so lucky.

My father also called and left several voicemails. I can imagine the inconvenience my death would have caused him, and wouldn't it have been ironic if it had been Blaise's doing?

I speak with the producers of the show, and they give me the out I want to skip filming tomorrow. I don't suppose they would look very nice if they had pressured me to work, not after Bridgeport's newspaper calling me a hero for saving Gracie and Ted Brewster, the president of Bridgeport State Bank, the largest banking chain in the Midwest. He won't shut up about me tripping over him and stopping to help, but I wish he would.

He wants me to come forward and publicly accept his thanks, but hell will freeze over before I do that. The producers give me the day off, but it doesn't matter. I won't show up on Tuesday, and I don't plan to tell anyone a damned thing.

Raff dropped me off on his way to *Talk of the Town*'s offices, and I said my goodbyes. It will be the last time I see him, and I'll remember today for the rest of my life.

I lie in bed, my dress in a heap on the floor near my door where I dropped it. I should eat. Raff and I did our best to live on love and nausea and hunger painfully churn in my stomach. My phone rings and I grimace. I don't want to answer it, but I flip it over to see who's calling before I let it go to voicemail.

It's Zoey, and curiously, I answer to ask what she wants. Out of any of the girls, I would have expected Emma to call, but she's silent, I suppose too busy locked in the bathroom peeing on sticks to care about anything else. "Hey, what's up?" I try to sound cheerful, but my question comes out strangled and too high-pitched.

"I know it's late, and you probably have your show in the morning," she starts in a rush, "but Gracie's having a hard time falling asleep and she's asking for you. We talked to a pediatric psychologist today, and she said Gracie might have formed an attachment to you since you rescued—"

"Zoey, hey, slow down," I say, interrupting her. She's talking so fast I can barely understand a thing she's saying. "What can I do?"

"Can you come over and talk to her? She's scared our house is going to catch fire in the middle of the night, and she's so anxious. We're going to set up family therapy sessions tomorrow, but she's so tired and Heath and I have tried everything."

"Oh, honey, of course. I'll be right there. Text me your address for the car, will you? I was only at your house the one time and I was with Raff."

"Thank you so much. We'll see you soon."

"Okay."

I hang up, and a second later Zoey sends me her address. I order a car with my transportation app and change my clothes from the pajamas I packed to sleep at Raff's (though little did I know I wouldn't need any clothing) to a nicer set of loungewear.

The car double parks, and I match the license plate to the text the app sent me. God knows the shit Blaise could try to pull between now and tomorrow night when he forces me to leave with him.

Zoey's waiting at the door, standing on her stoop, her face pinched in stress and worry, her arms wrapped around herself.

I hurry up the sidewalk to her brownstone.

"I appreciate this so much. I am so sorry," she says over a sob. "The past twenty-four hours have been so difficult."

I squeeze her arm. "They have been for everyone, Zoey. Whatever I can do, ask." The words stick in my throat. After tonight, she won't be able to ask me for help, and I want to scream about how unfair life is.

Upstairs, Heath's waiting in the hallway with a woman about my age. I think she's the psychologist, but he says, "This is Sheila, our nanny. She's been a big help keeping Paige and Hilary calm."

I nod at her, but all my attention is on Gracie's room. Her door is open, and I don't like that everyone is congregated outside it. "Gracie will be more comfortable if you do what you normally would do," I suggest mildly. "It's probably upsetting her you're all standing out here."

Heath's jaw clenches, and he has a right to be upset. I have no knowledge of how to raise a child. I can only express my opinion on how I would feel to have everyone loitering outside my bedroom as if I were a freak people couldn't stop gawking at.

Zoey nods and blows out a breath. "I could use a glass of wine. Heath, come downstairs. Sheila will sit with Paige and Hilary."

Reluctantly, Heath follows her, and Sheila and I share a "men" look before I enter Gracie's room. She's a shivering lump on her bed.

"Hey, sweetie," I say and sit on the edge of the mattress. "Having a little bit of trouble?"

She pokes her head out and she nods.

I scoot onto the bed, and she crawls into my lap. She's too big for it, but we make it work.

"What's going on?" I whisper, adjusting a pillow behind my back. We might be here a while.

"I'm scared. Are you?"

"Yeah, I am. Of a lot of things, but thinking my apartment is going to catch on fire in the middle of the night is not one of them."

She lifts her head off my shoulder. "It's not?"

"No. Do you want to hear a secret?"

"Is it a bad one?"

"Yeah."

"Okay."

"Someone set that fire, Gracie. Someone mean, someone who wanted to hurt me. The fire never would have happened if it wasn't for me. You would have had fun, eaten cake, and danced with your dad. You would have stayed up past your bedtime and had a glamorous story to tell your friends. It's my fault you don't have that now."

Tears drip down my cheeks, and in an act of surprising maturity, she wipes them off my face. "Who would want to hurt you?"

"Someone who's jealous I'm with Raff. He's dangerous, but this isn't about me. It's about you. You don't need to be scared. Sometimes bad things happen, and you would have been fine if you hadn't had to go pee right at that second."

She giggles a little. "You were there at a bad time, too."

"No, I was there at the perfect time. I helped you get out of there and that was what I was meant to do."

She snuggles into me and wraps her arms around my waist. "What do you do when bad things happen?"

"What do *I* do, you mean?"

She nods, her hair rubbing against my neck.

"It depends on the situation, I suppose. Sometimes, like the fire, you do what you have to do and then break down later. Sometimes things really aren't as bad as they seem, and after it's over, you realize things could have been a lot worse. Honestly, so far that fire has been the scariest thing I've experienced, and I hope that it will be for you. That you can go through the rest of your life without any more scary things happening to you."

The fire might have been the scariest thing to have happened to me, but I won't be as lucky as Gracie. I have a lot of scary things ahead of me now.

"Are you going to stop seeing Mr. Clark?"

"No. When someone wants to frighten you, it's important that you show them they haven't succeeded. I love Raff, and I can't let that mean guy win." I pause. "Your parents are going to set up a safe place for you to talk about your feelings, and I don't want you to be scared when they bring you there. If you have bad thoughts or nightmares about the fire, you have a lot of good people to talk to, okay?"

"Okay." She crawls off my lap and I tuck her in. "Can I have hair like yours? It will make me brave like you."

"Being brave doesn't come from the color of your hair, it comes from what's inside," I say, pressing my hand to her heart, "and from the people who love you. Raff made me brave during the fire. All I could think about was finding him. But, silver hair never hurts. As a very wise woman once said, put some lipstick on and get your shit together."

"I love you, Veronica," she says in that innocent and sincere way children have.

I lean over and kiss her cheek. "I love you, too. Go to sleep. You have a house full of people who are worried about you."

"Okay."

She burrows into her pillow, and I think she's sleeping by the time I reach her door. I leave it open, a nightlight shining in from the hallway, and I go downstairs.

I find Heath and Zoey in the kitchen, and he's leaning against the counter. She's sniffling into chest, his arms tight around her.

"Hey," I say, not wanting to disturb them.

"Oh, hi. Is she all right?" Zoey asks, reaching for a dish-towel and wiping her face.

"Yeah. I told her the fire at the hotel was arson, and I think that helped."

Heath stiffens. "It was?"

"Yeah. News got around today, and I heard the fire department is investigating. I might have only slapped a bandage on it, but she's sleeping now."

"Who would want to set fire to the hotel?" he asks, digging his phone out of the back pocket of his jeans. "We've been offline helping the kids adjust."

"Raff and I were offline most of the day, too." I blush. "There are no leads as far as I know," I lie, not comfortable telling Heath and Zoey what I told Gracie. Maybe Gracie will keep it a secret, maybe she won't. It won't matter. By the time she thinks to tell anyone what I said, I'll be long gone.

"Thanks. Did you want to stay for a glass of wine?" Zoey asks.

"You're welcome to," Heath says, but he's distracted, scrolling through his phone.

"No, thank you, though. I was lucky and I have the day off tomorrow to rest, and I need to go home and get some sleep. I told Gracie you arranged for her to talk to someone and to not be scared. I hope it helps her open up."

"Thank you so much." Zoey hugs me, her arms tight, and I have to nudge her away to break her embrace. "I'll order you a car."

"I appreciate it."

Needing the air, I wait outside, sitting on the top step of their brownstone. The light is a shimmery haze of pink and purple and I hate thinking this might be the last sunset I'll ever see, but how can I not? I know where Blaise will hide me—he owns a huge house on Cavern Lake where he lived with his other two wives. He'll lock me up and I'll spend my days doing God knows what until he decides to give me attention.

I may not be enjoying my last sunset, but this is my last few hours of freedom, and I breathe in the warm evening air and revel in the quiet that blankets the residential street.

I wish I would have stayed the night at Raff's, but I know there's no use prolonging the inevitable. I should have told him at least, the trouble I'm in, but I don't want him to try to go up against Blaise and his family. I love him too much to put him in harm's way. He almost died last night because of me. I'm doing him a favor, really, walking away.

That's what I tell myself.

The car stops in front of Heath and Zoey's brownstone, and I double check the license plate. I try not to let tears get the best of me, but by the time I'm locked inside my apartment, I can't hold them back any longer.

I don't have anyone to hold me and tell me my nightmares won't come back, and I lie awake for a long time, watching the lights smear against my bedroom walls, reliving Raff's gentle touch.

Sometime during the night my heart flips off, and when the sun shines through my window, I'm not the same person I was yesterday.

Raff interrupts me packing later that afternoon. I haven't eaten, haven't showered. Along with my heart, my body and mind shut down, and I walk around my room aimlessly, throwing random things into my suitcases. I must have really been out of it not to lock and chain my door, yet, what good would it have done? Blaise can break into my apartment, and no one can do anything worse to me than what he'll do driving me away from a life that I knew a long time ago I wouldn't be allowed to keep.

He steps into my bedroom, and my first thought is we've never made love on my bed. Is that strange? He's been here plenty of times planning coverage for an event or during the days and weeks he was saving my reputation, yet that was all long before I knew he loved me, when I thought he and Emma were together but keeping it a secret.

"You weren't on the show this morning," he says, standing in the middle of my room. I pause, trying to remember what I was doing. My suitcases are both open on my bed and one is half full, the other empty, waiting for me to fill them with things that I won't need. It's useless to pack anything. I'll belong to Blaise and he'll remind me at every decision that won't be mine to make, down to the clothes I wear.

I lift a shoulder. The show is far from where my thoughts are.

"What are you doing?"

"Packing," I say. Can't he see what I'm doing?

"Where are you going?"

I don't answer. I don't want him to know for one thing, and for another I can't force my lips to form words. He's so handsome dressed in khaki pants and a blue dress shirt, open at the neck, a blue and yellow tie knotted loosely under the second button. I've seen him in a suit plenty of times, but I think I like him best in sweats, sipping coffee and paging through the newspaper.

"Nic, you have to talk to me."

"I don't have anything to say. You should go. Don't make this worse."

His face sets and his eyes harden. "Then before I let you chase me out of here, explain this," he says, slapping a still of a video onto my bed. My eyes sweep over the picture of Blaise in the hallway of the Bridgeport Hotel talking to the employee who wasn't really an employee.

"I don't know."

"Yes, you do, and I want to know the truth. I want to know who Blaise Barker is to you. I want to know why he tried to burn down the hotel. I want to know why I can't find anything on you that's not older than seven years ago, and I want to know where the *fuck* you're going."

I lick my lips. "If I tell you, will you go?"

"Nic—"

"That's not my name."

He frowns. "What do you mean?"

If I tell him, he'll leave me alone. He won't want to deal with me, and he'll be safe. All my friends will be safe. Friends. I have friends now. Had friends.

Had.

Friends.

I sift through my closet. There's nothing here I want.

"That's why you can't find me online. You know some of it

already. I told you the night we had dinner with Tamara and Damian. I *did* grow up in a tiny town quite a few hours from here. My mom left when I was little and it was just me and my dad. My name isn't Veronica Chapman. It's Annie Johnson, poor little Annie Johnson from Littlefork, Minnesota, population seven hundred and twelve." I glance at him, but he's only standing in the middle of my bedroom, frowning. "My dad was, is, a CPA, had a good job, a legal job, doing bookkeeping for a grocery store, until booze caught up with him and they fired him for working drunk. Somehow, Mollie Barker found out and asked if he wanted to work for her family."

"Who's that?" Raff asks.

I stare at him, incredulous. "Mollie Barker? Ma Barker? She's only head of one of the Midwest's most dangerous crime families."

He shakes his head. "That's a myth."

I laugh bitterly. "To you, maybe. To me, the Barkers are my life. Mollie hired my dad, sobered him up, actually, and he's kept her books for the past fifteen years. He liked the power, the prestige working for them gave him, but he wants to retire and you don't retire from a job like that."

"What does that have to do with you? The fire?"

"My dad wants out," I say, running my fingers over dresses and blouses I used to wear to events when I pretended I had a life. "They won't let him go unless I trade places with him. My dad promised me to Blaise, and Mollie accepted. She said I'm lucky I'm beautiful, but sometimes . . . I don't feel so . . . lucky." Maybe I should pack a blue dress.

"And you're just going to leave?"

My hands fall to my sides. What does he want from me? "They'll kill my dad if I don't. I owe him. He could have left me in Littlefork, but he didn't. When Mollie hired him, he brought me to Fairfax with him, and I worked my ass off for a better life so I could leave them behind. Only, you don't leave the Barkers behind. Blaise watches me, probably has a man on me so I can't try to run. I wouldn't. My dad depends on me marrying him."

"What about the fire? People died, Nic."

Yes. I think I need a blue dress. And a green one.

"He was warning me. If I didn't do what he said, he would hurt my friends. Hurt you. He was watching us in the garden. He knows how I feel . . . felt . . . he knows how I felt about you."

Raff's not stupid. "Right. So this thing we had, it died because you want it to go away. The words you said to me, only lies, right, *Annie?*"

My name sounds like an expletive. I'm sure he'll say it that way many times until he forgets about me.

"Yeah," I whisper, looking at the floor. Maybe a white dress. Blaise says I look good in white.

"That's what this whole thing was? Why you wanted to marry Durand?"

I slowly slide a white sundress off a hanger. "I always knew at some point my father working for the Barkers would hurt me. Somehow. He told me he wanted out and said he offered me in exchange for his freedom. I was scared and didn't know what to do. I thought marrying Jack would make it all go away, that's why all of a sudden I wanted him to propose. He didn't, and I realized it was for the best. If I would have married Jack, the Barkers would have hurt my dad. They kill people who don't want to work for them anymore. I kept myself from falling in love with you. I always thought you and Emma were together."

"Imagine my surprise, *Annie,* that I haven't been with anyone."

That should have hurt me, but it doesn't. Maybe one day when I'm alone and I allow myself to feel, I'll cry over what we could have had.

I tilt my head. "No, I guess you haven't."

"When are you leaving? Can you tell me that?"

"Tonight. He's coming for me tonight." I turn back to my closet. Maybe not a navy dress. Maybe a black one. Or a skirt and a blouse.

"You're just going to leave all your things? The show? Me?"

"This was only temporary."

"Yeah, well, thanks for the heads up. He's a handsome guy. I guess it won't be too hard letting him fuck you. You're not that particular."

I drop the dresses into my suitcase. I've tried not to think about Blaise and what he'll want to do to me in bed. He's already threatened me, and he'll follow through. He doesn't love me. In the end, no one did.

"If all you have left are insults, you can go." My voice is thin, barely a whisper.

"Good luck, Nic. I mean that." He walks out of my bedroom, and I don't hear another thing.

"That's not my name," I say, but there's no one around to hear me.

———

I shower and dress. Blaise texts and tells me he's on the way and I better be waiting downstairs. I don't know when or where the exchange will take place. I don't know if this is a trap or if they'll let my dad go. The more I think about the likelihood they'll let him walk away with the knowledge he has, the less faith I have they'll do as they said.

I straighten my apartment and leave my cell phone sitting on the counter. I won't need it anymore. It connects me to this life. To Felix, to Emma, to Gracie and the other girls. I'm glad I don't have a pet. I couldn't bear to leave it alone. Raff will be okay. He's sexy and rich. Emma will introduce him to one of her new friends, and he'll forget all about me.

Before I go downstairs, I glance in the mirror one last time. I can play the part of an ice princess well. Silver hair, stoic face, frosted light pink lips. I dressed in a white sheath dress, silver belt, and silver sandals. Blaise will expect me to look perfect and there's no point in starting off on the wrong foot. If I do what he says, at the exact moment he says it, maybe life won't be so hard.

I wish Raff would have kissed me goodbye.

A light brush of his lips over mine.

I slide sunglasses over face to hide my bloodshot eyes and carry my suitcases downstairs. God only knows what I'll end up with, but I won't need anything I packed for very long. Blaise Barker's wives are treated to the best of the best. Diamonds to match the silver key he'll use to lock me up.

He's driven himself and double parks a black Range Rover in front of my building. Fairfax is hours away, and he's already spent time on the road to drive here. The exchange is important to him. Maybe the Barkers will keep their promises.

Blaise stores my suitcases in the back of the truck and opens the passenger door for me. Staring at the sidewalk, I climb inside, his hand hovering near my shoulder. He slams the door shut and rounds the hood dressed in his signature black suit and blood red tie.

He settles into his seat and twists in my direction. "Look at me."

I slide the sunglasses off my face and meet his flinty gaze.

"Good. You're a fast learner." He grabs the hair at the back of my head and kisses me, pushing his tongue into my mouth. I let him. There's no point in fighting against it. I even press my hand against his stubbly cheek. He pulls away and lets me loose with a ragged breath. "I think I'll like being married to you. For a while," he taunts, wiping a bit of saliva off my bottom lip with his thumb, and the motion reminds me so much of Raff that I choke back a sob and push the sunglasses back onto my face. I can't let Blaise see me cry, and if he suspects I'm crying over Raff, he won't be safe.

Play the part, Annie.

Fake it 'til you make it.

It's been my motto for a long time, and now, it might even save my life.

Blaise merges into the traffic on my street, and I don't look back.

CHAPTER TWELVE

Rafferty

L
ike fucking hell I'm going to let her go off with some psychopath arsonist. If she doesn't want to be with me, fine. If she were leaving with him of her own free will, that would be something different and a kick to the teeth I would tolerate because that's how life works.

But not this fucking shit.

Over my dead body, which is what I'm sure Nic was afraid of after Barker set the hotel on fire.

She's terrified, and I'm going to put a stop to it.

I pull out my phone and connect to Emma's number. I can't do this alone. "Are you and Jack at home?" I ask, striding down the block toward my car. People are at work, and I was able to snag a place around the corner from Nic's building.

Annie Johnson. No fucking way.

"Actually, yeah. I got my period this morning. He was disappointed and said he wanted to hide with me today. I told him no one gets pregnant on the first try, and it will be fine. Why? Are you okay? What are you pissed about?"

"I'll explain when I get there. Ask Jack to tell the concierge to let me up."

"I'll let him know you'll be downstairs. The code for the elevator is 1020. See you in a minute," she says, reminding me she lives in Durand's penthouse now.

Durand reserves two parking spaces for guests in the parking garage underneath the building, and I tell the parking attendant I'm here to visit Emma. He lets me pass, pushing a button and lifting the gate allowing me to ease forward. I park next to a black SUV I've seen Durand drive around the city. Normally, I wouldn't have bothered with the frou-frou, but time is slipping away and Nic's safety is at stake.

Emma greets me at the elevator and steps into my arms.

"I'm sorry, baby girl," I say, addressing the first concern. She was hoping she was pregnant, too. It wasn't only Durand.

"That's okay. False alarm—maybe stress. It will work out. Come sit in the living room. Jack's finishing up a phone call in the study."

I'm too restless to sit, and I wander around a penthouse I've never been invited to before. Durand and I weren't friends when he thought Emma and I were dating, and the shift in the dynamic of our relationship will take some getting used to. But, shifting it is. He was the first person I thought of with any real power who could do something to get Nic out of her father's mess.

"Clark," he says, stepping into the living room also dressed down in a pair of lounging pants and a t-shirt. "Emma pour you a drink? You look like you need one."

"No. I mean, yes, a drink would be welcome. Thank you."

Emma serves me herself, looking right at home in a pair of silk lounging pants and a matching camisole that I've seen her wear hundreds of times. It's nice to know that while we can't stop change, there are some things that never will.

Holding the glass, I perch on the edge of a couch cushion, and Emma curls into my side knowing I need the support.

Durand doesn't say anything, simply pours a drink and sits opposite us in an armchair. "What's going on?"

"What do you know about the Barkers?"

"You mean Mollie Barker and her family?" Durand asks, his eyebrows rising.

"Yeah. I thought they were rumors, stories that were exaggerated. I tried to dig a little and came up empty."

"Probably because in the past few years they've gone underground. They've had their hands in a lot of mudpies and aren't a lucky family. Mollie Barker's husband died a few years ago, and the cause was never confirmed. Some say a heart attack, some say from a broken heart. Their youngest boy was shot to death drinking and playing pool at the wrong bar and the wrong time. Some say poison, someone finding their revenge, but an autopsy didn't reveal anything, or so one rumor goes. Their two middle sons took over after that happened. The oldest, and the one who was set to step into his father's shoes, died in a boating accident. That's also a story told with unconfirmed facts. Some say he faked his death to hide from his family. His body was never found, nor the woman's he'd been sailing with that day."

"What about Blaise Barker? Where does he fit in?"

"He's one of the middle sons, helping Mollie run things."

"How do you know all this?"

"Blaise Barker met with me a couple years ago, wanted to see if my father and I were open to doing business. We weren't, and after an expensive lunch I paid for, we parted ways. Why? You run a story they're not happy with?"

I tighten my fingers around the lowball glass, and Emma

covers my hand with hers. I loosen my grip. "One of my guys was watching the hotel's security footage at the time of the fire—"

"How did he get a hold of that?"

I grimace. "Don't ask. I didn't. The camera caught Barker spreading gasoline around the hotel corridor that runs parallel to the ballroom. He's slimy. Kept his head low and avoided showing his face, but Justin matched him up to a clip he filmed of Nic a couple of weeks ago. Barker met with her the night of the fundraiser."

"That's the trouble she's in," Emma says, straightening.

I smile ruefully. "Yeah, well, her father. He's done some work for them, but they won't let him out unless they have her."

"Makes sense," Durand says, nodding. "They won't hurt him as long as she does what they say, and he won't blab if Barker's holding a knife to her throat—"

I stand in fury.

"—figuratively speaking," he adds quickly. "Barker told me Mollie has cancer, and that was a while ago now. She can't be doing well. None of her boys had kids, and I'm sure she's nervous about what will happen to the business once she passes away. She might even be hoping Veronica will take her place."

"Is their business really that shady? Nic seems to think they'll kill her father if she doesn't do what Barker wants."

"There have been instances of people disappearing, but nothing substantiated. I'd be more concerned about Veronica than her father. Barker's gone through two wives already."

I growl.

"Jack," Emma says disapprovingly.

"What? It's better to know than not, but if Mollie has her eye on Veronica as a successor, she's safe until she tells Mollie to go to hell, which she wouldn't do if they have a noose around her father's neck."

"Then what can we do? We can't let him kidnap her."

"When did she say she was leaving with him?"

"Tonight. I came straight here from her apartment. She's packing."

"Did she break it off with you?"

"Yeah. I was angry and called her a whore. Said she couldn't leave me because we weren't together." I set my glass on the bar and rest my forehead against the cool surface of the window. "What if those are the last words I get to say to her?"

Durand stands and rests his hand on my shoulder. "They won't be. We'll get this figured out. What's your end goal?"

I frown. "Getting her the fuck out of there. That's it."

"No. That can't be all. She loves her dad enough to do this, so factor him into the equation. The Barkers might be little league, but they're dangerous, and they'll protect what's theirs. They're dangerous enough I'd have put a detail on Emma if Barker had approached me while we were together."

"Jack," she says, standing from the couch and padding over to us.

He wraps his arms around her. "What? He might not have walked away as easily as he did. I love you and searched for you my whole life. I'm not letting some whack job take you away from me." He sighs. "Shit. I'm sorry."

I wave a hand. "Forget it. It sounds like they won't let him go, even if they have Nic."

"It's not likely. Do you want the whole family to go down?"

"I don't give a shit about the Barkers. I want Nic and her dad out from under Barker's heel. That's it."

"Okay." Durand pauses and sucks in a deep breath. "What do we know? Barker set the fire. A lot more people could have been hurt or killed. I want him for that, Clark."

"Agreed." The son of a bitch should pay for that. Nic and Gracie almost didn't survive.

"He'll kidnap Veronica," he continues, musing to himself. "There's no way she'd testify she went willingly. The police can storm their headquarters—"

"Jesus Christ, we aren't talking the mob here. Headquarters," I grumble. "Do they meet in the basement of an Italian restaurant?"

"Office, homebase, whatever the fuck you want to call it and when I had lunch with Barker, he ordered a bloody steak, so make of that what you will. Barker does the bulk of his business in Fairfax, near Cavern Lake. He owns a warehouse attached to a highrise sitting on the shore by the docks. If the cops bust up the place, her dad will go down with them."

"I don't see a way around that. Better off in prison than dead."

"If he wants out, he might accept a plea deal. He won't last long if word gets out he's a snitch."

I rub my forehead. I have a headache starting and I have a feeling it won't go away until I know Nic is safe. Even if she doesn't talk to me again after what I said, at least I know she'll be free to live her life the way she wants.

"How badly does the county's office want this guy? Do you know?" I ask. If Barker's been doing illegal shit, maybe they've had their eye on him.

Durand rests his hand on the back of Emma's neck. "I don't. What are you thinking?"

"The best I can come up with is getting him into a witness protection program. Nic said he's been working for them for fifteen years. If that's true, and I doubt she'd lie, then he'll know the business from the ground up. It will be enough to put them all behind bars for a long time. The problem is, I don't know if the Barkers are worth it. Hiding someone for the rest of their lives requires a helluva lot of resources and they may not care enough to go through the work."

"Would Veronica go for that?"

"That's another thing. His safety might not be enough for her. I don't know the kind of relationship they had before he offered the trade."

"You know for sure this guy set the fire?"

"Yeah."

"Okay. We need to sit on this for a couple of days—"

"What the fuck?" I ask, my mouth dry.

"Jack—" Emma says at the same time.

"No, hear me out. You're the one with the hotshot law degree. You know you have to gather the evidence first, and you need to give this guy time to believe he's gotten away with it. You don't think he's going to have his guard up waiting for you to go running to her rescue? The things you said to her will play in nicely. She'll tell the bastard you aren't coming for her—give it a couple days for it to sink in. Maybe they do what they said they're going to do and let her dad go. The cops can pick him up."

I chew on it, and I understand every bit of logic in his words, but I can't go along with it. "All that does is give him time to hurt her."

"Then what do you suggest? If you go in tonight, the second the cops make a move, it will be all over. She can take care of herself. She got away from them, didn't she?"

"Technically, no."

Durand spreads his fingers, palms up. "Then, I don't know. You know Veronica better than I do."

I scoff. "Yeah, right."

"*I* don't call her Nic."

"I have a nickname for everybody. You don't want to know yours."

"Stop it," Emma says, resting her hand against my chest. "There's no way I'm letting her be there with him alone. If he's not picking her up until tonight, they won't make it to Cavern Lake until midnight. I'm going to see her in the morning."

"Like hell you are. How would you explain that?" Durand asks, crossing his arms over his chest.

I don't like the idea of Emma within ten feet of that son of a bitch, yet I want more than anything to have someone watching Nic to keep her safe. We need the element of surprise on our side, I'll give Durand that, but I don't want Barker to have the chance to put one hand on her.

"I'll say the paparazzi followed them."

"That would be even worse. Barker hears that and they'll close ranks. Then we'll never find her." Durand meets my eyes and begs me to tell Emma not to go—he knows she'll listen to me.

"I hate to admit it, Em, but he's right. We need to give it a couple of days to cool off and think of a plan."

"You're taking a risk putting her father into witness protection—you don't know if he'll testify against them."

I roll my shoulders trying to release some of the tension. "I'm hoping his loyalty to his daughter outweighs the loyalty he feels toward the Barkers, but from what Nic said, they pulled him out of the gutter. He could still feel he owes them for that, and this will all be for nothing."

"It won't *all* be for nothing. Veronica's dad will go to prison, yeah, but even if the Barkers are a two-bit crime family, they should pay for what they've done, too. No one's had the evidence or the resources to go up against them, and now we do. No matter how this plays out for you, you need to do the right thing."

I like how my relationship with Nic is reduced to collateral damage because I did the right thing, but if her dad goes to prison or if he enters witness protection and she can't see him ever again and she hates me for either of those things, then that's how it's going to have to be.

He traded her freedom for his. She'll have no choice but to trade his for hers.

"What are you going to do?" Durand asks.

"What do you do when you want results?" I help myself to more whiskey.

"Go straight to the top."

"Exactly. I'm not going to waste time asking the county's attorney's office if they want the Barkers. I'll call the one person I know who can get shit done."

Emma sighs. "Are you sure?"

"Who are you talking about?" Durand asks, hating to be left in the dark about anything.

"Raff's going to call his mom. What will she want for helping you?" she asks, knowing how my mother operates.

"Only the blood of my firstborn."

"If Veronica forgives you," Emma says, tangling her fingers with mine, "that might be closer than you think."

———

I don't call my mother until I'm at my house, traces of Nic everywhere. I should have stuck to my rule about not letting women sleep here. To keep my mind off her, what I said, and what that bastard could do to her once he has her, I clean. I wash the dishes in the sink, pick up the scattered newspaper with us on the front page. I boot up my laptop, open the backend of *Talk of the Town,* and edit the posts my newer bloggers have submitted and approve them to post. Most of them are about the fire, interviews with people who were there. The banker can't shut up. It's amusing, but in a way, I don't know what the right word is . . . sweet, maybe, that he's secure enough in his own masculinity to thank a woman, and repeatedly, for saving his life. He had a come-to-Jesus moment in that corridor filled with smoke.

I think a lot of us did that night.

On a Monday evening, my mother will be home, and I wait until it's ten o'clock her time to call. If she's home and not attending an event, she's in bed by ten-thirty reading the latest political memoir, and I'll have a half an hour of her time. That's all I need and all I want.

She answers her cell, and I hear the disapproval across the line without her having to say a single word. "Rafferty," she says, her voice full of admonishment, "when you almost die in a fire, you call me. Why do I hear news like that from my sister?"

I want to say because her sister raised me and not her, but it's not the best course of action to piss off the person you're going to ask for a favor. "I'm sorry. I've been a little busy."

"I saw exactly who you've been busy with. A woman with silver hair. Are you in love with her?"

"Yeah." I sigh. "Yeah, I am."

"You don't sound happy about it. Invite her to meet us. Reese told me he asked you to fly in for drinks, but I haven't heard when you plan to do that. Melinda's pregnant. Did you know?"

"I did, but you weren't. It was supposed to be a secret."

"It can't be a secret if she's running to the bathroom every five minutes to throw up," she says, but she doesn't sound angry. "She needs to slow down and rest."

There is so much I could say, but all I do is sit down on my couch, rest my feet on the coffee table, and push back the sick dread that Nic's more than halfway to Fairfax. God only knows how Barker's going to treat her.

"I'm sure you're her role model," I say, veiling the insult inside a compliment.

"That's kind, but I wasn't sick when I was pregnant with either of you. Maybe she's having a girl. Anyway, that's not why you called me. You only call when you want something."

"I must get that from you. You seem to only call me when you want something, too."

"It's not my fault we've grown apart. You chose to stay in Bridgeport."

You chose to send me here, is on the tip of my tongue and I clamp my mouth shut. Christ, it's so difficult to stay calm whenever I talk to her. "Yes, I did. I like it here. But you're right. I need to ask a favor."

"I'm open to negotiations, Rafferty, but you know as well as I do nothing comes for free. I'm hoping you called prepared for that."

"I did."

"What is it you want?"

I explain the trouble Nic's in, and I don't hold back. My mother will need every detail to do what I want her to do. What Nic's real name is, what her father has done for the Barkers and for how long. That he offered her in trade, and that even as we were speaking, Barker was driving her toward Cavern Lake, expecting her to leave everything behind. I tell her we have evidence he set the fire, what Durand said about his wives.

She's quiet, writing down her notes. That's something I have to give my mother credit for. Well, she's not my mother right now, she's in full attorney mode, and I've never appreciated it as much as I do at this moment.

"If I understand you clearly, you want Veronica's father taken into protective custody and for Blaise Barker and his mother arrested on counts of, of what? You might not get everything you want if we can't find anything on this Mollie Barker."

"I know."

"You'll need to give me a couple of days, Rafferty. I'm sorry. I know you're worried about her, but I've never heard of this family. I need to make a few phone calls, lean on some people if they're not willing to cause a stir. So far, it sounds like they've managed to stay under the radar. That's skill on their part . . . or they've had help. I've yet to find an entirely clean police department. That might slow us down." Her pen scratches across paper. "I'll need the video clips. Send them to my email. I'll get in touch with the arson investigator. Do you know her name?"

"No. I'm sorry."

"Find out and forward me her phone number. It will save me some digging."

"Yes, ma'am."

"Providing I can get you what you want, are you willing to give me what I want?"

I grit my teeth. I knew asking my mother would give her the upper hand. Ensuring Nic's happiness will be at the cost of my own, but I will do whatever my mother wants me to do if Nic can live her life without having to look over her shoulder.

"You said this is a negotiation," I say.

"It is. What is the one thing you won't back down on?"

With or without Nic, I like it here. I don't want to move away from Aunt Caro, and I have friends here whom I would desperately miss, like Emma. She knows this. "I want to stay in Bridgeport."

She pauses. "I should have expected that, but I can work with it. You'll give up your rag mag, Rafferty. I mean it."

That was inevitable. "Okay."

My mother sucks in a breath. "You really love this girl."

"She's everything to me."

"I'm happy for you. You may not believe it, but I am. I want you to do something meaningful with your life, something your children can look up to you for. Don't squander your law degree, please."

"What if I ran for mayor? The current mayor is moving on to bigger things. He said he would endorse me. I have a good rep in this city, and I don't think it would be a difficult win."

"You won't get elected if you're not married. That's how politics work. Is Veronica going to marry you?"

"I don't know, Mom. If her father chooses to go to prison rather than turn state's evidence and enter the witness protection program, she might hate me for interfering."

"If that happens, you won't get elected no matter how hard you campaign. Bridgeport's residents want a first lady. She's gorgeous and it seems she's already well liked. I did a little research on her after the photo of you two came out. She'd help you win, that's not a question. But, she'll need to compromise. She won't have time to co-host that talk show if she's married to the mayor of Bridgeport."

"I know. There are a lot of contingencies."

"If she doesn't want to marry you, for whatever reason, then you'll move back home. I miss you, and besides your relationships with Caroline and Emma, there's no reason for you to stay."

I swallow a lump in my throat. "If Veronica marries me but I lose the election?"

"That likely won't happen if the present mayor is popular and is willing to endorse you, *and* you have Veronica on your arm, but even I know not everything is guaranteed. If Veronica marries you, but you don't win, I'll allow you to stay in Bridgeport, but *Talk of the Town* is over, Rafferty. You'll find some other means of employment. Something more respectable."

"You mean hanging out my shingle." Opening my own office used to put a bad taste in my mouth, but with Nic by my side, it might not be so bad.

"Not necessarily. This is a negotiation after all. Find something that will fulfill you. Pro bono work if that's what you want. Legal aid. Non-profit. Whatever fills your heart."

I sit back, stunned. "You'd let me do that?"

"Rafferty. I'm your mother. I know you think I'm an old dragon blowing smoke out of her ass instead of her mouth, but I do want you to be happy. We don't work for the money. Okay, not only for the money. We come from scads of it, and you've made your own. You don't have to work for a paycheck. Do what will get you out of bed in the morning and put a smile on your face at night. But do *something*. You started your rag mag to spite me. Consider me spited and move on."

"I don't know what to say."

"Say you won't hate me if it turns out honoring your part of our bargain means moving here. If Veronica doesn't want to marry you, please don't punish me for it. I've made a lot of mistakes. Sometimes I think sending you to Bridgeport was one of them, but it's turned you into the man you are and I admire that man. I would appreciate it very much if this could be a new start for us, even if I am forcing your hand."

"I would like that, too." When all is said and done, I can give Boston a couple of years, and if I hate it, I'll move back to Bridgeport. I can honestly say I tried, and my mother won't be able to argue.

"Try to get some sleep. From what you've told me, Veronica's a tough cookie. She's made it this far and if she loves you as much as you love her, she has a reason to stay strong."

"Thanks. I mean it. Thank you. I don't think this would be possible if you weren't the one doing it."

"Hmmm, well you've never appreciated what having money and power can do. I hope now you can. Having power for power's sake has never been what we're about, but you've never wanted to consider that. You're too busy trying not to be one of us. This might change your mind. If you win, you won't be sipping on scotch in the mayor's office with your feet propped on your desk. You'll be in a position to create change, make a difference. Perhaps keep your mind busy by building your campaign. What do you stand for, Rafferty? I think we all want to know. Goodnight."

"Thank you. Goodnight." I disconnect and find my own pad and pen.

What do I stand for? What kind of change would I want to see in this city? What could Nic and I do? Dennis Iverson has done a fine job over the years, but there still some areas where there's a need.

I write a page or two of notes, but I stop. There's no point pretending I'm not worried about Nic. If Barker forces her, will I still love her? Could I still touch her knowing she'd been with him? Damned straight I could. I said those things at her apartment because I was jealous of Durand and I hadn't let those feelings go.

When this is done, I'll have a clean slate with more than only my mother.

It will be a new start in every aspect of my life, and I would be lying if I didn't admit that it scares the hell out of me.

CHAPTER THIRTEEN

Veronica

We crossed the city limits sometime after midnight and drove for another half an hour to his lake house. Blaise carried my suitcases from the truck, but a housekeeper intervened the moment we stepped across the threshold and disappeared with them.

The house is made of glass and sits above the lake on a rocky incline. It's a beautiful view, and I'm surprised Blaise has it in him to appreciate something like that. He escorted me to a bedroom himself, a hand to my back.

"I'll give you time to get to know me. I promised your father I would treat you well, and I will. But don't mistake my generosity for weakness. Once we're wed, I will expect you to fulfill your duties as my wife and that means sharing my bed. Do you understand me, Annie?" he asked, standing inside the bedroom where the maid deposited my suitcases.

"Yes," I whispered, grateful I have time to resign to my fate.

"Good girl," he said, tipping my head back and brushing his lips over mine.

I tried not to tremble, but he felt it and angrily pushed me away. "You're not to leave the house unless you're with me. The staff know to report to me if you try. So don't bother. Now that I'm back in the city, I have things to take care of tonight. Tomorrow morning we'll talk to my mother and complete the exchange with your father. Dress appropriately. My mother wants to see the woman you've grown into."

He left me shivering in the empty room, the silvery moonlight shining through the enormous window that looks over the lake.

The housekeeper who carried my suitcases into the bedroom returned and asked if she could draw me a bath. I don't need a lady's maid, or I suppose in this case, a security guard, as I'm sure she knows ten different kinds of self-defense, can hit a moving target with a handgun from five hundred feet away, and kill a man with her bare hands. Maybe I'm exaggerating, but if his house staff have orders to keep me here, they have the skills to keep me here.

"No, thank you. It's been a long day, and I'm going to bed," I said, wanting to be alone.

"The en suite is stocked with everything you need, and the phone on the nightstand is connected to the kitchen. Press zero at any time if we can be of assistance, Miss Johnson. Someone will always be available."

I'm sure they are, I thought and tried to smile. "Thank you."

She nodded and retreated, closing the door behind her. Curious, I checked the lock, but I opened the door in time to see her round a corner. I'm not locked in, but I can't leave.

I undressed, brushed my teeth, and wiped my makeup off in the large bathroom.

I crawled into bed and couldn't stop the tears. Was it only yesterday I spent the day in bed with Raff? Nibbling when we were hungry, on food and on each other?

Lying in the dark, I let the truth wash over me. He won't come for me. The nasty things he said and the hard look in his eyes told me that. Never once did he say, how can I help you? What can I do?

He let me pack, let me go.

He never loved me, and lying in bed, shame filled me. I'm ashamed I ever loved him, trusted him, gave myself to him even while knowing he thought I was a piece of trash for jumping from Jack's bed to his.

All I ever wanted was for someone to love me, only a little.

It seems it was too much to ask.

This morning, after falling into a restless sleep, the maid who hasn't introduced herself opens the blinds and lets in the sun that's sparkling over the water. "Mr. Barker said he will be arriving in two hours to drive you into the city. He asked that I see to it you're showered and dressed. There's also coffee and breakfast in the dining room if you wish."

"Thank you," I say, lying there, blinking against the sunlight.

This is my life now, where time is not my own, where privacy is assumed but nonexistent. Blaise will know my every move, either by the spies he employs or bugs in my room.

She leaves, and I shower using the expensive luxury soaps and hair products, shave with a razor that's the same as the one in my bathroom. I wonder what will happen to my apartment and the rest of my things. I built a refuge, a place to escape a busy day, the paparazzi. That security was shattered the night I found Blaise sitting in my living room. That too, was an illusion.

Maybe my whole life hasn't been real.

A woman with silver hair. I'll be a myth, like Raff thought the Barkers are.

Blaise walks into the bedroom uninvited just as I'm finishing putting on my makeup. He crowds me between his body and the vanity, and he meets my reflection's eyes. We would be a striking pair if he wasn't so mean. Something turned him, greed for money and power, his need for his mother's approval. I don't know and don't care enough to ask. Maybe one day he'll tell me, or maybe I'll disappear before he reveals any of his secrets.

He's dressed in his suit, the blood red tie. I wonder if it's a warning, a red flag.

"You're very beautiful," he says to the mirror, rubbing his thumb over my jaw. He's hard, and his erection presses against my butt. He's strong enough to bend me over the sink, to take what he wants from me, and one day, he will.

"Thank you." What does beauty matter? It won't save me.

"Are you ready?"

"Yes."

I don't carry a purse—I don't have anything to bring with me. I don't have a cell phone and may never be permitted to use one. I don't need to touch up my makeup, don't need a spare lipstick. Blaise will drive me back when the meeting is over—we won't go anywhere else until he trusts me not to run. I don't chew gum, I'm not on my period.

He wraps his hand around mine and leads me out of the bedroom.

The housekeeper opens the front door for us, and we step into the warm summer morning.

We drive into Fairfax and out again to his warehouse located in the industrial park. It's connected to a huge office building, and Blaise catches me widening my eyes.

"Yes, we've made significant progress. It's a shame your

father wants to retire. We need him more than ever. Come, he's waiting for us."

"And your mother," I say.

He doesn't respond, only leads me through the parking lot with a firm hand to my back. I pause to look around. The docks are busy, teeming with people unloading and loading cargo ships. Exporting and importing is only a small slice of what the Barkers do, most of it illegal, some of it legal to hide what's not. Out of the corner of my eye, I think I see a woman who looks like Emma wearing a white sundress standing by a lamppost, her dark hair blowing in the breeze, but I do a double take and she's gone.

There's no reason for her to be here. No one knows I'm not in Bridgeport anymore. I doubt Raff will tell anyone. He's probably at his office, thinking of how to spin our breakup. Everyone will want to know why we aren't together anymore. Maybe he'll say I left him for another man, and one day someone will see me in Fairfax with Blaise, his lies will become truth. He can call me a whore on his website the way he did to my face in my apartment.

The producers of the show are probably livid, wondering what to do. I wasn't given approval to take today off, and my phone will be jammed with angry voicemails and messages asking me where the fuck I am. Felix may even stop by my apartment, though he's never done that before. The friendly rivalry that used to be a wedge between us fell away the night of the fire, turning us into true friends. It would have been pleasant working with him going forward.

Going forward.

Well, none of that, now, Annie. My life will forever be at a standstill. Suck it up.

Blaise opens the glass door and we walk through the lobby

to an elevator. It's already at ground level, and silently, we step in together. He punches the button to the top floor.

There's no one sitting at the desks, and the hallway we walk to reach Mollie's office is empty. This isn't a real business. The Barkers don't employ anyone they can't trust, and they wouldn't work here, out in the open.

I step into a large corner office. It's empty, like I suspected. No plants, the bookshelves empty. No artwork hanging on the walls. The docks and Cavern Lake are framed by a huge window at my father's back. "Annie," he gushes.

"Daddy," I say, my eyes skimming over him. Breaking the law on a daily basis agrees with him. He's fit, his skin a healthy tan. The suit he wears is similar to Blaise's, the cut impeccable across his shoulders. "You look good."

He nods, but doesn't answer, and it's then I see the frail older woman sitting behind the desk. She's thin, and her hair, what remains of it, has lost any shine. Her face is lined by stress and illness, and a lot of grief. "Mollie," I say, my heart going out to her as a woman who is giving up her life for her father to a woman who has given up her life for her husband and sons.

"Annie," she says, struggling to her feet.

Blaise swiftly crosses the room to assist her, and she reluctantly leans into him. Ghosts of the formidable woman she used to be are there in her stance, the unrelenting planes of her face. Loss has hit her hard, made worse by the knowledge her remaining children haven't had any of their own.

"You have grown into a beautiful woman. This exchange pleases me very much. My son knows it's time to settle down, to produce heirs to the business. You will be a fine match," she says, nodding at my dad. "Skinny, but a pregnancy will change that."

Dad grins from ear to ear, secure his freedom is eminent with the proposal accepted.

Blaise wraps his arm around my waist and nuzzles my ear with his nose. "Soon," he threatens, his voice low.

"There are papers to sign," Mollie says.

The contracts don't concern me, and I drift to the window and gaze across the water. Is it stupid I miss Raff? Even though I know what he thinks of me?

My dad shakes Mollie's hand and Blaise says, "You're irreplaceable."

"I appreciate everything you've done for me, the resources you gave me to help me get back on my feet. I don't think Annie would be where she is today if you hadn't cleaned me up, and I will always be thankful."

"And this is how you repay us," Blaise says, and my heart skips a beat. This won't go as smoothly as my father hoped.

"I'm giving you my daughter. I would think that proves my allegiance whether I'm actively working for you or not," Dad says, his eyes nervously dashing between Mollie and Blaise.

"Blaise, that's enough," Mollie says, fighting to stay on her feet. "The exchange is adequate along with the agreements he signed promising us his silence. You are free to go, Mr. Johnson. Billy is downstairs. He'll escort you out of Fairfax."

My dad licks his lips. "What do you mean? You said I could see Annie."

"And you have. Either you work for us or you don't. You are choosing to sever ties. Good luck to you, Mr. Johnson, with whatever life holds in store for you."

My father scoffs and closes the several feet between us. "I'm sorry, Annie. I thought this would be different, but we have to do what they say. Don't make Blaise unhappy." He lowers his voice. "Pop out a couple of kids and he'll leave you alone."

I want to slap him for the dispassionate way he whittled my life down to nothing but infants and heirs. There is so much more to me. There is so much more to me than my capacity to be a wife, to be a mother. My eyes fill with tears. I promised myself I wouldn't cry—all it will do is turn Blaise's temper toward me—but I can't keep one from dripping down my cheek.

He kisses it away like he used to do when I was a child and I hurt myself, and on his way out the door, shakes Blaise's hand, the final piece missing from the exchange. I belong to Blaise now, and there is nothing I can do.

"I'd like a few words with my soon-to-be daughter-in-law. Blaise, see Mr. Johnson to the car."

"Okay, Ma. Then I think we should go to lunch and celebrate."

"Yes, and I'll need to lie down after that. You and Annie will have the rest of the day. Help her settle in."

"Yes, ma'am. Let's go," Blaise says to my father, a firm hand to his shoulder, security escorting a fallen employee off the premises. Blaise shuts the office door.

"Would you like a drink, Annie?" Mollie asks, her voice losing the strong authority now that we're alone.

"No, thank you." If I start drinking, I'll never stop. Drinking, to me, will always mean sharing a whiskey with Raff while we spend time together. We never had drunk sex, though I believed with all my heart he'd never hurt me.

He might always print the truth, but he's a good liar.

She pours herself a glass from a metal cart near the desk. "It's the only way I can get through a day anymore," she says, her hands trembling.

"I'm sorry. Blaise didn't tell me you were sick."

"It happens, and I'm not sorry to go. I loved my husband, and I'll see him and my sons again one day. It's what I live for now."

"That's nice." I would think so if my situation were different, but now I say it because it's expected. I don't give a fuck how Mollie Barker perceives death.

"I don't believe you appreciate your role in your father's, shall we say, retirement, and I don't blame you. Women are treated as a commodity, and I admit I had a hand in that with my own sons. Blaise didn't cherish his first two wives, but he knows you're the end of the line. He won't hurt you."

"That depends on your definition, Mollie. I'm hurting just by being here, so for you to tell me he won't hurt me, that's already a lie."

"Are you in love with him?"

I blink. "Who?"

"Rafferty Clark. Bridgeport news travels this way, and I've scrolled through his website a time or two. You're a celebrity there, and we saw the photos. That's why I wanted to talk to you. Are you in love with him? We need to understand the risk we took accepting your father's proposition."

I tell her the truth. "I loved him. He didn't love me back."

"He won't come looking for you?"

I wipe more tears off my cheeks. "No."

"Then I am equally sorry and relieved. As women, we hope to be appreciated and respected for who we are. So rarely does that happen. I can promise, for as long as I'm still alive, to see to it Blaise respects you and treats you properly."

That's small consolation, and I don't put any trust in it.

Mollie continues, "To ensure that happens, I'd like to take you under my wing. Let me teach you the business. If Blaise values you somewhere other than his bed, you will have a much better chance of thriving in your marriage after I'm no longer here to protect you."

There is nothing she could give me that would persuade me to accept her offer. "I think I would rather have him kill me."

Her eyes harden. "I'm sorry you feel that way." She picks up her cell, connects a call, and says, "We're done here."

Immediately, two men dressed in suits, their jackets bulging, barely disguising their weapons, barge into Mollie's office. They flank me and one pulls me roughly away from the window.

"See to it she's confined to the lake house. She's not to go anywhere," she says to the one gripping my arm. "No one leaves, Annie. Not you, not your father. Blaise's wives tried to escape. Learn from their mistakes."

I stiffen. "My father? What are you going to do to him?"

"Something we should have done the minute he said he wanted out."

"No!" I scream.

The two bodyguards drag me out of Mollie's office. One shoves me into the elevator, and his partner draws his weapon, his finger curled around the trigger. The threat is blatant. I do anything, and he'll shoot me.

My legs can't hold me up, and I sink onto the scratchy floor. The elevator carries us down to the lobby, the prickly industrial carpeting stabbing into my palms and legs. They're going to murder my father. They never planned to go through with the exchange. Tears drip from my eyes. The door opens, and he grips me by my hair, forcing me to my feet. I have to trot to keep up with him, my heels scraping the pavement.

In vain, I search for my father, but he's gone. The kiss he gave me to wipe away my tear turned into his last kiss goodbye. I'll never see him again.

He shoves me into the back of an SUV, and the thug holding his weapon slides in next to me. He rests his handgun on his knee, his finger never leaving the trigger. I cower against the door until we reached Blaise's lake house.

The driver slams on the brakes and parks, rounds the hood, and opens the door. "Get out. Don't try to run away. All that will get you is a bullet in the back."

I think about running, but I have nowhere to go, and a bullet to my back might not kill me.

The housekeeper meets us at the door.

"The meeting didn't go as planned. Don't let her go anywhere. Mollie's orders."

She nods, and the three of them walk with me to the bedroom I slept in last night. I sink onto the middle of the bed, and she locks the door. I don't know if they'll feed me, and I don't care. Let them starve me to death. It's not like anyone cares.

Blaise is going to kill my dad, if he hasn't already, and eventually, he'll kill me too.

I lie there until dinner, and the housekeeper serves me a tray. I don't eat, and after an hour, she returns and carries it away.

I don't move. I don't even cry.

Sometimes I think about Raff and what he's doing. If he's with another woman. He always seemed so angry when we had sex. I can't call it making love because that's not what it was. He was always so rough, like he resented wanting me. I guess he did and took it out on me. Jack's leftovers.

No one disturbs me all night, and when the housekeeper serves me breakfast, I'm in the same spot I was in when she fed me dinner.

I don't hear a word from anyone. I don't know if my dad is dead or alive. I don't know where Blaise is. Planning our wedding, more than likely, so his mother can be there before she passes away.

The sun casts shadows on the walls, buttery yellow, turning to bright gold, then pink and purple, and then nothing.

I'm sick from hunger, but still, I don't move from the bed.
I don't move, hoping, that like the sun, I can fade away.

CHAPTER FOURTEEN

Rafferty

"They picked him up a hundred and forty miles outside of Fairfax, down a dirt road that led to a hunting shack," Durand tells me.

It's been three agonizing days since I brokered the deal with my mother.

She ordered me to keep my head down and my mouth shut, and that's exactly what I've been doing.

Emma had been insistent they didn't leave Nic alone, and Durand drove her out to Fairfax himself. They parked near Barker's warehouse and office building where he does business. Emma's lucky she isn't pregnant—Durand never would have indulged her if she was. Pretending to be tourists, they strolled along the docks and she caught sight of Nic, a man matching Barker's description leading her into the building. It wasn't long after that Emma and Durand watched two goons drag her out of there, and ever since she's been a captive at a lake house sitting on the rocky shore of Cavern Lake.

She's safe.

That's what I'm choosing to believe.

"It was supposed to look like a hunting accident," he says. "Witness protection has him in custody at an undisclosed safehouse. He's squealing, happy to be alive, worried about Veronica. He keeps calling her Annie. Do you know anything about that?"

"That's her real name. She changed it to distance herself from her father and the Barkers. Worked for a long time. No one had any idea who she really was."

"The Barkers always knew, and her dad's saying they were watching her the whole time she lived in Bridgeport."

"How much longer is this going to take? She's been there for longer than she needs to be."

"A detective with the Fairfax PD arrested the two who drove Veronica's dad out of town. They're waiting until he tells them everything he knows, and it's a lot, Clark. After fifteen years, it's a lot. Money laundering, murder. Arson cases that weren't solved. Your mother sent them copies of the hotel's security and the clip your guy filmed. They're looking for the fake hotel worker Veronica spoke with outside of the ladies' restroom. Your mother gave the county's attorney's office a head's up, and they wanted in. It shouldn't be too much longer now."

"Thank you for going out there, for letting Emma go out there." I try to keep my voice from cracking.

"Anytime, and I mean that. I care about her, too. I know you don't like hearing it, but maybe the four of us have bonds that will never be broken. That shouldn't be broken. Veronica and I didn't end well, but that's both our faults. She didn't ask for help, and I didn't offer it. This would have turned out very differently if she'd trusted us."

"She didn't, Durand. Right until the last, and my filthy

words proved her right. She didn't ask me for help either, and I didn't tell her I would protect her. I let her go."

"Make it Jack. I think we're close enough for that now. And you didn't let her go. You came to me and Emma, and you called your mom. You did everything you could. Her dad's alive because of you. Don't dismiss that."

I blow out a breath. Maybe Dur—Jack's right. "If we're getting all warm and fuzzy, call me Raff. I honestly don't know what my mother was thinking."

"I like it. It has a nice mayoral ring to it."

"What? How do you know about that?"

"Your mom's been keeping me updated. Oh, did I forget to mention that? She's a nice lady. Eats nails for breakfast."

I laugh, but it's weak and full of worry. "You're not wrong."

"The Fairfax PD will move in soon. They've been eyeing Barker for years and they're drooling for this, but they're going slow. They don't want to fuck it up. Factories, warehouse, office buildings, ships, and his lake house. Barker has staff watching Veronica. She's probably safer there than anywhere else."

I don't know if I want to let Jack know what I'm scared of, but I ask, "Has Barker, do you know if he's . . ."

Man to man, he knows what I'm trying to say. "He hasn't been there. My guess is, he wants to keep her isolated to freak her out. He hasn't touched her."

"Thank you."

"Hang in there. You're doing the right thing by holding back. So far, the Barkers don't have any idea what's going on, and that's the way the cops want it. I'll check in soon."

Jack hangs up, and I toss my phone onto the coffee table.

Yeah, sometimes no news is bad news, and I can imagine what Nic's going through alone, thinking the worst. About her dad. About me. I might as well have agreed to move to Boston.

Nic's not going to want to marry me after this. Why should she? I called her a whore and all but pushed her into Barker's arms.

All I can hope is that she loves me enough to forgive me.

And even then, that might not be enough.

CHAPTER FIFTEEN

Veronica

The minutes melt into hours and the hours into days. I don't do anything but lie on the bed. My father's dead. I know that with my whole heart.

We were fools to think they would let him go with all he knows, and when Blaise is tired of me, I'll be next.

I don't cry.

I could break down if I let myself, but no man I ever met was worth crying over, and that includes Raff.

People thought I was crying over Jack after he dumped me at his party, but what I was really crying over was knowing I'd end up here. Like this.

Earlier this morning, I gave in and drank a couple cups of the coffee the housekeeper brought to my room. I had stomach cramps so painful I thought she poisoned me. I've never felt that sick before—not even when I had food poisoning after dinner one night with Jack and I ate contaminated seafood. I spent the rest of the morning in the bathroom throwing up.

I realized later it wasn't poison, only my empty stomach rebelling what little I put into it.

I'm hollow, and I wish it would go away.

All of it.

I'm so tired, and I miss my dad. He was the only family I had left, and he's gone.

I miss Raff.

We never danced at the fundraiser. I never stepped into his arms like I've seen Emma do so many times. I wanted that. To be welcomed there. Wanted. Comfortable. Let him whisper gossip into my ear while I hold back giggles of disbelief.

Raff knows everything about everyone.

Except how much it tore me apart to hear the last words he said to me.

The little hands of the old-fashioned clock sitting on the nightstand slide to midnight. I don't know when Blaise will finally show up. I've never been alone this long. I try to find comfort in the solitude, but I'm waiting for something to shatter the silence.

I can't sleep, and I sit on the window seat counting stars and wishing on satellites. Out of nowhere, a scream pierces the air, and I jerk unsteadily to my feet.

"Open it," a rough voice commands from the hallway, and someone unlocks the door to my prison.

It swings open, and I tense. A slim woman wearing pumps, black dress slacks, a white camisole, and a black blazer, her hair pulled into a severe ponytail, steps into the room, two uniformed policemen behind her. Our eyes meet and she stops. Tentatively, she brushes back her blazer and reveals a gold badge attached to her belt. "I'm Detective Mason, Miss Chapman. Are you hurt?"

"N-no. Where's Blaise?" I stutter, wrapping my arms around myself. This has to be a trick. Blaise is testing me to see if I run. If I do, he'll kill me, but what's worse? Living a life alone, or dying? There's no difference.

"We've taken him and Margaret Barker into custody. You're safe now, Miss Chapman. We'd like to have a doctor look at you and ask you a few questions, and then you can go home."

Home? What is that? *Where* is that? Is it the little house where I grew up, in Littlefork, Minnesota? Is it my apartment? It's not Jack's penthouse. I've never been up there. It's not Raff's house. I didn't spend enough time there to consider it anything but a place where he used me for sex and then had the audacity to accuse me of using him to repair my reputation.

Home isn't anywhere I've ever been.

"I don't understand. How did you know where I was?"

"Your father told us."

At this, I sink to the floor and cover my face with my hands. "Mollie said they were going to kill him."

Detective Mason settles onto her haunches and rests her hand on my shoulder. "He's under police protection now, Miss Chapman. He's told us everything in exchange for leniency."

My hands fall into my lap, and I stare at her. Her eyes are deep brown, and even in the middle of the night, she's wearing makeup. "How did you know they took him?"

She smiles. "Let's just say you have some very concerned and connected people worried about you, but we had to verify a few things before we could do anything. We can go into further details, but I would prefer to do it at the station and take your statement. It's late, and I'm sure you'd like to go home."

"I never thought I'd get to go anywhere."

"Let's go. After we speak, you'll be free to do whatever you like."

I don't know how I'll get back to Bridgeport. I don't have a car, no way to pay for a ride. I want to ask her, but she's striding down the hallway, the two officers waiting for me to pick my ass up off the floor and follow. I'm dressed in lounging pants and a tank top, a cardigan thrown over them, slippers on my feet. I don't stop to change, and Detective Mason didn't give me time or permission even if I had wanted to.

I leave everything behind and join the detective in the living room. She's waiting by the front door.

"What happened to the housekeeper?"

"She's under arrest." Detective Mason flicks a glance at me. "Did she hurt you?"

I press a shaking hand to my stomach. "No, I don't think so. I was worried she poisoned the food, and I haven't eaten since Blaise brought me here."

The detective nods at a police officer. "We'll check it out, and you can have something at the station. Would you like to stop at the ER first? A doctor can give you an exam and you can speak to a social worker or a counselor. It's okay if you don't want to tell me why you do."

She tilts her head, and I realize she's talking about rape. "No, I'm okay, he didn't, he didn't hurt me like that."

"Okay, but you can change your mind anytime. This is Officer Lavigne. He's going to drive you, and I'll meet you there. I have a few phone calls to make before we talk."

"Thank you."

I huddle in the backseat of the cruiser, his dash lit up. He turned down the radio, but I can still hear the dispatcher's voice requesting an available officer in the area to check out a domestic dispute.

Someone told the police Blaise took me, but the only person who knew was Raff, and he didn't care. Who else knew? Did a reporter see him drive me away? None of this makes sense.

I step into the police department's lobby, and I'm even

more confused . . . Jack and Emma are sitting in the waiting area. They spring to their feet, and Emma rushes across the gleaming tiles and pulls me into her arms.

"Thank God you're okay," she says, her voice full of tears.

Jack approaches us at a slower pace.

"What are you doing here?" I ask, hugging Emma back.

"We weren't going to let you go through this alone," she says, holding me at arms' length, her eyes searching my body for signs of abuse. "We're going to sit with you and drive you home."

"How did you know what happened?"

"Raff told us."

"But he didn't—" I start, but Detective Mason joins us and leads us to a comfortable sitting area decorated with water-colors hanging on the walls and potted plants sitting on the floor.

I sink onto a brown leather couch, and Emma sits next to me, our thighs touching. It's on the tip of my tongue to tell her not to crowd me, always used to the insincerity of people who only pretended they cared, but Emma does and I would hurt her feelings if I told her to give me space. Jack sits near us in a matching chair, never moving too far from Emma's side.

Detective Mason pours us coffee into real mugs and offers me a prepackaged blueberry muffin that I accept but am too sick to eat. She settles onto the coffee table in front of us and says, "Tell me what happened. From the beginning, if you can."

I start from when Mollie approached my father and offered him a job, and I talk for over an hour. Detective Mason scrawls notes as quickly as she can. Emma holds my hand, and Jack listens to every word I say, growing angrier and angrier until I think he's going to blow like a teakettle.

"What's going to happen to my dad?" He deserves to go to prison for trading my life for his, for working for the Barkers for so long, but I don't want that for him. I think he's always tried his best, even if that best was never going to be good enough for what I needed him to be.

"He'll go into a witness protection program, Miss Chapman," she says, her mouth twisting. She doesn't like he's getting away free and clear. "Unfortunately, William Barker slipped through the cracks. It's imperative for your father's safety that you no longer have contact with him, especially before the Barker's trials. Your father's testimony, and yours, will be crucial for a guilty verdict. I'm sorry you didn't get a chance to say goodbye in person, but if you'd like to write him a letter, I can ask that it be forwarded to his location."

Jack bristles. "With Billy Barker out there, is Veronica in danger?"

Detective Mason shrugs. "At this point, I don't think so. He's smart, and he'll know Miss Chapman didn't play a role in putting his mother and brother away. Her father did that, and that's where William Barker will focus once he's back on his feet."

"Mollie's sick." I don't know what made me say it, maybe some misplaced sympathy that she'll spend her remaining time in prison away from her sons.

"She is. She'll likely pass away before her trial. After this, she doesn't have much to live for." Detective Mason touches my knee. "If you're interested in your things, we'll have them sent to you, but for now they're part of the evidence he kept you there."

"No. I was in shock, and I don't remember what I packed. Donate my clothes or throw them away. It doesn't matter."

"If you change your mind, contact me," she says, handing me a business card. "Otherwise, that's all I need. The county's attorney's office will reach out about the trial, but until then, you're free to go."

Just like that. I'm free to go. But go where and do what? I grapple with the idea that my life is free to do with what I will. The Barkers were always a nightmare that followed me from bed to bed. What will I do, now that I can finally rest?

Jack stands, furious energy radiating off him, his face set in grim determination.

Emma nudges me to my feet but doesn't let my hand go.

Detective Mason disappears, her heels clicking against the tile toward a room we can't see. If she's in charge of this case, she has a lot of work ahead of her.

We step into the parking lot, the sunrise pretty, but I'm too confused and tired to appreciate it. The air is heavy with heat and humidity, my cardigan too much for the temperature even this early in the morning.

Jack rounds on me the second we reach a familiar black SUV. I expect him to yell at me for putting Emma in danger, for putting him in a position where he had to come to my rescue, but he pulls me into his arms and tangles his fingers in my hair.

"I am so sorry," he says.

Emma watches, her face filled with relief. I look for jealousy or contempt, but there's nothing.

"For what?" I ask, reluctant to hug him back.

"For not forcing you to tell me the trouble you were in. For not being present in our relationship. I dated you for two years, and I didn't get to know you, didn't appreciate you as a person. I should have known all this about you, and I'm sorry you felt like you couldn't come to me."

"I didn't feel like I could go to anyone." I've never had someone constant in my life. My father wasn't—I spent all my time trying to distance myself from him. I saw Felix every day, but we were never friends. Jack and I were nothing but friends with benefits, and even the friends part was stretching it.

He pulls away and frames my face between his hands. "You will always have Emma and me. We'll see you through this, and if you and your father need an attorney, I'll pay for the best. Don't worry about anything. Annie? Is that what we call you now?"

Taken aback, I blanch. There's no reason why I can't go back to being Annie Johnson, but that little girl isn't who I am. Maybe Veronica Chapman isn't who I am, either. "That doesn't sound like me."

Jack studies me. "Maybe not. Maybe you like Nic better."

Raff. I'll never hear him call me that again.

Goodbye, dollface.

"I have a lot to think about," I say, twisting my head out of his grasp. Emma will tolerate him touching me for only so long, though, all she's doing is leaning against the truck watching us, her eyes gritty with sleep. We've been up all night.

"That's your way of saying shut up and let's get on the road," Jack says, huffing a laugh. "I got it. Those two years weren't a complete waste. Sleep if you can. We have a long drive ahead of us. We should've flew."

He opens the back door for me, and I crawl inside the stuffy interior.

Emma slides in on the passenger side and she smiles at me. "We're really happy you're okay." She turns toward the front, and Jack settles behind the wheel and starts the engine. He shifts into Drive, but before he navigates out of the parking lot, he seals his lips over hers in a long kiss.

I peel my cardigan off, the material and my skin damp with sweat, and I fold it into a makeshift pillow. I doze the entire way to Bridgeport, but I'm aware enough to know Emma constantly looks over her shoulder to check that I'm okay. I don't know where her sense of loyalty toward me came from, I'm only grateful she has it. Out of spite, she could have kept

Jack from helping me, but instead, she helped, too. Friendship, real friendship, like what she has with Mia and Haisley, Zoey, and yes, Raff, is foreign to me, a concept I never let myself consider could be mine.

We drive into the city limits, and I'm on the verge of throwing up from hunger and motion sickness by the time Jack double parks in front of my building. I don't have a key, didn't bother to lock my door behind me when I met Blaise.

"Go up with her, Jack," Emma says. "I'll wait here."

"That's not necessary—" I start, sitting up, my stomach doing queasy flipflops.

"Yes, it is. Jack and I had to wait for permission to drive to Fairfax, but I couldn't sit and do nothing. Zoey helped me empty your fridge and we put fresh food in it. We cleaned a bit, and I washed your sheets. I hope you don't mind. You left your phone behind, and I plugged it in. You've missed a lot of calls," she says, grinning sheepishly.

"I don't know what to say." Her generosity leaves me speechless.

"Don't say anything. Get some real sleep, and if you change your mind and need to go to the clinic, *call me* and I'll go with you. I'm not working today."

"Okay. Thanks."

Jack lets me out of the truck and walks with me up the concrete stairs. Somehow, he found a key to the front security door, and we're silent in the elevator. I need something to eat, a shower, and a lot of sleep, in that order.

He unlocks my apartment door and drops both keys into my hand. "I told him I wouldn't interfere, that I would let you two work it out, but Raff's worried about you. Even if you decide not to forgive him for what he said, a quick text to let him know you're okay would mean a lot to him."

I quirk an eyebrow. "He's Raff now? You never liked him, Jack."

"You're not the only one who's made friends." He kisses my forehead. "We're glad you're all right. Text or call if you need anything. Nothing is too big or too small."

I smooth my hand over Jack's tie. "Thanks. You weren't the only one to blame. I kept myself from getting close to you, too. I never thought a normal life would be possible for me. Not with my dad working for the Barkers."

"I appreciate that. Maybe we can put this behind us now."

"That would be nice. I'm going to, ah," I say, not knowing how to end this conversation. Jack might harbor a lot of guilt because we weren't close enough I could feel comfortable asking him for help, but that was my life, and oddly doesn't have much to do with him.

It was just the way things were for me.

"Yeah, yeah. Sorry. I'm fuzzy. It's been a long night. We'll see you later." He squeezes my arm in goodbye, and he lopes toward the elevator. I'm not sure which he's more excited to see —his bed or Emma. Luckily, Emma will be *in* his bed, and if I found that, I would be excited, too.

I push the door open and step into my apartment.

The refrigerator is full of food: fruit, vegetables, lettuce for salad, and milk that's not expired. My phone is sitting where I left it on the counter, and it's done charging. I don't turn it on, instead I drop my keys next to it and unplug it. The show and the producers are the least of my worries. Jack and Emma seemed to have taken control of things here, maybe one of them reached out to *Rise and Shine, Bridgeport!* and let them know what was going on. I'm not sure if I want to go back. I wanted the high-profile job as a way to stay in the public's eye, the attention giving me a false sense of security. I don't need that now, but it's all I know.

There's canned chicken noodle soup in the cabinet and though it's a strange thing to eat for breakfast, I sip on the broth and wander around my apartment. It's different being here knowing nothing will force me to leave. Everything I did in my adult life I did believing it would be only temporary, and being able to look toward the future is a different feeling for me.

I sip on the soup until my stomach calms down, and afterward, I stand under a hot shower and wash my hair and shave. That feels better than having food in my belly, but what would feel best of all is if Raff were waiting for me. If I could fall asleep with his arms around me.

My stupid heart won't let me forget how much I love him.

I sleep better than I have in months, maybe years, but I wake up muzzy, my usual pattern off. I think about changing into clothes, but I leave my pajamas on and brush my hair. My evening looms long and empty in front of me, another thing I'll need to get used to and possibly learn to enjoy. No hectic nightlife.

Someone knocks on my door, and my heart skitters. Maybe Raff came to apologize and beg forgiveness for the nasty things he said. Maybe he wants a life with me, maybe he wants to marry me . . . no. If he truly loved and wanted me, he wouldn't have let me leave.

Nervously, I open it, hoping it's Raff, needing to see him, needing to feel his arms around me, but Emma's standing in the hallway along with Mia and Haisley, Zoey, her girls, and . . . Claire.

I gape stupidly. "What are you doing here?"

"We thought maybe you wouldn't want to be alone tonight. Are you up for a slumber party?" Emma asks.

Graciela peers around the doorjamb. "Please?"

"Oh, honey," I say, loving this brave and spunky girl, "yeah, sure."

"Cool!" Hilary exclaims and pushes past me into my apartment.

Zoey rolls her eyes. "Hilary."

"I guess I'm being too slow. It's a lot to process," I say, opening the door wider and letting them inside. I don't know Claire well, and I smile timidly at her. "Hi."

She yanks me against her chest, hugging me for the first time since I've known her. "Jesus Christ, and I thought I was the drama queen around here. I've got nothing on you," she says, laughing.

"I'll let you have it," I say wryly. "I've had enough."

Mia and Haisley unload bottle after bottle of wine, and the girls beg for Chinese takeout. Zoey logs into a streaming service on my smart TV and queues up *Frozen* (the girls' favorite movie), and Emma unpacks large air mattresses that Claire helps her blow up.

We sit and eat Chinese in my living room in a heap of limbs and wine. Gracie is too big for my lap, but she tries her best, resting her head on my shoulder, her arms tightly wrapped around my waist. Emma sits next to us, Paige cuddling in her lap.

Mia and Haisley sit together on my loveseat, and Claire is sitting on the floor, Hilary in front of her, while Zoey teaches her how to braid hair.

"Thanks," I say to Emma over Gracie's head.

She sighs in contentment. "You're welcome."

———

The rest of the evening flies by in a haze of chicken chow mein and wine. The girls last through *Frozen 2* before succumbing to the late hour, and they fall asleep in my bed. Everyone is on a regular sleep schedule and settles onto the air mattresses not long after the girls, but at midnight, I'm wide awake and crawl onto the fire escape needing fresh air. I'm not used to being around so many people in such a tiny space. I appreciate Emma's good intentions, but I need a few minutes alone.

Minutes I'm not granted, but I won't argue.

"Here, I brought you more wine," Emma says, sneaking onto the fire escape with me, holding two wine glasses filled to the brim.

"Are you trying to get me drunk?" I ask, my eyes widening.

"Haha, no. I emptied a bottle, and that's what was left."

I *tsk* good-naturedly. "Don't lie to me. That's not what was left. You emptied a bottle, period."

She laughs. "Maybe. God, it's beautiful out here."

I look over the city. We're not high enough to see everything, not like the view Emma is treated to in Jack's penthouse, but we're high enough for my tastes. "Yeah, it is. You have a new appreciation for things like this when you think you won't have them anymore." I sit on the wrought iron staircase, the cool breeze brushing over my face.

"That can be a good thing," Emma says, standing, her elbows resting against the railing, her hands gently cradling her wineglass. "I never thought I'd be where I am right at this second with Jack, my friendships with Zoey and Claire. Not when I thought he was going to marry you. I think about it a lot, and I'm grateful he loves me." She looks at me. "Don't ever think I would be mad if you needed Jack for anything. I don't ever plan on not being friends with Raff, and it goes both ways."

"Raff and I don't have anything. I thought we did, but what we had was a lie."

Emma tips her head. "He drove straight to the penthouse from here and told us what he said. I'm not going to defend him, but I've known that man since he was twelve years old, and he doesn't have a cruel bone in his body. He was scared and lashed out."

In agitation, I fling my arms into the air, and wine sloshes over the rim of my glass. "I told him what my father did, I told him what I had to do. He called me a whore and left me there, packing, my heart breaking. I love him so much, and he, he threw me away like garbage all because I used to date Jack." I set my wineglass down and cover my face with my hands.

I almost don't hear her over my sobs. "It's really difficult to be in love with someone who's with someone else."

I wipe my eyes. I said I wouldn't cry over Raff. "I don't care."

She places her glass on the step near mine and kneels in front of me. "I'm not asking you to forgive him. I'm not asking you to give him another chance. All I'm going to ask you to do is go by his house tomorrow, listen to what he has to say, and properly break it off if you don't like it. He's been a mess while you were with Blaise, and even if you're there to tell him to go to hell, seeing that you're okay will ease his heart."

I open my mouth to repeat that I don't care about Raff's heart, not when he can so easily break mine, but she says, "You don't care about how he feels, I get that. But there's a lot you don't know, a lot I'm not going to tell you because it's not my place. I promised Jack I wouldn't get involved. He's still a little nervous sometimes, and I think the four of us are going to feel that way for a while. It's what happens when life gives you something that seems too good to be true. We're taught it usually is."

I stare at my hands.

"I'm here because I'm your friend. I always will be no matter what happens between you and Raff." She pauses. "I saw the photo of you on the front page of the paper. He was scared because he wants to keep that. Don't you?" She kisses my cheek, and with her wineglass, slides through the window and inside my apartment leaving me alone with nothing but an empty heart, an empty future, and after I chug all my wine, an empty glass.

———

While Emma and I were talking, Paige slid out of bed to sleep next to her mother, leaving room for me in my own bed, which I gratefully took advantage of. Gracie was whimpering in her sleep, and I don't know how Zoey and Heath will feel about it later, but I tucked her next to me and she stopped. Can you believe that in all this, I forgot about the fire?

God, my life is so fucked up.

The next morning, Zoey pulled me aside and said in a low voice, "Gracie's been having a tough time, still. She's embarrassed but she wanted me to ask you if you'd go to therapy with her. If that's not your thing, don't worry about it. Therapy isn't for everyone, and it's okay if you don't want—"

I rested a hand on her arm. "I'll be happy to go with her. She went through a traumatic experience with me. Whatever I can do, let me know. And we still have those hair appointments, right?"

She sighed in relief. "Thank you. Yes. The girls haven't forgotten, but I wasn't sure . . ."

"Make the appointments and let me know."

"Thank you."

"It's no problem, really."

Emma didn't say anything more about Raff, and I helped her carry the mattresses and bags downstairs to Zoey's minivan.

They left a little before eleven, Emma and I holding everyone up sleeping past nine.

I putter around straighten up, and I think a lot about what

Emma said on the fire escape. I do want to know the whole story. I want to know why Raff would say those things and then immediately go to Jack for help. Was he only lashing out like Emma said? If he was, he knew exactly where to hurt me.

My phone is so bogged down with texts and missed phone calls, I don't know where to begin, and I call the producers of the show first. I'm still not sure if I want to keep my position there, but I might as well until I find something else to do. Most of the other messages are from reporters, the good ones and the bad ones, asking for exclusives, like they don't know if I give anyone my story it would be to Raff for *Talk of the Town*. I might be angry, but I owe him, and I dislike being in debt.

Detective Mason called and left a message, asking if I was settling at home okay and if I needed anything. She reminded me I could forward a letter to my dad, but that's another thing I'll have to mull over. Thanks to Jack, he's alive and if he's not stupid, he'll stay that way, but for him to offer me in trade is something I don't think I can forgive him for, no matter how alone I am in the world.

You know what? I'm really tired of men letting me down.

I'm tired of shaking it off. I deserve better.

Fueled by the resentment, I shower and dress in a slinky ice-blue barely-there sundress that matches my eyes. I style my hair and apply my makeup. I'm going to tell Raff to go to hell, and I want him to see what he'll be missing for the rest of his life. I don't own a car, and I have to order one, leaving me stranded at Raff's until I can order another to pick me up. I could ask the driver to wait, but Emma said I don't know every-thing, and I want to.

I want to know every dirty detail.

I meet the car downstairs.

The driver stops in the parking lot in front of Raff's house, and he's already gone by the time I pick my way across the crushed rock and concrete in my sandals. I wore the perfect fuck-me heels because he's never getting any of this, ever again. I know his true feelings, and like hell I'll ever let him touch me.

I rap on the door, three quick knocks with my knuckles. I wait, my heart pounding. My fury is seeping away to dismay. I shouldn't be here. I shouldn't have let Emma talk me into this.

He answers, cracking the door open, and any chance I had to run away disappears. I meet his eyes and stumble backward. His skin has a grey pallor I've never seen before, his jaw covered in scruff. He smells as if he hasn't showered since the afternoon he saw me at my apartment.

He looks like Mollie.

"Are you sick?" The question pops out of my mouth.

The corners of his lips slightly lift up. "No, not in the way you mean, I don't think. What are you doing here, Nic?"

I lift my chin. "Emma said I don't know the whole story."

He scoffs. "Of course she did. Come in then, let's get it over with."

"Get what over with?"

Looking over his shoulder at me, he says, "All of it."

CHAPTER SIXTEEN

Rafferty

She's gorgeous. I ever tell you that? She's simply gorgeous. It won't take long for her to replace me, I can guarantee you that.

"Do you want a cup of coffee or something?" I ask.

She walks past me and stands in the middle of my kitchen. Well, if my kitchen had walls. It's too early to drink, but I haven't let that stop me. I doubt she'd want a drink if I offered her one. She looks like, for the first time in her life, she has her shit together. Well, good for her.

"No. I want to know why you said what you said." She sets her purse on the stool she sat on while I finger-fucked her. She hesitates, remembering that night, how ferocious I was because I couldn't get enough. I better have now. Should have saved it up.

I shrug. I can't defend myself. I was a prick. "I was hurt, angry. You told me you were going to go off with some guy, and I was supposed to, what? Accept it? Ask you not to go? You didn't ask for my help, and I didn't know what I was up against. I'd never heard of those assholes before."

"And that gives you the right to call me a whore? Especially since we'd already had that conversation, up there," she says angrily, pointing to my bed upstairs.

"Jesus Christ, Nic. Do you think I like the idea of another man touching you? Fucking you? I told you I love you. That means something to me, but you rolled over, showed your belly. It didn't mean a goddamned thing to you."

"I grew up with the Barkers breathing down my neck. You have no idea what that's like, what I've lived with for the past fifteen years. I didn't think I had a choice, and I did what I thought I had to do."

"And I did what I had to do."

Crossing her arms over her chest, she asks, "What *did* you do?"

"I pulled a favor. It doesn't matter." It sure as hell doesn't matter anymore.

"What favor? Jack did everything."

Pain pierces right through my heart, but Christ. I wanted her to believe that. "Yeah. Yeah, he did. Listen, let's just say we had a few good days and leave it at that. I'll call for a taxi."

Grabbing my arm she says, "No. I want to know what favor you asked for."

I sigh. "I called my mother. She threw her weight around and she's the one who placed your dad in protective custody, otherwise the cops would have arrested him along with everyone else. If he would have pleaded for a lower sentence, word would have gotten out the second they locked him up. He would have been dead within a week for being a snitch."

Her throat works and her fingertips dig into my skin. Finally, she says, "The police wouldn't have let him go. My dad's free because of you."

"Yeah, well, turns out it was better all around. They got a lot out of him, and he brought down the whole business from what I've heard. I stopped listening when Jack told me they picked you up at the Fairfax police department. All I cared about was that you were safe."

She pauses, her beautiful blue eyes searching my face. "Favors aren't free. What did you promise your mom?"

I jerk my arm from her grip. "Nic, it doesn't matter. You hate me for what I said. I was out of line and I deserve it. I was pissed, for a lot of reasons, but I shouldn't have taken it out on you. Especially since we already *had* hashed it out, and I don't think of you that way. You weren't a virgin, neither was I, and I should have left it alone."

Steadying herself with the back of the stool, she kicks off her heels and wanders into the living room. Every second she stays is another glass shard slicing my heart open. I wish she would go.

"It matters to me. What favor did you give your mom in exchange for hers?" She stops at the window and stands in the buttery light shining through the glass. Her hair gleams like a newly minted nickel, her dress hugging her curves in all the right places.

I'm never going to get her to leave if I don't answer her questions. She's tenacious like that, and one of the things I love best about her. "*Talk of the Town* is dead. I told her I'd give it up. I can't decide if I want to sell it or shut it down."

"Raff, no. You love your e-zine."

"Not as much as I love you, and it was my choice. She hated I started it, she hated I wrote for it, and it was the first thing she asked for. I'd do it again, so don't bother feeling sorry for me."

She narrows her eyes, not missing a single thing I said.

Fuck.

"The first thing she asked you for. What else does she want?"

It's barely noon, but I meet her halfway and pour a drink at the bar. Swirling the whiskey around the glass, I say, "At the fundraiser, before Barker set the hotel on fire, Mayor Iverson approached me. He said he wasn't running for re-election and asked what my thoughts were about running if he endorsed me. I haven't given one fuck about politics, but it's all my parents care about. I told her I would run. I'm pretty much a shoo-in— my reputation around here is already decent. I don't need to convince anyone I'm a good guy, well, except you."

"You won't win if you're not married. People like to know they're voting in a family man."

"Yeah. I got that."

"Then why would you tell your mom you would run?"

"I was going to ask you to marry me, but you'd say no, so I'm not going to bother." I search for some indication I'm wrong, that she would say yes if I asked, but her face is smooth, not betraying any hint to what she's thinking. She's been in front of a camera too long to let her emotions go unchecked.

"What are you going to do? You won't campaign if you won't win."

"No, you're right. That would be a waste of time and money. Mom wants me in Boston, so I'm going to pull up stakes. It's fine. I miss my family, and she misses me too, or she wouldn't play hardball to get me up there."

"Do you want to move?" she asks, staring at the floor.

"Not particularly. I'll miss Emma and my aunt. I like this area, but shit happens, you know? It's not your problem, Nic. I placed a lot of bets, and I lost. It's not a big deal."

Her head snaps up, her eyes flashing. "It is to me. Just because you said some crappy things doesn't mean I don't still love you. Love doesn't work like that, and all I could think about when I was locked in that bedroom at Blaise's lake house was how much I missed you and if you ever really loved me. You left me there, packing, letting me think you were abandoning me, but you were never going to let me go through that alone. That's the part Emma said I didn't know, isn't it? Jack didn't do anything. It was all you."

"I don't need your gratitude." I want her love, not her obligation.

"What if I want to marry you?"

I scoff. "Right. You don't get it, do you? Campaigning, then when I win, you'd be a mayor's wife. With a city the size of Bridgeport, you wouldn't have time to work, that means bye bye *Rise and Shine, Bridgeport!*. You'll be too busy hosting luncheons, doing volunteer work, and blowing me under my desk to hold down a job. I'm not going to ask you to give up your career for that."

A smile plays with her mouth. "I didn't realize blowjobs were part of the package."

"It's all part of the package. The kids or the two dogs and ten cats, whatever we decide on, City Hall, meeting my family. My mother won't let us have the ceremony just anywhere, you know. She'll want us to marry in Boston, and I'm sure you're scrambling to sign up for that."

"Would you like being Mayor Clark?" she asks, stepping toward me.

"Dollface, I run this town. It doesn't matter how I do it, as long as you're with me."

She wraps her arms around my waist and rests her head against my chest. "What if you don't win?"

I set my glass on the bar and rub my hand up and down her back. "If we get married but I don't win, we can stay here, but *Talk of the Town* is done. That's the only piece of the agreement set in stone. It's done. Mom wants me to use my law degree. Legal aid, opening my own office. Whatever floats my boat." I look down at her and she meets my eyes. "I have plenty of money, I don't need to work to take care of you."

"I'm sorry you gave up so much."

I cup her cheek in my palm. "I wouldn't change a single thing if it means you're standing here, safe, with your future wide open. I have to admit, you're never going to be an Annie to me. You'll always be Veronica. I hope that's okay."

Wrinkling her nose, she says, "I've never felt like an Annie Johnson or a Veronica Chapman, and I think it's because I wasn't either of those women. While I was Annie, I was running to a future I couldn't see but desperately wanted. While I was Veronica, I couldn't escape my past, and I was hiding. I think, what I really need to put all this behind me, is to be Veronica Clark. Stand by you while you do great things for this city, have babies or not, rescue dogs or not. I want to meet your family, and I don't care where we get married. I love you, and all I want is to start living my life with you."

It's what I want to hear, but I'm not the only one giving up something important to make this work. "But your show—"

"I don't care about the show. I wanted to be the center of attention because I felt safe there, but it didn't do a bit of good. Blaise still drove me out of town as easily as if I had been a nobody. I'm used to the spotlight, and I think you and I will be a good team. I'll help you when you're mayor, but I am not giving you blowjobs under your desk."

"How about you give me one now?" I joke, relief pouring through me. I thought I lost her. I really thought I lost her because I was a jealous bastard.

"How about you go shower? When was the last time you did? You smell."

I pick her up and she wraps her arms around my neck. "I can't remember. Shower with me?"

She laughs. "I know where this is headed, but we're not spending the rest of the day in bed. I want a ring, and the second Emma hears we kissed and made up, she'll want to see us."

"How about this," I say, carrying her up the stairs, "you shower with me and give me a blowjob. Then we'll nap . . . I haven't been sleeping well. Tonight, we'll buy you a ring, and to celebrate, we'll invite Emma and Jack to dinner."

"That, actually, sounds perfect."

"Good." I drop her onto the bed and kneel in front of her. She promptly closes her legs, and I laugh. She knows me too well. "I'm not here for that. That, and you, will come later, but I wanted to ask you the way a man should ask a woman he loves to marry him," I say, holding her hands.

Tears fall from her eyes, and they drip onto our entwined fingers.

"Nic, I don't know when I fell in love with you. I really don't. Maybe it was when you were dating Jack, or when I was helping you clean up that mess, maybe it was when you told me you were in some kind of trouble, I don't know. The night of the fire, I was waiting for the firefighters to find you, and I couldn't think about anything but how empty my life would be without you. The photo they took of us, that photo captured my heart and soul. I'm nothing without you. I want you to marry me, stand beside me for the rest of my life. Never think you can't come to me if you're in trouble. Never feel like you're alone. Whatever I have is yours, and you belong to me. I will keep you safe. I will love you until death parts us, and I hope you love me that much too."

"I do, Raff. I've been alone my entire life, and I never knew how it felt to have people care about me. My father didn't. He only thought of me as collateral, something to borrow against when he needed it. I've never had friends like Emma, Zoey,

Mia and Haisley, and Claire. I'm sorry I didn't tell you about Blaise, and I promise that from today on, whatever I need, I will come to you. I want you to feel the same. I'll give you whatever I can." She sucks in a deep breath. "I'm so sorry about *Talk of the Town.*"

I laugh. "Dollface, being Bridgeport's mayor will be a ride, and there's nothing in our terms that says I can't start another e-zine. My mother can hold me back, but she won't hold me down. I love you so goddamned much."

She falls into my arms, and yeah, I don't get my shower until much later.

Even with Nic cuddled into my side, as tired as I am, I don't fall asleep. I thought I was doing okay with Emma's friendship and my relationship with my aunt, but since Nic came into my life, she shoved right into my face how wrong I was. Maybe I lost my e-zine, but sometimes you have to let go of the old so you can grab on to the new. My friendship with Emma expanded to include Jack and Claire, and my lonely nights won't be so lonely anymore. I won't have to hide in Emma's spare room and if I attend an event, it will be because I want to be there, not because I don't want to be alone.

Nic might think I've given her friends and family, but we gave those things to each other. Tangling my fingers in her hair, I hug her close, and her breath fans against my skin. I press my lips to the top of her head and promise to be everything she needs because that's what she is to me.

CHAPTER SEVENTEEN

Roman

In a way, the clicking of all the keyboards is comforting, and my hands pause their fidgeting.

Clark's working behind a massive desk, three monitors sitting in a row, his eyes glued to the middle one as he types.

I step into his office, and he looks up and he tilts his head, considering. He and Claire have gotten close since Jack Durand asked his secretary to marry him, and Clark will keep an eye on me.

I don't mind.

Rolling an unlit cigarette between my fingers, I step farther into his office.

"Mansfield," he says, standing and walking over to a bar that's gleaming in the sun, the bottles sparkling. "Do you want a drink?"

Saliva pools in my mouth. "I shouldn't."

"I'll pour and you can decide. I heard you were back in

Bridgeport. Does Claire know you're here?"

I clear my throat. "Ah, yeah."

Clark raises his eyebrows and offers me the glass. I accept and sip, the alcohol doing its job. My muscles loosen and I relax, but only for a moment. It's all I can afford.

"What can I help you with?" he asks, leaning against his desk holding his own drink.

"I heard you're getting out of the business," I say, my gaze darting around his office.

"What you'll give up for love," he says wryly, a smile on his lips.

I pick up a framed photo of Clark and Veronica Chapman, Bridgeport's princess, locked in an embrace, fire blazing in the background.

"Fair trade," I say, though what I gained in return for letting Claire walk doesn't compete, not in the same way, but I wouldn't do things differently.

"I like to think so," he says softly, his eyes on the photo.

"Word is you're shutting it down."

He shrugs uneasily. "It's not what I want, but I don't want to sell. I don't want to see my reputation and all that I built go down the toilet. I'd rather pull the plug than let some fucker do God knows what."

"What if you had an honest buyer?"

He scoffs. "I doubt there's any such thing."

I lift my chin. "I think there is. Don't close up shop, Clark. Sell it to me."

———

Roman and Claire's story, *Safe & Sound*, is available now on Kindle, in Kindle Unlimited, and Paperback. Don't miss the exciting conclusion to the Lost & Found trilogy!

Want to keep up with news, special sales, and giveaways? Sign up for my newsletter and have exclusive access to that and a free full-length ugly-duckling billionaire romance novel, *My Biggest Mistake*. Sign up here: https://vmrheault.com/subscribe/

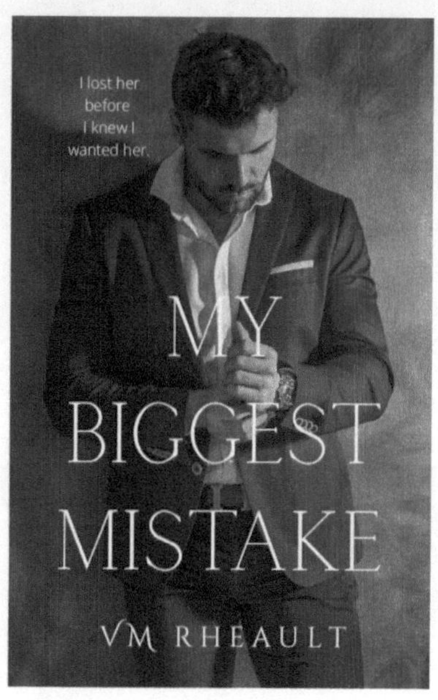

ALSO BY VM RHEAULT

Captivated by Her (Cedar Hill Duet Book One)

Addicted to Her (Cedar Hill Duet Book Two)

————

Rescue Me

————

Give & Take (The Lost & Found Trilogy Book One)

Lost & Found (The Lost & Found Trilogy Book Two)

Safe & Sound (The Lost & Found Trilogy Book Three)

————

Faking Forever

————

Twisted Alibis (Ghost Town Trilogy Book One)

Twisted Lullabies (Ghost Town Trilogy Book Two)

Twisted Lies (Ghost Town Trilogy Book Three)

————

A Heartache for Christmas

ABOUT THE AUTHOR

VM Rheault writes billionaire romance and contemporary romance under Vania Rheault.

She lives in Minnesota with her two children. When she's not writing, she's working her day job, sleeping, or enjoying the four seasons with a hot cup of coffee in hand.

Find her at vmrheault.com.